PLANTWISE
STEWARD'S WORLD, BOOK 1

MICHELLE L. LEVIGNE

www.YeOldeDragonBooks.com

Ye Olde Dragon Books
P.O. Box 30802
Middleburg Hts., OH 44130

www.YeOldeDragonBooks.com

2OldeDragons@gmail.com

Copyright © 2023 by Michelle L. Levigne

ISBN 13: 978-1-961129-02-3

Published in the United States of America
Publication Date: June 15, 2023

Cover Art © Copyright 2023 Ye Olde Dragon Books

CHAPTER ONE

That fall in Westerland, everyone attributed the lush harvest and perfect weather to the birth of Arden, daughter of King Alfred and Queen Elise. The stories surrounding the little princess's birth spread like the firegrass that sprouted rainbows of tiny flowers after the fields had been harvested and plowed under for winter's rest. The peasants of the farming kingdom said the sun shone when the princess laughed and rain only fell when she cried -- and there were few reports of rain all that harvest, until long after the last sheaves had been brought into the barns.

Plantwise Glynna felt Arden's birth when the roots of the trees all through Westerland twitched in their loamy beds. She felt it in the unripe grain when the milk of the kernel turned to rich ripeness in a flicker of thought. She tasted it on the harvest wind, warm and sweet and full of the sudden new abundance that flowed over the land.

Arden was the one she had waited for, so many long, weary years. Glynna would Gift the baby princess with her plantwise magic.

She didn't need to hurry to reach the princess before her christening, which was the most appropriate time for a Gifting of such importance to Westerland, and the surrounding kingdoms. Alfred was a wise man who listened to the heartbeat of the land, the breath of the wind, the tides of the air that controlled the rain. He cared about his people. He would wait until after the harvest was complete before holding the blessing and naming ceremony for his daughter and include all his subjects in his family's joy. Glynna had plenty of time to spread her plantwise magic through the land one last time, and bless the crops and farmers and their beasts in the rhythm and pattern that Yeshen had established when the Maker called her to this duty.

King Doyne of Stonemount, Westerland's ally on its eastern border, came for the festivities. He brought his only child, Maddix. After all, he had said in his letter responding to the invitation, his son was eight and Prince Alix of Westerland, was seven, and it was high time the two boys met. They would be allies when they took up their fathers' duties.

The people cheered as the tall, white-haired, red-faced king rode down the cobblestone streets of Port'ham with his golden-haired son. Those who cared about such things remarked on how alert the young prince was, watching everything with those sharp gray eyes, constantly turning to his father's advisers with questions. A boy like that, who cared about the world around him at such a young age, would make a large mark on the world. Or so said the old gaffers who sat in the doorways and smoked their clay pipes and passed judgment on the world.

~~~~~

"I've seen country estates larger than this so-called palace," Hirst, aide to Lord Jaygo of Stonemount, grumbled through a mouthful of spice cake. He washed it down with sweet cider and wiped the overflow off with his velvet sleeve. "It's a crying shame—"

"That you never learned table manners to go with your clothes," Jaygo whispered in that voice that could turn a hot spring into a skating pond. "Consider what you just put into your mouth."

"Spice cake and cider. So what?"

"It's very good, isn't it?"

"Everything in Westerland is good."

"Exactly. And where does most of the food in Stonemount originate?" Jaygo nodded to an aged couple meandering down the other side of the table.

Their faces were like rosy, ancient apples, gleaming with scrubbing above the pristine white and rainbow-hued embroidery of their festival clothes. In contrast to the abundance around him, Jaygo wore his habitual, gleaming black, which accented the silver streaks in his thinning hair and short-trimmed beard. He was a tall, emaciated crow towering over Hirst's slovenly, muscle-bound form.

"Here. That's why you keep prodding the king for a betrothal, now that these farmers have a princess. To keep the food coming."

"For far more important reasons than that. The old fool is a romantic. He's added to my work, insisting his son needs to win the heart of his bride." Jaygo rolled his eyes. "Not only do I need to protect Maddix from his father's weak-minded philosophy, but I have to tutor him in seducing a woman into willing servitude. A waste of my talent, if you ask me."

"Have you told Durmad that he's wasting your talent?" Hirst mumbled.

He flinched away when Jaygo cast a furious glare at him, and didn't see the terror under the fury. Durmad was not a master to question or criticize, even from five kingdoms away.

"Anyway, what does all that have to do with King Alfred living in a house Baron Kapron wouldn't go near?" Hirst reached for his goblet of cider to wash the last few crumbs of cake down his throat.

"This is a nation of farmers, my dense young friend. To a farmer, this ... cottage is a rich palace. Alfred believes he shouldn't hold himself too high above his own people. Don't mock those with limited sense. Pity them. They don't see the real world. They think they are happy."
~~~~~

Hirst responded to that with a grunt. Jaygo sipped at apple wine and turned to look for Maddix. Despite believing his talents were better employed elsewhere, he had some fondness for the young prince. He believed himself a far better father to Maddix than Doyne. He even allowed himself some pride in the boy. He was coming along quite nicely in his lessons on proper kingship and the role he would play in bringing the lower half of this continent under Durmad's thumb.

Near the center of the bustle of happy activity in the palace gardens, the two princes, Maddix and Alix raced each other in circles around their chatting fathers and the wide table that held the topic of their conversation. Alix was his father's son, with ruddy cheeks, hazel eyes and thick brown-black curls. From a distance, they were just two boys, blond and brunette, playing with that curious mixture of rivalry and friendship that waited for a turning point in their relationship. Arden's christening meant nothing to either boy, beyond speeches and having to stand perfectly still and not make faces at each other from across the wide aisle of the chapel.

Up close, the differences grew clear. Maddix wore velvet and silk and his belt knife had a gilded sheath. When he wasn't laughing and running and gasping for breath, his narrow mouth fell into pouting lines. Alix wore a fine broadcloth shirt, richly embroidered, with a leather vest. His knife had a plain grip of carved wood bound with leather. The sheath was scarred and stained, but he cherished it, a gift from his friend, Derrien, son of the Captain of the Guard.

King Alfred and King Doyne stood to one side of a table holding a map of the entire continent. Westerland and Stonemount fit together like two kidney beans from the same pod and were close enough in size the differences didn't matter. Above them, touching both their borders was Ambray, roughly a fifth larger than either of them. Curving around to touch Ambray on its eastern border, Stonemount on its eastern and southern borders and part of Westerland, was Brentonwald. It was nearly the size of the other three kingdoms combined.

On this pleasant day of festivities and sunshine and laughter, neither king much enjoyed the discussion that had prompted the map being spread out before them. The king of Ambray had written them both, asking for their opinion and advice on how to deal with a possible problem. Two kingdoms far to the north, beyond the nearly impassable, snow-clad, jagged peaks of the Cascade Mountains, had merged into one. No clear details had passed the mountains, beyond rumors that they had been forced together, rather than the time-honored way through a marriage alliance. The disturbing consistency among all the rumors was that Durmad, who controlled three-quarters of the land north of the Cascades, had done the forcing. Troops wearing his snow tiger insignia had been spotted in small clusters throughout kingdoms south of the mountain range, vanishing and reappearing like fever-laden fog. Ambray's king hoped he was being alarmist to suspect the troops of being spies.

Needing a respite from such dark concerns, King Alfred's gaze settled on his golden-haired wife, sitting among a circle of chattering, laughing noble women and their daughters. He had always believed Elise was a rare beauty, but today with their daughter in her arms he believed her the most beautiful woman in the entire world. She glowed, with no ornaments but her smile and flowers braided into her hair. Her green eyes sparkled as she looked up from the tiny bundle in her lap and saw her husband watching her. For a moment, there was no one and nothing in the world but the two of them.

Comyn, Alfred's most trusted advisor, stepped up to the queen with a bow and interrupted the communion of their hearts. His hair was purest white, but he still moved with strength and assurance. Alfred hoped the man would still be there, reliable and wise for Alix to lean on when he began his rule.

"Something wrong, my friend?" Doyne asked

"Hmm?" Alfred chuckled as he realized he had been staring, silent just a few seconds too long. "No. Everything is far too right today. On days like this, I wonder what I ever did to deserve such happiness. It's like a nursery fable."

"I hope it remains so, long after our children are grown. My counselors are pressuring me to request a betrothal. Nothing would make me happier than to seal our friendship by sharing grandchildren someday. Political maneuvering has always worried me. When does royal duty overrule the happiness of our children?" Doyne nodded toward their sons, who had stopped their games when approached by Lord Jaygo. "Yet sometimes we must sacrifice our hearts' desires for the good of the country. If that becomes necessary, I pray Yeshen that Maddix and Arden will be rewarded with great happiness together."

"I know any son of yours will make my daughter a good husband. That is enough for me." Alfred reached for the wineskin sitting on one corner of the map and gestured at their half-empty cups. "Come, let me refill our drinks to toast the future."

~~~~~

Glynna entered Port'ham at the River Gate, her sandals crunching on the gravel that lined the donkey path along the side of the river. She walked slowly, feeling the little princess's presence drawing her. Though this was the day she had dreamed of with eager weariness, she felt a
~~~~~

twinge of reluctance. And, she was wise enough to admit, some fear. She only knew stories of what would happen when she Gifted the baby princess with the full store of her plantwise magic and years of wisdom and experience. She had never met anyone who was Gifted, so she couldn't know if the stories were true.

The people of Westerland knew they were more than welcome to visit the palace gardens and catch a glimpse of the little princess on her christening day, to take a cup of cider and a share of the roasted boars and geese the king had provided for the celebration. Most kept their visits to just that, a glimpse, a taste, and a word of congratulations to the parents. Then they went back out through the palace gates to their own celebrations. Those who could left little gifts for the child; sweets, knitted stockings and little shoes, quilts with blessings stitched into the soft fabric, preserves and little wooden toys.

Glynna walked among the festivities that spilled out of every tavern and inn. People danced in every fountain square, where someone would play a fiddle or harp or beat a drum loud enough to give them a rhythm. She smiled, knowing Arden would love these simple, generous, happy folk as she had come to love them in the many decades of her service.

From time to time, someone turned long enough from their merrymaking to see Glynna and recognize her. Then she would hear her name called and someone would smile and wave. People called out thanks and blessings to her. Someone would offer a bit of good news, another would run up to her with a cup of cider. Someone else would give her a bit of fancy cake or a meat pie small enough for two bites. The constant halts to talk, nibble or sip slowed Glynna's journey, but she didn't mind. She was glad for one last chance to see the people she loved, and to make her farewells.

Three streets from the palace, magic tingled in her fingertips. Green-gold sparkles danced along her arms for a moment. Glynna turned to look.

"Ambrose!" Tears touched her eyes even as laughter rang in her voice. She hurried through the press of people, arms stretching wide.

The man who strode across the square and around the well with its garland-hung roof was taller than everyone there by nearly a head. His silver hair gleamed and the momentary silver sparkles of magic dancing on his fingertips had a slight tinge of purple. He was clean-shaven and let his hair grow long, though that small attempt at disguise did little to hide the resemblance between himself and King Doyne, who wore his hair short and his beard full. Ambrose was uncle to the king of Stonemount. He should have been king, but because of his healing Gift, he renounced the throne in favor of his younger brother, Doyne's father.

Ambrose believed, as Glynna did, that Yeshan had granted Gifts to benefit the entire world, not individual kingdoms.

"My dear, it has been too long!" Ambrose flung his arms tight around her. She was two heads shorter than him, thin and weathered and topped with snowy hair, but for a moment as they embraced they were two raw children, meeting on their first forays into the wild world to test and share their Gifts. He laughed as he released her and twisted the vine leaves back into her hair where they had come loose. "Another good harvest, I hear. Thanks to you."

"When the people have good in their hearts and love for the land, there really is little need for me. Except to remind them, of course," Glynna added with a chuckle.

Then she noticed the quiet, thin, dark boy who stood like the old man's second shadow. It took but a moment to note the hawk's nose, the gray eyes, the air of gentle thoughtfulness about the boy. He and Ambrose were dressed much alike; sturdy, earth-colored roughspun and traveling leathers with large belt pouches at their waists, worn packs on their backs and walking sticks in their hands.

"This can't be Dylon, so grown up already, can it?" she said, smiling down at the boy. "So, how do you like apprenticing with your grandfather, young sir?"

"I like it very well, Lady," Dylon responded with a bow. He touched his brow with two fingers since he had no hat to remove. Glynna was pleased to sense that he had grown to be even more like Ambrose since she last saw them four years ago.

"He knows the basic healing herbs by sight," Ambrose was saying with fond pride in his voice. He smiled down at the boy, who grinned back up at him. "And only ten years old."

"I can see you're going to live up to all your grandfather's pride."

"Thank you, Lady Glynna," Dylon said, bowing again. "I hope so."

"Oh, dear, so formal already?" She chuckled and bent so they were eye-to-eye. "I'd much rather you called me Auntie Glynna, lad. Would you do me that kindness?"

"Gladly, Lady -- Auntie Glynna," the boy said, blushing a little.

"Thank you." She and Ambrose shared a smile of muffled amusement. "Oh, isn't it glorious at this time of year? I do so enjoy the harvest festivals, watching the people bring in all the crops. It feels wonderful to sit back and watch. Like what you feel when a patient is on the mend."

"Ah, now that's a wonderful feeling," Ambrose said, nodding. "But why are you here? I thought you'd be further north, preparing for winter."

"The princess. I felt her birth in the wind. She's the one I've been waiting for." She didn't miss the momentary parting of his lips as if he would protest her decision, and then the understanding that dimmed his eyes.

"I'll miss you, dearheart," he finally said.

"You're not going to argue?"

"I grow weary, too. Will you let us walk with you?" When she nodded, Ambrose gave her a sweeping, courtly bow and offered her his arm.

She laughed, remembering the few times she had let him talk her into visiting the Court in Stonemount; the fancy dresses his brother's wife laced her into; the silly times they spent on dances and fancy food and double-talk in Court. It had been a game; one she tired of quickly. Westerland was her home and it called her back. She had felt only a twinge of regret when she heard Ambrose had married an herb mistress. They remained friends, though years passed before they saw each other again.

Dylon bowed and offered his hand to Glynna. She smiled and laughed and the three set off again, strolling through the crowds. As they neared the palace Ambrose's hand rested a little more heavily over hers in the crook of his arm. Glynna didn't mind. Time was short, and she preferred to spend these last few moments with her dear friend.

~~~~~

Sunset wore bright fall colors as it spilled across the fading festivities in the royal gardens. Even the city-bound folk lived their lives in tune with the rising and setting of the sun.

Lord Comyn sat with the two princes on the step of the chapel in the palace gardens. Maddix fidgeted as Comyn regaled him and Alix with a story of a hunt for a ten-point buck on a snowy evening. Ordinarily, he would have found the story fascinating, but Lord Jaygo insisted Comyn was a weak-willed, overly cautious man who only held his post as King Alfred's advisor because the king owed him a huge debt. How could Maddix respect such a man? Despite the pounding of his heart and the tight excitement in his chest, the prince knew this story had to be a nest of lies. It was probably a yearling doe Lord Comyn chased through the mud, rather than a magnificent beast that turned and faced its pursuers before dying with ten arrows in its chest.

Alix leaned against the old man's knee, taking shallow, panting breaths, as if he rode with the hunting party. He never blinked and his body twitched a little from side to side as if he followed the wild ride of Comyn's story. Maddix envied his enjoyment, even knowing Jaygo would say this was the enjoyment of a little boy. He understood, with
~~~~~

some regret, that it was high time he grew up and put aside childish toys and games. His father was an old man and could die unexpectedly, leaving him in charge of the entire country. The young prince was grateful for Jaygo's advice and constant stories of how a future king should think and act.

Queen Elise sat in a sheltered spot, holding her sleeping daughter. A few noble ladies were making their farewells, talking quietly so as not to disturb the baby. Arden's nurse hovered at the queen's elbow, ready to take the child whenever her mother's arms grew weary.

The mayor of Port'ham stood with King Alfred and King Doyne at the map table, saying a last few words of congratulations to the two monarchs. His plump wife and five children waited on fidgeting legs for him to say in twenty words what most men could say in five. Still, the people loved their mayor and Alfred valued the man's wisdom -- once it was sifted out from his many words.

~~~~~

"Who's that?" Maddix asked, not two seconds after Comyn finished his story. At this point, most listeners would still be in a respectful silence for the grand animal that had fought so hard to live, but the boy just pointed at the main garden gate.

"Yes, who is that?" Jaygo asked, stepping from the shadows to join them. Hirst appeared at his side a moment later, holding a half-gnawed goose leg in one hand.

"Oh, my ..." Comyn stared as Glynna paused in the gate to look around the gardens. How many years had it been since she had come through the gates of Port'ham? As much as eight, or even ten, he thought. The woman hadn't changed, still with her gleaming white hair and weathered face, her brilliant green eyes and the vine leaves twined into her hair. She held sandals in one hand, treading the grass barefoot, and the grass in a wide circle around her waved in silent greeting.

A white-haired man and a half-grown boy waited in the gate, watching Glynna walk away from them. She looked back once. The man smiled sadly, bowed and spread his arms wide, as if bestowing the gardens on her to wander through at her pleasure.

The servants flitting through the garden, cleaning up the debris of festivities, paused and looked around. One by one, their momentary stillness and widening eyes marked the moment they saw Glynna and recognized her. The muted conversations dotting the garden died away as the little knots of people reacted to the growing anticipation in the air and looked up. Alfred and Doyne turned and saw her.
~~~~~

CHAPTER TWO

Elise stood, her smile hovering between pleasant surprise and disbelieving wonder. She took a few steps to meet the late-coming guest, then couldn't seem to move any further.

"Who is that old woman?" Jaygo asked, his voice pitched a little lower, responding to the ripples of silence and expectation washing across the garden.

"That is Auntie Glynna," Comyn said. He nearly laughed at the pride in his voice. Plantwise Glynna was indeed a national treasure. As proud as the people of Westerland were that she chose to make her home among them, he doubted any of them would be so foolish as to claim she belonged solely to them.

"Surely not Queen Elise's aunt. The woman should be better dressed."

"Auntie to everyone grateful for her talents," Comyn said, resisting the urge to snap. "She's plantwise. It is a great honor for her to come. She should be resting now that it's harvest."

"Another farmer." Hirst belched. "The smell around here must be terrible in the spring." He smiled woozily when Comyn glared at him.

"Lord Jaygo?" Maddix asked, moving over to stand closer to the nobleman.

"Hush and listen, lad. You might learn from this." Jaygo frowned, watching as Glynna stretched out her arms and Elise gave the baby into her embrace. He flinched when green-gold sparkles flared from her fingertips and danced up and down her arms.

The two kings started across the garden toward Elise and Arden and Glynna. Passing the little chapel, they brought the two princes and the other three men with them in their wake. They stopped short as a soft, green-gold glow flowed over Glynna, enveloping her and the baby, hiding them both from sight for a few heartbeats. Alfred let out a little gasp and his legs wobbled. Alix hurried to his father's side and the king clasped the boy's shoulder. He smiled down at his son, but his lips trembled, and momentary tears touched his eyes.

"Father," Alix whispered, "is she Gifting Arden?"

"Indeed she is." Alfred took a deep breath and his limbs steadied. "Your baby sister will be plantwise when she is grown."

"Fool, fool, fool," Jaygo muttered.

"What's wrong, Lord Jaygo?" Maddix asked.

"Nothing, my prince." He bared his teeth in a strained smile. "This is indeed a wondrous moment. You must join me in persuading your father that a betrothal between you and the princess is vital to the good of our country. Both our countries," he hurried to add, with a warm smile that chilled Comyn for a moment.

"Why? Girls are stupid."

"Oh, how much you have to learn," he said with a chuckle. He winked at Comyn, as if sharing a private joke with him. "She will grow into a woman. As beautiful as her mother. Show some wisdom and look toward the future." He gripped Maddix's shoulder and the boy grimaced, hinting that the grip hurt him, just for a moment.

"You have nothing to fear, Lord Jaygo," Comyn said, forcing a smile and a bright tone to his voice. There were undercurrents to this conversation that worried him, although he could not figure out why. "Westerland and Stonemount will be allies for generations to come. You have no reason to fear losing access to the bounty of Westerland. Especially now that …" He sighed, turning back to watch Glynna and the baby princess, wrapped in golden-green magic. "Now that Arden is Gifted to be plantwise. Yeshan truly has blessed us."

"Father!" Maddix stomped over to where Doyne and Alfred watching the green-gold glow fade from around Glynna and baby Arden. "I want a Gifting."

"When you've earned it." Doyne exchanged a grin with Alfred, very clearly meaning: *He will never earn it if he keeps this up.*

"Arden got a Gifting, and she's just a stupid baby."

"My sister isn't a stupid baby!" Alix flung himself at Maddix. Alfred lunged forward, catching his son by his belt. Doyne swung Maddix out of the way before the boy did more than stick his tongue out.

~~~~~

A soft sigh swirled around the gardens as Glynna handed the infant back to Elise. The moment her fingers left the silken quilt, translucence washed over her. Her hair grew brighter. Her feet vanished into the grass. The tips of her fingers grew transparent. The edges of her skirt evaporated, with nothing underneath them as they grew shorter. Glynna turned toward the gate and pressed her ghostly hands to her lips to waft a kiss to Ambrose. For a moment she remained, a figure of softly shining glass. Then she faded like mist touched by a fresh morning breeze.

Ambrose stepped into the gardens and bowed deeply, one hand pressed to his heart. As he straightened, tears made his face shine. He was aware of all the people looking at him because Glynna had turned to him before she vanished. He didn't care what they saw or thought.

"Farewell, old friend," he whispered, voice breaking, and blinked
~~~~~

away tears.

~~~~~

"Doyne?" Alfred murmured, suspecting something special about the white-haired, tall man who had shared that final moment with Glynna before she faded away. "Who is that?"

"My uncle, Ambrose the healer," King Doyne said, just as quietly. "If not for him ... we would not be here today. He gave the throne to my father for the sake of sharing his healing Gift with all the world."

"Ah. A wise and generous man." He bowed deeply to Ambrose as he turned to rejoin the dark-haired boy standing in the gates. He contemplated asking them to come be his guests, but something about the exchange between Ambrose and Glynna told him the man would not want strangers intruding into his thoughts.

"Very generous." Doyne watched his uncle walk away and lines of weariness settled onto his own face. "And truly wise."

"The duties of nobility, old friend," Alfred murmured, and they shared yet another smile of understanding.

"Uncle Ambrose will give me his Gifting someday," Maddix declared. "I'll be the greatest healer in the whole world!"

"That would be a great gift and responsibility indeed, Prince Maddix." Comyn rested a hand on Alix's shoulder. "Be sure you use your gifts for good. A magical gift used for evil turns to poison and harms the entire land." He tipped his head with a questioning look to King Alfred, who nodded, and led Alix away. Better to head off another argument before it had a chance to sprout.

~~~~~

"Don't listen to that old fool," Jaygo murmured, as he drew Maddix away in the opposite direction. He kept his voice smooth as cream, the slightest sneer in one corner of his mouth. "If you have magic, my wise young prince, you must use it only for your own people. There are limits to even the most wonderful gift. If you spend it foolishly on everyone who asks, you'll run out sooner or later."

"Prince Ambrose shouldn't be allowed to wander as he does," Hirst chimed in as he followed them. "If he dies far from home, his magic will go to someone outside Stonemount."

"Why doesn't my father keep him at home, then?" Maddix piped up, on cue.

"I don't know," Jaygo said with a long-suffering sigh he had perfected when speaking with the prince about his father. "I hope you will do better when you are king."

~~~~~

A swirl of magic, silver shifting to green to blue to purple, spun
~~~~~

through the air over the heads of the people dancing in the fountain square several streets away from the palace. Ambrose caught his breath at the sight and turned to follow it. He took five steps before realizing Dylon had continued moving through the dancing, laughing, rejoicing people. Shaking his head, feeling more excited and awed than foolish, Ambrose hurried after the boy and wrapped an arm around his shoulders to guide him out of the square. He watched his grandson, a knot of worry and hope in his chest, until the boy's eyes widened and he turned his head, visibly following the swirl of magic overhead. Good. The boy saw the magic as well.

He hadn't given much thought to who he would Gift his healing magic to, when the day came to lay down the burden and blessing Yeshen had placed on him. Not until he saw Glynna Gift her duty and magic and years of experience to the little princess. His son, Dylon's father, had inherited his late wife's gift for words rather than healing, and chose a life of scholarship, serving the Repository, a vast complex of caverns full of scholars and scrolls and the histories of every kingdom on the continent. Silver sparks had appeared when Dylon was born, indicating he had the potential for healing, but Ambrose had seen no further proof of magic. Until now.

The two wove their way through the laughing, singing, dancing throngs, down five streets and through another fountain square, until they came out into a quieter portion of Port'ham. A young man with gingery curls and a faint dusting of beard, wearing the simple clothes of a traveler, sat on a bench in front of a closed shop, and watched them come down the street. The swirls of magic faded as they spun down around him. When Ambrose got close enough, he saw the young man's eyes: fern green. A faint glow like a candle flame flickered behind them, just for a moment before the last of the magic faded entirely.

He stopped a dozen paces away from the young man, who had a simple traveler's pack tucked under the bench by his feet. A sturdy walking stick leaned against the bench. Ambrose bowed head and shoulders in silent tribute.

"Healer." The young man smiled. "I'm pleased to meet you."

"You honor me, Steward." Ambrose's lips twitched in a brief smile when Dylon caught his breath at the title.

"We are all servants on level ground at Yeshen's feet." The young man got to his feet. "I'm grateful we had a chance to meet. I feel I was guided here to warn you, as well as Auntie Glynna."

"Me?" He held perfectly still, thinking of Glynna, newly Gifted to the baby princess, and the damage that could be done to Westerland, to all the kingdoms touching the farming kingdom, if that magic Gift was lost. Other times when a Gift had been passed on, Durmad had struck, through physical attack or through subtlety, killing the new Gifted or taking them prisoner, or warping them to employ that magic in his service. Had enemy spies followed Glynna here, sensing she was about to Gift herself?

"The boy, your nephew's heir." Steward's expression turned grave. "Shadows are slowly gathering, and poisoned roots reach for him. He is a potential pivot point in our war. My dreams of him are hazy. Nothing is confirmed. No decisions have been made, but he is poised on too many knife edges. The enemy wants him, and he is vulnerable." He nodded to Dylon. "This one is young. I do not like to ask you to put him into the war, but a companion who isn't awed by his rank could be a good influence, a wall of protection." He shook his head. "And could come under attack for it. I don't want to ask it of you ..."

"You don't have to." Ambrose gripped Dylon's shoulder. "My nephew is already concerned about his son's attitude, since losing his wife. She was a defensive wall against the flatterers and bootlickers and liars. He suggested some time ago that Maddix needs a steadying influence, and someone who will stand up to him."

"Thank you."

"The princess ... is she in danger?"

"Not yet."

"But she will be?"

"When she starts thinking for herself, and lets her heart guide ..." The Steward sighed and shrugged. "I have dreamed too many branching paths ahead of her, and all of them vanish into the mist of possibilities."

~~~~~

Midnight in the palace nursery. Candles scented like springtime gardens glimmered behind shields of green and blue glass, keeping away the utter blackness. Arden's nighttime nurse worked on her knitting.

She didn't see the faint shimmer of green-gold magic swirling just above the princess's cradle. She didn't hear the soft murmuring of an old woman crooning nonsense lullabies to a sleeping child.

Arden woke from a happy dream, a baby giggle soft in her throat. Before she could do more than take a breath, she saw the shimmering just a few inches above her cradle and reached little hands to clasp it.

"Oh, I'm sorry, sweetheart," Glynna said as the shimmering coalesced into her features. She shook her head, smiling down at the wide, blue-green eyes staring up at her. "You can't touch me. Only my spirit is here. And only you can see or hear me. But we'll have a jolly time together, won't we?" She smiled and clapped her transparent hands
~~~~~

silently as the baby let out a bell-like giggle. "Everything I have is yours, my darling, all my knowledge, all my experience. I will be with you forever, just like the old tales promised. And together ... such wonderful things we will do together."

~~~~~

Little Princess Arden was a well-known figure in the farms and fields and forests surrounding Port'ham. She rambled everywhere her sturdy little legs would take her, usually escorted by her brother and Derrien, son of the Captain of the Guard. They rode trustworthy older horses from the palace stables and she had her furry, rascally pony, appropriately named Feathers. Only Arden could get the pony to behave. She was the only one who could refer to him by name without getting her fingers bitten off or a hoof shoved into tender anatomy.

The people of Westerland loved the sight of their princess scampering through the fields and markets, her hip-length red-gold hair flying behind her like a curly banner. She dressed like a peasant, as was appropriate for her outdoor venturing, but her hair clearly marked her for anyone to see. No one else had hair that particular shade that seemed to burn with a light of its own. They were rather proud she knew most of the dogs and horses in the city, and every farm animal she encountered, on a first-name basis. So what if Arden didn't look or act like a "proper princess," as some foreign diplomats were heard to complain from time to time? She was Westerland's princess and she loved her people and that was good enough for them.

At the moment, she was a wet little princess, crouched in the partial shelter of the chapel steps in the palace gardens. Arden was always in the palace gardens if she couldn't escape outside to the forests and fields. Today, Queen Elise had extracted a promise from her daughter that she would not go adventuring. They had very important guests expected by noontime, and she didn't want the guards hunting Arden for hours on end. Today, the girl was far too intent on her newest lesson to wander very far.

Her third-best frock and petticoats were damp from the rain that had fallen for the past three hours. What spatters didn't reach her in the doorway soaked up into her skirt from the puddles on the stone steps. Arden didn't notice the damp or the chill, though her bare legs were spotted with gooseflesh.

She held a brown and shriveled seedpod on her flattened palm and stared down at it. One hand cupped the other. A single raindrop slid down her cheek and dripped off her chin, unnoticed. Glynna hovered in front of her, slightly above her head, transparent and tinged faintly green.
~~~~~

"Very good, my dear. But you're trying too hard."

"How can I try too hard, Auntie?" the child whispered, never glancing up.

"Magic must flow like a stream, not squirt like a fountain." She chuckled. Arden grinned, keeping her gaze on the pod. "Think about happy, good things and let the magic come when it wants."

"But I have to make something grow *now*! Prince Maddix will be here soon." She sighed, concentration breaking despite herself, and blinked as she shifted her gaze to her teacher.

"If you're worried about impressing our guests, then hurry into the palace and change into dry clothes and put on some shoes," Glynna said with a sniff.

"Prince Maddix is a boy. My brother doesn't care about fancy clothes, does he?"

"You have a point." Her eyes narrowed. "You're not letting that silly letter he wrote influence you. Are you?"

"It's not silly. How many letters do you think little girls like me get from the princes of very important countries like Stonemount?"

"Hmm, that depends on your definition of important." She sighed. "You took his words to heart, didn't you? About how quickly you're learning to control your plantwise Gift, and how important it is for the futures of both our countries?"

"It is, isn't it? Westerland produces enough food we can export to all the surrounding countries, and still have extra left over."

"True." Another sigh. "Your brother will be responsible for dealing with other countries and their needs, and keeping our friendship with them strong. You need to focus on your plantwise Gift and performing your duties to please Yeshen. Other people's opinions aren't worth ashes if your heart isn't right and your soul isn't clean. Understand?"

"Yes, Auntie. I know that."

"You know that ... oh, this is ridiculous. Here I'm scolding you to concentrate and let the magic flow, and then I distract you. You, my girl, are a bad influence on me!" She leaned close so her transparent nose flowed into Arden's snub nose. The girl sputtered and jerked back, and then they both burst out laughing.

The sound of Arden's laughter echoed softly through the damp garden, attracting the attention of two adolescent boys as they stepped through the door from main wing of the palace. Alix was half a head taller than Maddix. He still wore the knife Derrien had given him and walked with the assured, long stride of a boy sliding easily into a man's responsibilities. He didn't do as much damage to his festival clothes at age fourteen that he did at seven, so today his best clothes were nearly a rival for Maddix's velvet and silk. Alix's head was bare to the drizzling rain, the drops giving a silver sheen to his dark, close-cropped curls. Maddix was dressed all in midnight blue dusted with silver. His flat cap with a long feather drooped in the damp. He had a rapier in a silver-embossed sheath and rested his hand on it as he walked. Nearly two feet of space separated the two princes and neither one looked at the other as they crossed the gardens.

"Arden?" Alix smiled when he spotted his little sister huddled in the damp shadows of the doorway. "Come on, you silly goose! Our guests are here. Auntie Glynna, are you here? Couldn't you have gotten her inside sooner?" As usual, he looked into the air high over Arden's head, though his little sister had told him quite often that Auntie Glynna usually hovered a few inches above the ground and slightly to her right.

"Of course I'm here, you nitwit," Glynna sighed. Her face brightened with a fond smile. "But Arden is a little too busy to listen to even me now." She reached out to caress the princess's curly, wet head with fingers that passed right through her.

Arden barely heard either one speak, all her attention focused on the grand, handsome figure striding toward her.

Maddix straightened his shoulders, reacting to the child's very clear fascination with him. He tugged on the hilt of his rapier, bringing it around a little more and struck a pose, so much like an illustration from a book of adventures, Glynna chuckled.

"Don't call her a goose. I'm sure whatever she's doing is very important." He bowed to the girl, then swept his cap off his golden curls.

Arden's mouth opened in a tiny 'o' of awe. Green-gold sparks flashed on her fingertips. The pod in her hand burst into life, sending out three shoots that sprouted leaves and then pale blue flowers. Glynna rocked back in mid-air as she saw it.

"Oh, my. You're going to have to learn a *lot* of control, my dear." She sighed, caught between delight and pride and a sudden overwhelming dread of the future.

"That's amazing, Arden!" Alix dropped to his knees on the steps next to his little sister and hugged her. "I didn't know you could do that."

"Of course she can. Arden can do anything." Maddix bowed again and offered her his arm. "Didn't I tell you that in my last letter? My sweet, clever princess," he added, his voice dropping to a purr. Arden's cheeks pinked and her eyes went starry. Over her head, he sneered at Alix's groan of disgust.

CHAPTER THREE

Glynna sighed and wished her foot was solid enough she could stomp in vexation. She stayed hovering above the wet chapel steps, watching as Arden walked back to the palace arm in arm with Maddix. The little girl hardly blinked, all her attention focused on the prince. Alix walked next to his sister and their guest, his fists jammed into his pockets, shoulders hunched, scowling.

"She's not going to listen to a word I say until that overdressed poser is gone," Glynna told the stone roses carved into the lintel of the chapel door. "Oh, my. We are going to have trouble. I can just tell."

~~~~~

That evening, Princess Arden was permitted to stay up past her bedtime to attend the dance given in honor of Prince Maddix's visit. This was his first visit to Westerland since the christening. He had been busy since his arrival, impressing the nobles and the members of the king's council with his heavy courses of study over the last seven years, and how much he had traveled to other kingdoms on behalf of his father, whose health, unfortunately, was declining far too quickly. It was a pity, he confided to anyone who expressed concern, that the Gifted healer Ambrose couldn't be in constant attendance in the palace. Of course, Maddix understood completely that his great-uncle had an obligation to share his healing Gift with everyone, but was it really so selfish to want that Gift to be focused on family, first? Especially when that family was the king of Stonemount?

Comyn and King Alfred and several others had already noted how often Prince Maddix seemed to echo his counselor Lord Jaygo's phrasing and intonation, and sometimes even his solemn expressions. Both prince and counselor commented frequently on what a good match Maddix would make for Arden, and how Westerland needed a much stronger bond with its long-time friend and ally. Neither one had said the word "betrothal," yet the impression of many of the nobles in the small ballroom was that both royal families had an unofficial agreement regarding the union.

Tonight wasn't the time to confront Lord Jaygo or meet with the council to clarify the situation, and begin tracking down the rumors to their source. Tonight was a time for enjoyment, relaxing, and socializing. And hopefully wiping those hints of sneers and condescension from the expressions of many Stonemount representatives.
~~~~~

By the second dance of the evening, Arden hadn't made her entrance. Queen Elise confided in Alfred and several of their closest friends that their daughter had insisted on a new arrangement for her hair tonight, to go with her new dress, and thus was running late.

"She's growing up too quickly," Alfred murmured, and shivered with a sense of impending doom. He managed to smile when several of their friends made appropriate remarks of sympathy, and then offered humorous stories of their own trials and tribulations as parents.

~~~~~

Maddix had learned well how to hold up a mask of interest and to pretend to be grandly entertained when he wanted to scream from boredom. He sat with Lord Jaygo on the small dais where Westerland's royal family watched the celebration. He tapped one foot in time with the music and held the same slightly heroic pose that had enchanted Arden that afternoon. He smiled as if nothing in the world was so pleasant as watching the "farmer nobles," as Jaygo sneeringly referred to them, having a simplistic good time. Occasionally, the corner of his smile twitched as he made a disparaging comment under his breath to his adviser. Jaygo, in his habitual black, uttered a short, soft chuckle and add his own fillip to the criticism of Westerland's people.

Late flowers and garlands of greenery and brilliantly colored leaves decked the walls and the tables of refreshments and adorned the cuffs of the musicians who provided lively dancing music. Maddix supposed Westerland used such things because they simply could not afford the silken sashes and banners and semi-precious stones that served as decorations in Stonemount. He enjoyed the cider and spiced ale offered along with the fruity wine, and then told himself it must be because simplicity was so odd and rare to his mature palette. He knew, and Jaygo assured him, he would grow bored with it in a very short while. Maddix promised himself he would be long gone from Westerland before that happened.

The doors opened at the far end of the long, oak-paneled ballroom and though no announcement was made—very bad Court etiquette, Maddix noted—people moved aside, creating an aisle even as they continued dancing. A small figure in blue appeared in the shadows just beyond the doors, hesitating.

"That is undoubtedly your blushing bride-to-be," Jaygo murmured, barely moving his head to indicate the doorway.

Maddix opened his mouth to make a disparaging comment about the bedraggled figure he had so easily enchanted in the palace gardens. At times like this, when he contemplated the long-range plan he and Jaygo had worked out together, something in him raged at the sacrifices
~~~~~

he would have to make. Yes, he could see the necessity of conquest through subtlety, rather than wasting resources on war, but the thought of courting simplistic girls like Arden to win them as brides, the distasteful task of begetting sons on them, and then ensuring those sons were heirs to their grandfathers' thrones nauseated him. How long until he could take and then keep a bride who was worthy of him, rather than encouraging her to die in childbirth? He had only agreed to focus on winning Arden because his father was so dead set against a purely political marriage. So what if his parents had married for love? What good had it done either of them? His father had lost half his wit when his mother died. Maddix vowed he would never let his heart be tangled in a wife. He resented his father for not taking more brides and fathering rivals to the thrones of other countries, to start the grand campaign of unifying the entire continent under Stonemount's rule. Why did all the work have to rest on him?

All those complaints raced through his mind as he watched the tiny figure entering the ballroom. He concentrated on keeping his expression pleasant, when he was sure in another few steps he would see whatever that silly child considered an appropriate dress for tonight's festivities.

Then something caught his attention. That sharp, predatory element in his spirit sat up and took notice. The tiny figure seemed to glide across the floor with uncommon grace. A faint glimmer of gold touched with green hovered around her head like a halo as she passed from the dark doorway into the sweet-scented light of hundreds of candles in the chandeliers.

Tiny Arden seemed to dominate the ballroom. Maddix was barely aware of the many courtiers who stopped and turned to look. Many ladies and lords bowed and curtsied and the child nodded acknowledgement to them with the poise and grace of a grown woman. Her long hair had been pulled it up into hundreds of curls, each held in place with tiny blue and white flowers that made her blue-green eyes seem larger and brighter. Maddix could almost smell the perfume wafting about her in a delicate cloud. Her dress shimmered a dozen shades of pale blue, and a tiny edge of lace petticoat appeared at the bottom where she held up her skirts. She skimmed across the glossy wooden floor, not seeming to hurry yet reaching the bottom of the steps in a heartbeat's time.

Her face glowed with happiness. Her mouth was set in a tiny rosebud of a smile. A delicate blush touched her cheeks as she made a full, deep curtsy to the royal company. She darted a glance at Maddix, all innocent grace and excitement, and looked away.

She dazzled him, just as he had worked to dazzle her that afternoon,

Maddix realized. She had transformed herself into a miniature enchantress — just for him. It was a heady sensation and he lapped it up.

"Well, what a surprise," Jaygo murmured. "Who would think farmers could produce such a rare flower?"

"Indeed," the prince murmured, and swallowed hard.

He bowed to the princess, delighted when her blush deepened. He straightened his coat and stepped down, bowed again and offered her his arm. She was his, he could tell. Whatever he asked, she would do. He ached with a fleeting stab of regret that she would have to be crushed and tossed aside under the spiked wheels of his conquest. Well, at least no one else would enjoy her sweetness.

"My lady, will you honor me with your first dance of the evening?"

They could have been a ridiculous couple, the small seven-year-old dancing with the fifteen-year-old prince in the middle of a growth spurt. His gravely serious gracefulness and her glowing happiness made them an image that caused many old married couples to sigh and smile, remembering the first days of their courtship. Maddix bent in the graceful way the fencing and dancing masters had drilled into him and led the little princess around the room at a slightly slower pace than the rest of the dancers. To his delight, the musicians changed their tempo to match his. In the exhilaration of power, he gladly exerted himself to charm the little girl in his arms.

It would not be so hard, married to Arden someday, he was willing to admit. With the plantwise Gifting she would give to their son before she died, and such a beauty to enjoy for however long she lasted, perhaps this part of his plan wouldn't be quite so onerous as he had feared. And of course, in the end, Westerland would be his.

That was another pleasant aspect of his plan. He hadn't liked Alix when they met seven years ago, and he loathed the farmer prince now. Taking Westerland away from the clod would be a delight. If only he could be sure Alix would know whose hands had brought about his destruction in the end.

~~~~~

By her tenth birthday, Arden could hold a leaf in her hands and blindfolded know what tree it came from. She could taste a leaf or flower or twig and know the health of its plant. She could take seeds or clippings or bits of roots, hold them in her hand for a few seconds and make them sprout. She dreamed of the day she could dig her bare feet into the soil and feel the life and health of plants beyond arm's reach. Someday, she would be able to sense for miles around. Glynna promised if Arden applied herself and worked hard and the need in Westerland was great enough, someday she would feel the health of the land and
~~~~~

plants inside her own country's borders. As it was, Arden couldn't even feel the health of a tree if she planted her bare toes right against the roots and wrapped her arms around the trunk. But someday, she would.

On the morning of her tenth birthday, Arden rose before her nurse and dressed in one of her sturdy, plain dresses, made for roaming and doing all sorts of plantwise work. Barefoot, she slipped down the stairs and out the garden door and scampered across the dewy grass, scattering silver drops and shivering in the chill. She tasted fall in the air, though not a leaf had changed color yet. That much she could do, and her teacher admitted it was a sign of far greater feats and strengths yet to come.

Her family and the palace servants left her alone because this was her special day. If Arden didn't want to eat breakfast or take her lessons, that was her decision. The cook and her staff put out special treats to wait for when the princess did want to eat. There would be a grand feast in the Great Hall at sunset, with all the nobles and their children invited. There would be mummers and minstrels and tumblers. This day, Arden would graduate from faithful old Feathers to a full-size horse.

The day couldn't be more perfect, except for one thing: Maddix couldn't come for her celebration. He had written a long letter explaining all the work he had to do. Ambray was causing trouble for Stonemount, spreading lies. Even worse, Maddix feared Ambray had plans to cause trouble for Westerland. He felt it was his duty to not just protect his own father's kingdom, but look out for the interests of Westerland, and investigate all these ugly stories. After all, Westerland was Stonemount's most loyal ally. Even more important to him, Westerland was her home and it meant everything in the world to him to keep her safe and happy. She did understand, didn't she, that royalty had a great burden to carry? She did understand, didn't she, that royalty always had to serve the good of their people, and make daily sacrifices? He promised her that when he was free of straightening out Ambray, he would come to Westerland with her birthing day present and deliver it himself, and they would have an entire day together. She could show him all her favorite places in the countryside. He quite looked forward to it, and seeing for himself all the brooks and fields and other places in the countryside that were precious to her. Because of course, everything she loved, he knew he would love too.

Arden had put the letter under her pillow five nights in a row after she received it. When she woke up one morning and found it on the floor, she feared it would be damaged if she kept it there. She put it in the stained-glass box Maddix had sent her for her eighth birthday. She kept all his letters there. Auntie Glynna sniffed like she always did when

Arden received the letter and skipped around her room in delight. And like always reminded her that fine words were just that, words, and actions were far more valuable and real.

Today, though, she didn't want to think about such things, because today was her day, for fun and freedom. She refused to mope. She especially refused to think about Maddix spending time with that fluttery, whispery little Princess Bianca of Ambray. She was all pale feathers and spun sugar, and Arden was dismayed by how her brother went starry-eyed and blushed and lost his words whenever Bianca was in the room. If Alix could be an idiot over Bianca, then no young man had a chance of holding onto his common sense. Including Maddix.

"Stop it," she scolded herself, and raced out into the countryside. She had her new horse, a lovely little roan mare, to put through her paces. She could visit all her favorite places so much more quickly now, racing the wind on her mare's long legs. This was a day for fun and freedom!

~~~~~

Mid-afternoon, Alix and Derrien caught up with Arden in the palace gardens. She had thoroughly enjoyed her morning, delighted to the point of being flustered by all the townspeople who made a point of looking for her, to offer her a treat and good wishes for her birthday. She had ribbons for her hair and lace to trim her petticoats, seeds saved from trees and flowers that had been in family lines for decades, sweets and small meat pies and fruit pies, pots of colored ink and journals, and several satchels for her ramblings, to store cuttings and roots and seeds. All sorts of treasures that filled her heart to bursting over this proof of how much the people of her father's kingdom loved her. Now, she was tired, and needed to be alone, to think. And to try a few dance steps, practicing for that evening. Her new dancing slippers were light and soft on her feet and the color of ivy drenched in morning dew. Still, she preferred being barefoot.

The two young men paused in the gate from the palace into the gardens and watched her slowly spinning and turning and curtseying.

At seventeen, Alix was as tall as King Alfred, just as wide of shoulder, and weathered with long days spent outdoors. He had the grace of a dancing or fencing master, though he only danced when Court etiquette required and only practiced swordplay because it was necessary. He had great skill with all sorts of weaponry, but no love for it. His first love was for the land, like his father and grandfather. He believed as they did, that the best way to know the people he would someday rule was to know how they earned their living. He could plow and sow and reap with the best of Westerland and his people loved him
~~~~~

for it. He earned their admiration and awe by his skill with horses. Riding, whether races or trick riding, was the kind of dancing he loved.

Derrien, son and heir of the Captain of the Guards, stood a head taller than his best friend. Crowned with a short-cropped thatch of red-gold hair, tanned dark and weathered by storm and sun, he took seriously his future duty to defend Westerland. Though they had known no need for the army since Alfred's youth, he believed as his father did that the need would come when their country was least prepared. To ward off danger, Westerland needed to be prepared. His storm-gray eyes sparkled as he watched Arden daintily dancing her way across the garden, her steps so light she barely left a mark in the grass.

"Arden!" Alix called after only a few moments of watching. The princess flinched but otherwise showed no sign she had heard. She bent, one dirty damp foot lifting into the air, and plucked a rose petal from the ground.

Glynna faded into view just to the girl's right. She smiled even as she shook her head and tsked a few times. "Your brother is calling, dear."

"I know ... " Arden sighed and glanced over her shoulder.

"He knows how much you love being out here. He wouldn't call you unless it were important. Go on."

Glynna scooted over closer, pushing out her hands as if she would give the girl a shove. It was an impossible effort and looked slightly ridiculous, bobbing ever so gently in the air, knee height above the ground, with rose bush limbs and leaves sprouting through her gown. Arden chuckled, conceding defeat with good grace, and turned to cross the garden. If anyone were to call her in from her play, she preferred that it be Alix or Derrien.

"And put your shoes back on," the woman called. "You're a princess — at least, when you're indoors."

"Auntie Glynna!" Arden was very happy that only she could hear and see Glynna. She hated it when she was reminded to act her station. It was such a bore.

"Auntie Glynna told you to put your shoes on, didn't she?" Alix said, chuckling as she joined them in the gates. "I wish I could see and hear her, little sister. Could you tell her something for me?"

"She can see and hear you, even if you can't see or hear her." She wisely refrained from remarking that she had reminded him of such things dozens of times.

"Forgive us, Auntie Glynna, wherever you are," Derrien said, bowing in the general direction of where Arden had been moments before. "If there is anything I can do to assist you, please let me know."

"Oh, I like him more every time I see him. Where was he when I was young enough for courting?" Glynna chirped as she flew over to join the three.

"Auntie Glynna!" Arden was very sure Derrien would be embarrassed by that particular remark, and she found herself angry for his sake. She liked him and was very glad he was her brother's best friend. He had trained her roan mare for her, so she could ride bareback if she wanted, in perfect safety. Arden was quite sure that was their special secret.

One thing she especially liked about him was that Bianca didn't fluster him. He also didn't let Fiera of Brentonwald make him stammer when she was snappish or sulky.

Arden didn't tell anyone, not even Glynna, but her idea for a perfect life would be to stay in Westerland all her life, roaming with Derrien from sunrise to sunset on matching roan horses, tending to the farms and orchards of the kingdom.

"I don't know what is worse," Derrien remarked as he offered an arm to Arden, "not being able to see her or not being able to hear her."

"I have this feeling we don't want to know what she said," Alix remarked under his breath, and glanced back over his shoulder, as if Glynna would suddenly become visible.

"You two are horrid!" Arden tugged her hand free and stomped her little feet.

"She's always with you, isn't she?"

"No ... not all the time." A shiver traveled up her back that drove away her pique. Arden let both young men take her by the hand. They turned to go into the palace. "When she's not with me, she goes somewhere she won't tell me about," she admitted, her voice softening.

Arden had heard some of the more fantastic tales of what happened to someone who had Gifted their magic to another. Glynna had told her most of them, just to show rumors and folk tales were not always reliable or even sensible sources of information.

"I tried to explain to you, dear, but it's beyond your understanding." Glynna sighed and swooped around so she floated ahead of them, flying backward, and managing to dodge around obstructions without really looking. Arden envied her that ability, until she thought about what it must be like to have no body and only one little girl who could hear and see her. She rather thought Glynna was lonely.

CHAPTER FOUR

"Why do I have to come inside?" Arden said with a sigh, simply to change the subject.

"There's a letter for you -- from Stonemount," her brother added, before she could open her mouth to ask.

"I already got my birthday letter from Maddix. Who could it be from?"

"Prince Ambrose, the greatest healer in the entire world."

"Why would he write to me?"

"Come inside, silly goose and find out!" He tousled her hair with his free hand and refused to release her when Arden tried to tug free. She laughed with them when Alix and Derrien broke into a run.

~~~~

Twenty minutes later, her hair brushed and braided and shoes on her feet, Arden stepped into her father's study. King Alfred and Queen Elise waited at the head of the long council table, Comyn standing just in front of the king, to his left.

A tall young man with tousled, curly dark hair and gray eyes, dressed in sturdy traveling clothes, stood on the queen's right. He held a packet sealed with green wax, which had to be the letter from Ambrose. Arden wondered only for a moment why he wasn't wearing the green and black livery of Stonemount. Shouldn't a courier from the royal family be in livery?

She forgot that question when the young man's eyes widened and he looked past her. Right at the place where Glynna hovered. He could see her. That meant he had magic.

As if in confirmation of that thought, several silver sparks hovered around his head for a few heartbeats. Silver magic was healing magic. That made sense now. He was another healer like Ambrose, so he had brought the letter instead of sending it by courier.

All three adults smiled as Arden curtseyed very prettily.

"Arden," her mother said, gesturing at the young healer, "this is Dylon, grandson to Healer Ambrose."

"Oh, my, how he's grown. He looks so much like his grandmother, rather than Ambrose," Glynna said.

Dylon grinned and gave a head-bow to Glynna, and Arden's heart sputtered a few beats in excitement. He could hear her, as well as see her. She had yet to meet anyone who could see and hear her beloved
~~~~

teacher. This was quite the best present for her birthday. She couldn't wait to talk to him. And have Glynna talk to him.

"I bring you wishes for a blessed and joyous tenth birthday, Princess Arden, from the royal family of Stonemount." Dylon bowed in a full courtly bow so his shaggy curls flopped forward into his eyes, prompting a giggle from her. He winked as he straightened up. "And especially from my grandfather. He had so hoped to be here, to see you." His gaze slid to Glynna. "Unfortunately, an accident has kept him bound, indefinitely, to the palace. King Doyne is relieved to have him close at hand, where he can be protected –"

"Protected?" Glynna blurted. "That's ominous. What healer needs protection?"

" –and tended to, while he heals," Dylon finished, after a brief pause. He bent again and picked up a sturdy leather travel sack from the floor. He withdrew a journal bound in bright green leather with silver lacing, and a clear bottle of green ink, and two silver pens. "My grandfather knows how Auntie Glynna teaches, and he sent these to help in your continuing lessons and observations." He held them out to her.

"Oh, they're wonderful." Arden stepped forward to take the gifts. "Please, give him my thanks and my prayers for a speedy and full recovery. I know Auntie Glynna would be so pleased to see him again. Perhaps we could make a journey to Stonemount, to visit Healer Ambrose, Father?"

"That wouldn't be wise," Dylon hurried to say, as King Alfred smiled and nodded. "If the roads between kingdoms aren't safe for a revered healer, who should be sacrosanct, can they be safe for a princess who could be kidnapped, perhaps taking all the farming wealth of Westerland in ransom?"

From the frowns the king and Comyn exchanged, Arden had the clear impression they weren't aware of such danger. Then again, Ambrose's injury was news for them.

"My grandfather fully intends to come visit you as soon as he is well," he continued, and held out the sealed parchment packet. "I will leave you to read in private."

"You will stay and enjoy the festivities this evening, won't you?" Queen Elise asked, as Dylan bowed and turned to head to the door.

"Thank you, Highness. That is very kind." His gaze locked with Arden's, and she flushed as she realized that her answer was important to him.

"Yes, please. Do you like to dance?" She nearly giggled when Dylon flushed and he gave a tiny shrug.

"I don't get many chances, but yes, I do." He grinned. "I'm not sure how good I am."

"Then I will save a dance for you." She nearly crumpled the letter packet when his grin widened and he bowed again before hurrying out of the room.

"You've quite made a conquest," Alfred murmured, once the door clicked closed behind Dylon.

"Papa!" Arden's voice squeaked.

"You couldn't do better than to choose Dylon as your partner for the rest of your life," Glynna said. "And not just for the benefits of pairing plantwise magic with healing magic. He has his grandfather's kind heart and generous spirit." She chuckled. "Granted, I quite favor young Derrien for you ..."

Arden pulled a chair out and sat down quickly, praying her face wasn't as bright red with blush heat as it felt to her right that moment.

"Do you want to see Ambrose's letter, or don't you?" she whispered.

"Do you want to be alone, dear?" her mother asked.

"No. Let me read it once myself, then I'll share it with you."

After all, this wasn't like the letters that Maddix sent to her, sometimes as many as two in a month. Three out of four letters came by private courier, delivered by stealth into the hands of a serving maid who hid the letters under Arden's pillow. She took the letters Arden wrote in response and left under her pillow. The courier waited two days for Arden's answer each time. At first, she hadn't liked keeping those letters secret from her family, but Maddix had said in his first letter how much he hated having his entire life lived out on a public stage. He wanted something sweet and private and precious, safe from the ugly, interfering gaze and judgment of the world. He wanted to protect her and enjoy their courtship in utter safety and purity.

The word *courtship* had quite taken her breath away. She had nearly made the mistake of asking Glynna what it meant. The only dark spot on the lovely secret of Maddix's letters was that visions of spending the rest of her life with him clashed with her daydreams of riding and exploring and adventuring with Derrien. Yet as Maddix had told her, she was a princess and her royal blood demanded duty of her. She didn't have the right to marry for any reason except the good of her kingdom. Besides, he reminded her at least every third letter that both their fathers wanted them to marry, to strengthen their kingdoms' alliance.

Arden was sure that just like the official letters Maddix sent through proper channels, this letter from Ambrose wouldn't be anything she would need to keep deliciously secret from her family. Why would a man as important as Ambrose, one of the most powerful magical healers in the world, have anything to say to her that couldn't be public record? She felt quite grown up, receiving what was most likely a royal birthday greeting.

She settled back comfortably in the chair and carefully cracked the green wax seals on the packet, so they didn't break off and fall to the floor.

"Oh, my—Ambrose, after all these years," Glynna sighed. She positioned herself just above the corner of the table, to look over Arden's shoulder.

> *My dear Princess Arden:*
>
> *Felicitations on your tenth birthday. That's fancy royal talk to say I hope you have a wonderful birthday party. I've waited ten years to write to you, and I hope you and I will become good friends. I was friends with Glynna, and I was there the day she Gifted you. It would please me very much if we could be friends as well. I hope that as you grow, I may be of help in your training. My intentions were to come for your birthday, to meet you and give you the journal Dylon has delivered to you. However, highway brigands had other plans for me. I do not want any shadows to darken this joyous day. Think of me as you enjoy your celebration and ask Glynna to tell you stories of our youth together. She will make you laugh, and I will laugh as I remember as well. I hope to come visit you next year on your birthday, and every year after that. There is so very much I wish to teach you, to help you in your duties to your father's kingdom, and in the service of Yeshen.*
>
> *Pray for my recovery. It is a sad truth that healers are the worst patients. And even more sad truth that our magic makes us resistant to the healing magic of other healers. I see a long recovery ahead of me. Please, write back to me, and make an old man very happy.*
>
> *If it isn't too much trouble, could you include a message from Glynna when you write?*

Glynna leaned forward, resting her hands on Arden's shoulders and sinking into them slightly. She sniffed and smiled and blinked away nostalgic tears.

"He always was a thoughtful dear," she murmured.

"He knows you're with me, Auntie?" Arden whispered.

"Of course he knows, dearheart. That's what it means to be Gifted. The spirit of the one who gave you her magic stays with you, for always."

"Then when he Gifts someone with his magic—" The idea made

Arden shiver. She had never really considered the import of Glynna's presence and the sacrifice that went into her Gifting.

"Ambrose will be with him forever."

"Dylon?"

"That makes the most sense." Glynna frowned faintly. "We really do need to talk to that boy and find out what exactly happened. Highway brigands? They would have to be insane and desperate to attack a healer. The curse that rebounds on anyone who does a healer harm ... it is beyond imagining."

~~~~~

"Grandfather believes they were sent by Durmad," Dylon said, when Arden and Glynna met privately with him that evening, before the festivities started. They had seen him walking through the gardens and hurried from Arden's room to intercept him. "There was warning. An old seer Grandfather visited several times a year warned him that black clouds were following him, and he should take a different route home. We tried, but then a boy came from the next village, begging us to come, there had been a dreadful accident at the mill. The brigands attacked us in a valley just outside the village, rolling huge boulders down on us, separating us. Grandfather broke a leg and several ribs, and he was bleeding badly enough, he lost consciousness. When help came ..." He shuddered and his eyes were shadowed while his face went pale.

"You've never seen the vengeance meted out on those who violate the laws of magic and charity, have you?" Glynna asked. She rested a hand on his shoulder, lightly enough it didn't go through him.

"Grandfather told me such things have happened." Dylon shook his head and his throat worked, as if he fought sickness. "Birds dove down from the sky and from the trees, and the trees themselves twisted and lashed out at the men, and I thought for a moment they would uproot themselves and come running. And there was a bear —" He caught his breath. "Those men didn't seem to notice as the bear ripped into them and the animals overpowered them and they were beaten unconscious. And they died. They shouldn't have died. There was more magic at work, killing them, to keep them from betraying who sent them. And when we asked at the village, no one sent for us. The boy wasn't one of theirs."

"What is this world coming to, when healers are attacked with impunity?" Glynna's light dimmed and she floated away from Arden and Dylon a few steps. "What kind of a fool is Durmad, that he thought his magic was strong enough to overpower Yeshen's laws, and his tools wouldn't suffer?"

"He doesn't care about his tools. Grandfather is convinced the
~~~~~

attack was to kill him, perhaps us both, not to capture and enslave us."

"Perhaps ..." Arden shuddered and the grass under her feet waved as if a breeze blew hard against it. "Auntie, what if that was the goal, to kill Prince Ambrose? What if there was someone waiting to take his Gifting before he died? Can someone steal a Gifting, if the holder is so badly injured they're about to die, and ... I don't know ... they're tricked into giving the Gifting to the wrong person?"

"I've never heard of such a thing, but that sounds like something Durmad is nasty enough, desperate enough, arrogant enough, to attempt." Sparks snapped around her and she shuddered. "What is this world coming to?" She reached out to Dylon again. "Tell Ambrose to be doubly careful. Not just of himself, but you. After all, you are his obvious heir, and whoever wants to claim his Gifting when he is gone has to get you out of the way. If not kill you outright, then at the very least separate the two of you long enough to finish their plan."

"I will never leave his side," the young man promised.

~~~~~

King Doyne and Prince Maddix agreed with Glynna's reading of the situation and insisted that Ambrose no longer travel outside the borders of Stonemount. As Ambrose wrote to Arden, he chafed against the restrictions, but he understood his nephew's and great-nephew's concern. His worry for Dylon's safety was stronger than his fear for his own. Besides, he had evidence of some inimical magic at work behind the attack, because his convalescence dragged on far longer than it should have. The Court healer at the palace of Stonemount examined him and couldn't give him any clear answers, other than yes, he sensed some magic at work, like a pinprick leak in Ambrose's energy, a constant slow drain. When he was finally up on his feet again, he was hobbled by a severe limp, and his bones protested damp and cold weather.

Maddix begged for Arden's help in persuading his great-uncle to stay home and protect himself, and not risk one of Stonemount's greatest treasures in foreign lands. After all, hadn't Yeshen distributed magical Gifts throughout the entire continent? Shouldn't the other kingdoms be happy with the healers and other magical Gifts born to them, rather than expecting elderly men like Ambrose to risk their lives to travel to them?

Arden thought there was some sense to Maddix's reasoning, but Glynna just sniffed and commented that he most certainly didn't know Ambrose very well, if he thought the man would be content to limit his Gift to one kingdom.

"Magic and Gifts that are hoarded start to rot and go bad. Eventually they turn to poison that spreads to the entire kingdom, and then to the rest of the world, if they aren't shared. Gifts need to roam
~~~~~

freely, not sit in a treasure box, locked up in fear. The more they are shared, the stronger they grow, and the more benefit they do everyone," she had said. And repeated herself over the next several years, every time Maddix's letters returned to the subject.

Arden didn't like Glynna's criticism of Maddix. Wasn't he justified in wanting to protect his great-uncle? Wasn't family the greatest treasure of all?

She took to sneaking away to read Maddix's letters as soon as they came, and carefully choosing which ones she would share with Glynna. Making the decision wasn't hard, because Maddix had asked her from the very beginning to keep their correspondence secret. She had never told Glynna that her parents didn't know about most of the letters from Maddix, and now that her mentor grew more critical of him, she wasn't about to confess that little secret.

On Arden's fifteenth birthday, she was very glad she had developed that tactic, because Maddix announced that he was tired of waiting, of being discreet.

> *I adore you, my darling Arden. I live in torment at the exigencies of my duties, and the dangers that lurk along the highways between our kingdoms, which conspire to keep me from visiting you.*
>
> *I love you, with a devotion and passion that can no longer be denied. If I thought it was safe, I would beg you to run away with me, to be married, and if we must, live in hiding until your eighteenth birthday, when we can freely declare our love in the daylight. When no one can separate us.*
>
> *Promise me you will wait for me, though the years between now and that day of our union will feel like decades, and my heart will ache. Can you give me some assurance that you feel even a fraction of the delicious agony that drowns me? Show some mercy on my aching heart, and send me a token of affection, some hope that someday, you will feel the overwhelming passion that gives me the strength to endure in hope?*

Arden had a difficult time paying attention to her guests and thanking everyone who presented her with gifts at her birthday ball that night. Maddix's words made her feel dizzy and hot and a little frightened. But yes, she had to admit, adopting his phrasing, it was a delicious kind of fright. She knew Maddix considered their friendship something special and precious that needed to be guarded. He wanted something private, something he didn't have to share with the rest of the world. It was the burden and the duty of royal blood to have so very little that wasn't shared with their people, the kingdom, the world, and he didn't care who condemned him, he wouldn't share her and their precious friendship with anyone.

She simply hadn't expected that special friendship to turn to the passion that Maddix had confessed.

Her gaze strayed quite often that night to Derrien. She compared his sweet, sometimes adorably stumbling words to the eloquence and passion in Maddix's letters. He carved cunning figures of wood and ivory as gifts for her and brought her seeds and cuttings from plants she had never seen before, while Maddix sent her official gifts of lace and fine fabrics and delicacies. In the last year, her daydreams of a life of riding and laughing and exploring with Derrien had been tinged with guilt, and the awful sense that she might just be selfish. Maddix had been teaching her quite a lot about the duty royal blood had to their kingdoms. While she would love to stay here in Westerland and continue her plantwise duties in the fields and forests and meadows she had grown up loving, she did have a duty as a princess to strengthen the bonds of friendship with an ally kingdom. Marrying Maddix would accomplish that and please their fathers. Maybe ... this sudden confession of deep feelings from Maddix was a gift from Yeshen, a reward for doing their duty?

What was the right choice?

She regretted keeping Maddix's letters secret all these years. She certainly couldn't go to her mother for advice, nor to Glynna. The only other person she felt she could confide in, who seemed to understand her better than anyone was the last person she wanted to share this conundrum. Derrien. The last thing she wanted to do was hurt him.

Arden gnawed on the problem for days before common sense intervened. She was only fifteen, after all. She would be an idiot to even consider running away with anyone, no matter how romantic and exciting that might be. There was too much to do, too much to learn, before she was old enough to even consider marriage. In three years, who knew how the world would change? At the very least, she wanted to see Maddix face-to-face a few times before committing herself to running away with him. Romantic, secret letters were all well and good, and very exciting, but she would have to live with the man if she did marry him.

CHAPTER FIVE

"Arden is turning into a problem," Maddix said, and flung her crumpled letter into the overflowing basket next to his desk for punctuation.

"Not if you follow the plan." Jaygo turned away from the window that looked out over the palace gardens. "You're not getting squeamish, are you?"

"About what? Squeezing the dirty little farmer princess dry and tossing her aside when she's served her purpose? Nauseated at pretending to be stupidly in love, yes. Squeamish, no." He scowled down at the miniature portraits neatly arrayed on the far side of his massive desk, twice as large as his father's. Five pretty, feminine faces looked back at him. Contemplating all the work it would take to woo and seduce, marry and impregnate each of those targeted princesses exhausted him. And what were the chances he could ensure none of them would marry someone else before he could rid himself of the previous distasteful breeding stock and move on to her? How many husbands would he have to kill and widows would he have to console, before he had solidified his claim to most of the thrones on this continent?

Yes, exhausted.

"She's broken her promise to me, I just know it." Maddix gestured down at the letter he had tossed away. Jaygo had read it first, as always. Jaygo wrote his love letters to Arden, which he then had to copy over in his own handwriting before sending to her. They had no secrets.

A tiny smirk bent up one corner of his mouth, accented by a sharp, hot prick of anger. They had no secrets, although Jaygo didn't know that. Durmad had made contact less than two months ago, revealing to Maddix that he was the mastermind behind Jaygo's plans of conquest, the years of advice and guidance he had lavished on the heir to Stonemount's throne. Durmad had expressed some disappointment in Jaygo's slower pace. He blamed the many years of service Jaygo had given him. Thanks to Durmad's magic, Jaygo was nearly two hundred years old, but barely looked past forty. Maddix could look forward to twice as long a life, in Durmad's service. And all the power and wealth he could ever desire, as emperor, head of a dynasty that controlled all the land south of the Cascade Mountains.

After fury and a sense of drowning at learning that Jaygo had been manipulating him, rather than helping him, that his vows of loyalty and dedication were somewhat false, Maddix had felt relief. From the nagging sense of guilt every time he resented Jaygo's lectures and reminders about their plan. From knowing he would be justified someday, when he tossed Jaygo aside like another no-longer-useful tool. Or the too-mature letter from Arden. If Durmad was disappointed in Jaygo's performance of late, then that meant Maddix was justified in his disappointment as well.

"No, far from it." Jaygo chuckled.

Maddix wanted to slap that fond little smile off his advisor's face, maybe choke that amusement out of his throat as well.

"These farmer nobles mature a little faster than the pretty bits of decorative royal fluff in bigger kingdoms like Ambray. And they hold far tighter to a sense of honor than anyone with good sense would do. If she promised never to tell anyone about your correspondence, you can be sure she will go to her deathbed without telling. No, she's showing some good sense, that's all, in wanting to finish her education. That gives you more time to wrap her silly, simple little heart more securely in your net. And yes, you would be wise to delight her with visits. Dazzle her with your manners and eloquence and good looks. Get close enough to find out if you have any rivals."

"Rivals? Who or what is there in that kingdom, or the surrounding kingdoms, to steal her heart from me?"

"The fact that those young men are there, at hand, while you are far away, should give you some concern. Simple-minded folk like her will always value what's at hand over a far-off promise. Stop being a mere promise of delight, Maddix. Give her a taste of the reality."

"Reality." He snorted and clenched his fist against the urge to swipe Arden's tiny portrait off his desk. Right next to her was Bianca of Ambray. After her was Sylva of Sunderfield. Each a bride destined to fall victim to his charms and give him a son to someday inherit his grandfather's throne. After all other claimants were eliminated.

Maddix understood the order of attack, though he chafed. Arden had only one brother to eliminate, Alix. Bianca had three. Sylva had an older brother and sister, both of whom had a child each.

Assassins were already getting into position, carefully, slowly, learning the surrounding countryside and the habits of the people surrounding their targets. The barriers to kingship couldn't all be eliminated in one sweeping attack, though Maddix would have preferred it. Just like he would have preferred some of those obnoxious, too-noble-for-their-own-good princes to know why they had to die. Everything had to be done delicately, discretely, so no one would ever suspect the grand plan even after everything came together many years in the future.

Far too many years in the future.

He had to wait three years, apparently, before he could finish seducing Arden. Bianca would be eighteen next year. Why couldn't he dazzle her, first? It wouldn't be so hard to convince stupid, gullible little Arden that it had been a political marriage. Maddix thought it would be rather clever of him, to come to her with a broken heart and play on her sympathy. Silly farmer girls adored babies, didn't they? If she was reluctant, if she was stupid enough to feel a little betrayed by his marrying Bianca first, he could always trap her with his desperate need for a mother for his orphaned son.

Maddix pretended to accept Jaygo's advice, and nearly shrieked his impatience when the ridiculous, overbearing old traitor stayed in his office, talking, for another half hour. When the man finally left, he sat down and plotted out his new plan, to trap Bianca first. A chill finger raced down his back as it occurred to him that it would be wise to clear this plan with Durmad, first. Just because Jaygo had become a disappointment didn't mean he was entirely a fool and incompetent.

~~~~~

Arden's fifteenth birthday had been like a silent signal to other kingdoms with sons looking for brides. Two days before Maddix arrived on a surprise visit, Prince Brandon of Ambray came on a long diplomatic mission. He made it clear that he wasn't there entirely to discuss trade agreements and problems with brigands on the shared border with Westerland. He was a wonderful dancer and didn't even blink the first time he saw Arden riding astride, in trousers, rather than side-saddle. Prince Tomas of Zashenbourg had choked and stumbled when he saw her riding, but he had a lovely baritone voice and could compose funny rhymes at a moment's notice. Both princes made it clear they extended their stays to inconvenience each other, and Maddix. Arden was slightly ashamed to realize she liked how Maddix glared at the other two princes, and she felt a funny sense of gleeful pride when he lost his elegant manners and snarled at them.

He managed to meet up with her for a few moments of privacy in the gardens at dusk. Just long enough for one startling stolen kiss before her closest companion and lady's maid, Caitlyn, caught up with them. That was all they had, but it was enough to dream on for months afterward.

That sudden influx of suitors slapped Arden hard with a realization she hadn't fully considered, except as something far off and slightly unreal: when she married, she would have to leave Westerland. The
~~~~~

more she thought about leaving the fields and forests, the farms and villages she loved, the little ache deepened in her soul. How could she be happy in her new home if she had abandoned her first duty, her first love? The thought of Westerland having no one to guard the grasses and wild flowers and encourage the grain to grow tall and sweet saddened her. As the winter snows deepened, she confided her trepidation to Glynna. If only there were some way she could leave part of herself in the land of her birth.

They talked long into the stormy winter nights. That spring, Arden traveled everywhere across Westerland, and when it was safe, crossed the borders to the farming and woodland communities of neighboring kingdoms, seeking the old stories and half-forgotten and only rumored bits of the most ancient magic. She visited huts and cottages where the hedgelores were kept by word of mouth and herb mistresses stored their memories in tiny living trees. She spent days digging through ancient libraries full of dusty scrolls and newly printed books, looking for stories and theories. Glynna had never encountered another green magic-wielder during her decades traveling the continent, and Arden didn't dare cross the sea to another continent to seek out another plantwise with more knowledge and experience than Glynna. Until Yeshen heard their prayers and sent the Steward to talk with them, they could only work based on speculations.

Spring turned to summer and Arden was busy with her usual duties during the growing season. She sometimes wept in gratitude that she wasn't so distracted with her new quest that she shorted Westerland. The harvest was doubly bountiful that year, and all her travels served to spread the blessing of her magic, even into neighboring kingdoms. Glynna just chuckled when they received news of that and reminded Arden that magic and Giftings needed to be shared, and grew more powerful with the sharing.

Still, despite the bounty she had brought to Westerland, Arden was relieved to settle down after the harvest. She talked to herb wives and lore masters and ancient grannies and gaffers sitting at the fires as winter howled around them and tried to reach down the chimneys.

When spring came again, so did the Steward.

Arden sensed the thrumming of what she could only describe as joy, pulsing through the ground, spreading outward from the massive old oak where he sat. A new perfume filled the air, constantly changing, never lingering long enough for her to describe it. With Glynna close beside her, she followed that thrumming, that perfume, through fields bursting with emerald life, to her favorite stream, and the oak where she liked to sit on a wide branch and daydream and let the trees and fields and flowers sing to her.

She stepped around the oak and saw the man. For two heartbeats she was startled, but then she knew who he was. Outwardly, he was just a thin young man with a thick cap of nut-brown hair, skin a shade lighter, green eyes, a thin dusting of beard, and slightly dusty traveling clothes of roughspun and leather. His smile wiped away her momentary trepidation and made her feel breathless as she went to her knees next to him.

"Don't leave Westerland, dearheart," he murmured.

"I don't want to, but if my father ..." She flushed hot and couldn't meet his smiling eyes. "Am I being silly?"

"It's never silly to love, to join your soul in delight and abandon to another soul." He winked. "I've only recently been blessed with that gift, and it takes my breath away whenever I think of her. I'm constantly wondering how I could be so lucky that she loves me." He laughed, and Arden laughed with him.

"Her duties could send her away, though," Glynna said. She neatly folded her legs and floated down until she sat facing them, so they made a little triangle. "Those of us with great Giftings have greater obligations to sacrifice."

"Yes, and you show great wisdom and devotion in wanting to prepare against that day, Princess of Westerland. What I am about to show you is within your skills and strength. But be warned: the stronger the magic and the more powerful the blessing, the greater the danger of it turning to poison and curse. Your heart will be too tightly tied into this gift for your kingdom, and the heart can destroy when it is broken." He tapped two fingers to his breastbone, then gestured at Arden's chest. "You must be strong. You must be pure. And you must fight against bitterness, no matter how tempting."

What he told them to do surprised Arden with the simplicity. Glynna laughed, when she confessed that surprise to her on their long walk home to the palace.

"The most effective and useful magic is often the simplest," her teacher agreed.

The plan, however, could not be implemented now. Arden needed time to gather up the energy this task would require, a little at a time. She needed to weave together the life and beauty and purity of Westerland all through the growing season and the harvest.

Maddix visited three times, and each time he managed to steal a minute here, a minute there, to dazzle Arden with kisses and words of passion and poetry that often brought her to tears. A year ago, she would have gladly fled Westerland with him, to marry in secret and toss aside her duty to her family kingdom. Now, though, with the magic task awaiting her after the harvest, Arden refused to leave. She shivered when Maddix stormed at her and accused her of being a flirt and a minx and playing games with his heart. She finally confided her courtship heartaches to Caitlyn, and her friend told her she should feel flattered that a man was desperately in love with her to the point of fury.

Arden wasn't so sure. Especially when she caught Derrien giving her those sad, longing, hungry looks. He had drifted away once the princes started their courtships and envoys came to investigate the possibility of a diplomatic marriage. He was still there, still her brother's best friend, still her willing companion when she had to travel long distances to help farmers having difficulties with their crops. But the warmth and cozy sense of safety had fled.

Why did she have to be royalty, with so many obligations weighing on her? Would Maddix have ever noticed her if she wasn't the princess of Westerland? Sometimes she resented the task waiting for her after the harvest finished, because preparing her kingdom for the day she had to leave it somehow made that day seem close at hand, and dreadful.

Worse yet, Arden feared she wasn't ready for the massive release of all the energy and life she had been storing up since spring. What if she failed? What if her conflicting feelings and the twisting in her heart somehow blocked that release of magic? She was sixteen now. The pressure to marry would increase at her seventeenth birthday, and grow to the bursting point on her eighteenth.

"Trust in Yeshen," Glynna said, when Arden tried, with stumbling words, to explain all the questions and fears bursting to escape her. "Focus on the task in front of you and trust in Yeshen, put yourself in the Maker's hands ..." She chuckled. "And if all else fails, convince yourself you simply don't give two figs for all that ridiculousness waiting to pounce on you. You are plantwise, and guiding and guarding life is your purpose and your joy. Rest in that."

"Don't give two figs," Arden whispered, and somehow she was able to laugh. "You mean be a child again, don't you? Isn't that what you've been telling me for years? To dive into the magic and live in the now, focus on what I can do, and let Yeshen take care of tomorrow?"

"Of course. And don't sigh and roll your eyes and mutter how you know all that. Knowing and application are two distinctly different things, and as far apart as the east is from the west."

"Don't I know it." Another chuckle escaped her. "Yeshen, help me to let go?"

The first chill of fall crept across the land, bringing whispers of the sleep to come. The day finally came. Somehow, Arden had changed inside, and she looked forward to this day instead of dreading it, and all the changes it signaled. After all, what if she failed?

No, don't think about failing. I have to do this. For Westerland. For my family. For Yeshen.

With no more claims on her Gifting, Arden's magical strength increased, flowing through her in giddy waves. In previous falls, she had regularly poured the overflow of magic into bags of seeds, which were given as gifts at Winter Solstice, in anticipation of the spring planting.

Not this year. She waited, restraining the energy trying to spill out of her, until she felt as if her skin tingle-itched all over her body. Then Arden got to work, pouring everything she had, everything she had learned from Glynna, into an apple seed.

For six days she concentrated on the seed clenched warm and tight in her moist palm, pouring her energy, her love for Westerland, her magic into the tiny brown nugget of life. It struggled against her clasp, but she refused to let it burst into life. Not yet.

On the seventh day, she rose before the sun and went to her workroom. She filled a pot with moist, rich soil, filtering it through her hands so green-gold sparks of magic dusted into the pot. Then, as the sun rose, with Glynna hovering over her shoulder, Arden retrieved the seed from the protective little fold of cloth tucked under her pillow. She unwrapped it and held it between her palms, breathing on the seed and concentrating all her love and hopes and dreams for Westerland into the bit of brown hardness one-third the size of her pinkie nail.

Opening her palm so the light from the rising sun could hit the seed, Arden closed her eyes and begged Yeshen's blessing. Then smiled and whispered, "Now," to the seed and to herself. She let go all the tight bonds that held the seed closed despite the surging energy of magic and life that strained it to the bursting point.

Green-gold sparks of magic washed over her body, stirring her unbound hair that hung to her knees. It flipped up the lacy edge of her nightshirt and curled a cool breeze around her bare toes.

The seed jumped, nearly leaping from her palm. As it tumbled back down to its safe resting place, five thread-like green shoots burst out from all sides. Arden's eyes snapped open and she stared at the growing shoots in amazed delight. The pale green tendrils of life darkened and thickened and doubled in length with every other heartbeat.

"Quickly, child," Glynna whispered.

Laughing, Arden turned to stick her tongue out at the woman, then nearly stumbled over her own feet as she darted across her workroom to the long table full of pots and baskets of soil and watering pails, sticks and trowels and herbs. She caught up a handful of rich black soil from the pot she had prepared and gently tipped her other hand to let the growing shoots fall in. Hands trembling, she sprinkled the soil over the writhing, growing, bursting seed.

Before she had finished and reached for the watering pail, four shoots had merged into one long strand nearly a foot tall, straight up, before it suddenly shot out a dozen leaves. None of them was larger than the tip of Arden's thumb, and so pale green they were almost white. As she slowly sprinkled water into the soil, the leaves tripled in size and turned a healthy, vibrant green, deeper than emeralds.

"Well, Auntie?" she breathed, as the little sapling put out three branches, nearly scraping the tip of her nose before she could step backward.

Wrapping her arms around herself, ignoring her wet and dirty hands, she pirouetted around the room until she sprawled on the padded bench against the wall opposite the table. She giggled and reveled in the oddly dizzy, hollow feeling that pulsed through her. At the back of her mind, she was softly aware of the still-growing tree, as if it grew within her thoughts as well as in the pot sitting on her worktable.

"Very good." Glynna's eyes sparkled with delight. "This tree will be a blessing wherever it is planted. It will protect Westerland for decades after you have died."

"Oh, pooh! Who wants to talk about death on such a gorgeous day? I've done it!" She drew her knees up to her chest and rocked backward. The slight knock of the back of her head against the wall only prompted more giggles.

"Your magic will remain in Westerland and protect it no matter where you go. No matter how far away your father has to send you. I pray Yeshen you never have to leave. Who cares about politics and alliances? This is far more important."

CHAPTER SIX

Arden had a dozen answers to that, all of them contradictory. She wanted the adventure and wonder Maddix promised her, if she married him. She wanted the peace and safety and feeling of being securely rooted that would be hers if she stayed in Westerland and married Derrien. If he ever spoke what his eyes hinted. If he ever tore down that wall he had allowed to rise between them. How could she leave Westerland when Mistress Rose, his mother, was ill and likely would die soon? And what about all the other princes who wanted alliances with Westerland? What about the threats of wars spilling over the Cascade Mountains to them, as Durmad pressed to take over the entire continent? Who could plan for the future when nothing was certain?

Then she opened her eyes and gazed at her tree. The leaves had doubled in size and number just in those few minutes. It was two hands taller, and the thin trunk was twice as thick.

How could she feel any fear for the future when this wonder glowed softly green and vibrated with life in front of her?

Yeshen … help me trust and rest in you?

~~~~~

As her tree grew, Arden felt her own roots dig deeper into the foundations of Westerland. She felt the sleeping life all winter long, and fed it from her heart. When spring returned and crept across the land, she wandered through Westerland as far as her creamy brown mare or her feet could take her for a day's journey out and back again. She imprinted every field and tree and stream and person's face into her memory and heart. She thought about leaving and tried not to. Just as she tried to ignore the need to transfer the apple tree from its pot and plant it.

Glynna warned her that if she resisted much longer, if she went against what was only common sense, she would suffer for it. Arden knew she was right, but she delayed. If only to put off the visible admission that yes, Westerland was protected and blessed by her tree, making her just a little more free to leave.

She didn't want to leave.

Four days after spring equinox, she went to her workroom to check the tiny white knots of blossoms just starting to open on the apple tree and found a letter packet waiting for her. Another secret letter from Maddix. More poetry that made her squirm. More descriptions of the
~~~~~

glories of the palace gardens in Stonemount. As if they could ever replace her gardens right here in Westerland?

She hesitated to pick it up, and that hesitation made her shiver. A brief flare of anger at the maidservant who brought the letter prompted her to go to the head housekeeper and demand the girl be sent away. Other servants now cleaned the royal family's private quarters, so the maidservant had to deliver the letters somewhere else. Arden understood that, but seeing the letter packet next to the tree angered her. She felt threatened. She felt guilty.

Arden didn't want to read it, because every letter lately had a note of bitterness. Somewhere in the letter, Maddix would insist that they were foolish—meaning she was foolish—to wait until her eighteenth birthday, and more foolish to want the approval and blessing of her parents. Why did she continue to refuse to run away with him, to give a heroic, adventurous start to their marriage, and create a legend that would have all the surrounding kingdoms envy them?

She couldn't read that letter here, by the tree, the visible reminder that she would leave Westerland. It threatened this new, deeper unity with the land provided by the tree. She picked up the letter, slipped it into her satchel and fled the workroom without checking the tree. After a quick stop in the palace kitchen, to snatch some food for a long day of rambling and thinking and asking Yeshen for an answer, some guidance, she raced for the gates out of the palace grounds.

"There you are, dear," Glynna said, fading into view as Arden leaped across a tiny ornamental stream that marked the boundary of the farthest edge of the property. "Something troubles you. I could feel it in my sleep."

Arden fought down a sense of pressure in her chest. "Sleep" was what they called those periods when Glynna went away, to rest and commune with others who had Gifted themselves. She had never been able to describe that quiet, cloudy, drowsy place. Sometimes, like now, Arden resented the fact that Glynna had something she could keep to herself and not share. It felt entirely unfair, because wasn't her entire life open to Glynna's study and judgment?

No, not everything. She had managed to keep secrets from her mentor, hadn't she?

And look how bitter, maybe even poisonous, those sweet secrets had turned.

The pressure turned to tears, and a sick feeling squeezed her heart against her ribs. She ran. Fleeing across the meadows knee-high with crops. She ran until her legs shook and ached and her ankles threatened to turn, and she couldn't breathe for the banging of her heart against her lungs. Arden staggered the last dozen steps, until she reached the sanctuary of the little spring surrounded by willows and berry bushes where she and Alix and Derrien had come to sit and talk and laugh so many times after their rambling adventures. They hadn't come here together in years. She had never brought Maddix here.

And didn't that indicate something she had been ignoring until now?

She dropped down onto the flat stones she and the boys had placed around the spring years ago, for a comfortable sitting place. The heat of the sun baked into the stones stung slightly on her bare legs, and she welcomed the discomfort like a well-deserved rebuke.

"What's wrong, sweetheart?" Glynna faded into view again. She reached to frame Arden's face in her hands, and just for a moment, a sensation of coolness soothed the girl's hot, sweaty skin, and the throbbing of her blood that made her skull feel like it would burst apart.

"Oh, Auntie, I am such an incredible ninny!"

Then Arden drew her knees up to her chest and rested her head on her knees and spilled her secrets in between sobs.

Later, she laughed at how little time it took to confess what felt like an enormous, crushing burden. Her words ran out before her sobs did. Releasing both kinds of aching pressure was such a relief, she felt light and empty and exhausted, and she wouldn't have been surprised if she fell asleep, sitting there with her face half-buried in her tear-soaked skirts.

Slowly, birdsong and the whisper of the breeze through the leaves around her took the place of the thudding of her pulse in her ears and the rasping strain of her breathing. She raised her head, rubbed the last few tears out of her slightly swollen eyes, and turned to the right, where she knew Glynna would always be.

"Have I made a horrid mess of things?"

"Goodness, no." Glynna floated a handspan above the stones, her legs neatly folded with her skirts tucked underneath them. She smiled fondly and reached to cup Arden's cheek. Again, that brief sensation of soothing cool. "I think I'm relieved, actually."

"How?" Arden's voice cracked.

"Well, I'm a firm believer that every girl needs to experience at least one heartache before she's mature enough to find true love, real love. I think Yeshen was watching out for you. Most of the injury, you brought on yourself, instead of it coming at the hands of some pompous, too-big-for-his-padded-britches prince."

That startled a strained little giggle from Arden.

"It sounds to me like you were already taking your heart back, but you're so much an idealist, my dear, you felt like you were betraying someone who most certainly isn't and likely never will be worthy of your affection, forget about your love and devotion. What a selfish snot this Maddix is."

"You really think so?"

"Whiny, on top of it. And a sneaking schemer. The gall of him, teaching you to lie to your parents, and calling it romantic and heroic and something you had to do because of the heavy burden of nobility that denies you some privacy. If I still could, I would spit." She wrinkled up her mouth and shuddered.

"He didn't have to teach me to lie, I chose to do it." Arden caught her breath. "And I lied and hid things from you, too. I'm sorry, Auntie."

"Well, I'd be lying if I said it was all right, but you are forgiven, dearheart. And I must admit, from my own foolish days, I understand completely why you did it, why it felt right. We just need to thank Yeshen that you came to your senses."

"He's going to come for my birthday and try to get me to run away with him."

"Yes, well, Prince Maddix is in for a huge surprise. And high time he learns that he can't have everything he wants, when he wants it."

"I suppose we would be wise to cancel that trip to Stonemount."

"Oh, absolutely. That would be the perfect time for him to devise some foolishly romantic scheme. Like something from a ridiculous fable. The two of you go for a ride, and the next thing you know you're at a hidden woodlands chapel, standing in front of a priest, and some charm forces you to speak vows you had no intention of making." She shuddered again.

Arden knew Glynna was trying to make her laugh, but the idea felt entirely too real and possible.

"I was so very much looking forward to meeting Ambrose, at long last. Face to face."

"Hmm, yes." Glynna's smile faded. "So was I. The last time I saw him, spoke to him, was at your christening festival."

They sat in silence, until Arden felt the soft, whispering pulse of the land underneath her. She sighed, and a few more tears touched her eyes, as she realized just how much the tension of the last few months had dulled her connection to the land. Maddix's letters, full of increasing lectures and criticism, had done that to her.

"I don't suppose we can get away with just telling him flat out no, I've changed my mind, the last thing I want is to be his bride, stop writing to me, and please don't come to my birthday party?"

Glynna's laughter had a touch of bitterness.

"Before everything else, you are a princess and Stonemount is your father's strongest ally. Maddix can't do anything to strike at Westerland right now. Not while his father is alive and his council supports his actions and decisions. But the moment the crown is on Maddix's head, everything could change. He can install his own advisors and supporters into positions of power and justify every unjust action he takes. From what you've told me, how he's carried out this campaign to get you to follow his plans, do things his way … this young snot is a schemer, and sees nothing wrong with twisting the truth to suit his vision and his goals and his standards."

"I need to take this to my father, don't I?" Arden said, her voice dropping nearly to a whisper.

"The sooner, the better." She brushed her misty knuckles across the girl's cheek. "I'm sorry."

"Bitter medicine is best taken swiftly." She braced her hands on the stones to get to her feet but slumped a moment later. "In a little while? I'm so tired."

"Of course. Hard lessons can be exhausting." Glynna floated backward, over the spring. "I hope I'm being an alarmist, dear, but you should consider changing your habits for a while. Until Maddix understands you aren't going to run away with him, a guard might be wise."

"Soldiers, tramping through the fields, as harvest approaches? That won't be welcome by the farmers." Arden's face warmed.

"Not a troop of soldiers. Just one … very dedicated guard." Glynna's smile twisted into a smirk. "That darling Captain Derrien comes to mind."

"Auntie!" Her face warmed even more, and her heart thumped extra hard against her ribs, so she had to press her hand against the spot.

~~~~~

Confronting her parents and confessing the secrets she had been keeping wasn't nearly as hard as Arden had feared. Perhaps because she had already done so with Glynna and faced the worst of the shame. She didn't cry as much as she had feared. At least, until her mother sighed and enfolded her in her arms and kissed her. Glynna was right, she realized, as more tears came. Her parents understood. They were disappointed, but they weren't furious. Arden almost laughed when her father remarked that she had certainly punished herself enough that he didn't need to do anything. He didn't even need to lecture, because she had figured out what she did wrong already.

The hardest part was facing Derrien. Especially after she overheard him stammer and struggle to politely refuse to be her escort as she
~~~~~

continued her rounds through the kingdom. The first three times he rode out with her, he wouldn't even look at her. She had to carry more than four-fifths of the conversation, and his responses were as short and neutral as a man could get, almost on the point of making her think he wasn't even listening to her.

Finally, she took the problem to Alix. If anyone could understand what was going on in Derrien's head, it was her brother. The two had been best friends all their lives.

"You adorable ninny," Alix said, after she stumbled through what she had thought was a carefully prepared statement of her worry, and examples of Derrien's actions.

"I did hurt him, didn't I? How do I make it up to him? I didn't mean to—" She squeaked when her brother pressed his hand over her mouth.

"First of all, he blames himself. He's been putting distance between the two of you because he believes, as we all do, you'll have to make a diplomatic marriage. Despite Mother and Father insisting they want us both to marry for love. All right?" He waited until she nodded before he lowered his hand.

"Derrien didn't do anything wrong." Her face warmed, and she wondered if she had been lying to herself. Maybe she had been hurt, a little hurt, by the distance?

"Well, he's been kicking himself, thinking if he had been a little bit selfish, you wouldn't have fallen for that fancy-dressed rotter in the first place. He's in love with you, you know."

"Do you really think so?" She pressed her hand over her heart, startled at how it raced. "But how can he trust me, if I—if we—I know I'd be worried if this happened to him, if some girl broke his heart, and then he smiled at me and asked me to dance again and looked at me like … well, I'd think I was second choice. I don't want to do that to him. What if I'm already doing that to him?"

"Look at it this way. You've both been hurt by Maddix. You're both sensitive and hurting, and it's going to take a while to heal. Tell him that you're just like every other girl in the world, easily fooled by pretty words and you're considering joining a cloister for a few years, to find out if a life of holy service suits you."

She squeaked and pulled back a hand to punch him, then burst out laughing. She could always depend on Alix to shock her out of her silliness.

"I love you. You are my favorite brother."

"Lucky me." Sputtering, he wrapped his arms around her.

She buried her face in the front of his jacket and wrapped her arms tight around him. Even as they both laughed and he rocked them from side to side, she prayed silently that Yeshen would make sure she never had to leave Westerland. How would she survive without her brother looking out for her?

"How do you know all this?" she said, when they were both quiet again. "Did Derrien … tell you how he felt?" Arden wasn't sure if she felt embarrassed or grateful the two men had discussed her, so Alix knew how to advise her.

"Hmm, not in so many words." He squeezed her tight, then caught her shoulders and moved her back to arm's length. "It's more the things he doesn't say, the way he reacts when some subjects come up."

"Will you tell him … " She groaned and covered her face with her hands. "I can never look him in the eyes again."

"No. Nothing in the world will convince me to step into that mess!" Alix laughed and gave her a little push in her shoulder. "Talk to the man. How are you going to survive being married to him if you don't learn to talk now?"

Arden's face flamed. "Who said anything about—" She couldn't force out the word. The next moment, her rising spirits plummeted. "How can I do that to him? To both of us? Is it fair, to give him, give us both hope … if I do have to marry and leave Westerland?"

"I don't know," her brother admitted after a few moments of just starting into each other's eyes. "Maybe you haven't thought about it, but I have that problem too."

"Is there anyone here you could … be sweet on?"

"Have I showed you the literal art gallery I have in my study room? All the miniatures of princesses and daughters of nobles, all lined up and ready for choosing. Along with entire books written on their virtues and talents and the diplomatic benefits of each of them strengthening the alliance with Westerland."

"Oh, Alix … I've been rather selfish, haven't I?" She reached out and wrapped her arms around her brother again.

"We'll get through this." He groaned and held her tight, and picked her up so her feet dangled, like he used to do when she was very little. That made her sputter laughter. "And I promise you, the last thing I'd ever want to do is force you to marry someone you don't really like, for the politics and diplomacy. Because I know exactly how it feels for me."

"You really are my favorite brother."

~~~~~

The next several outings with Derrien as her guard were even more awkward, as Arden tried to apologize without embarrassing them both. She thanked him for his loyalty to the crown and trying to protect her feelings. Then she told him about Maddix's secret letters, and Derrien's
~~~~~

quiet anger at the prince's duplicity and scheming seemed to crack, if not break down the wall between them. She was able to laugh about some of Maddix's more poetic, extravagant language by the time Princess Bianca of Ambray arrived with a trade delegation, late in the summer.

Arden needed to laugh at Maddix a little bit, because another letter had come from him, more demanding and critical. He wanted her to promise that when he came to Westerland for her birthday, she would be ready to flee with him. He refused to wait a day longer. A princess's seventeenth birthday was a magical turning point in her life, and he considered Westerland extremely backward in designating the eighteenth birthday the moment of maturity. Everyone knew from lore and fables that the seventeenth birthday contained more blessings and potential for disaster than any other point in a girl's life. Especially a princess. Especially one with a Gift.

"He wants my Gift for Stonemount, and I wouldn't be surprised if he expects me to use it *only* for Stonemount's benefit," she confided to Glynna the morning after Bianca's arrival.

The welcoming festivities for the Ambray delegation hadn't gone into the early hours of the morning, as Maddix always boasted about Stonemount's celebrations. After all, Westerland was a nation of farmers, and most of the nobles and guild leaders were involved in the preparations for harvest. They couldn't stay up until nearly dawn if they needed to rise at dawn to fulfill their duties. Arden rose every day before dawn, to ride as far as she could every day, spreading her plantwise magic and warding off any disasters that might strike at the worst possible time in the harvest.

Still, the dancing and socializing had lingered far longer than Arden had felt comfortable because her sensible, reliable, honorable brother had turned into a somewhat dazed idiot from the moment Bianca stepped out of her carriage. Alix's mouth hung open so often, Arden feared he might start to drool. Yes, Bianca was stunning in a feathery, sweet, first-snowfall-of-the-winter sort of way. She blushed prettily every time Alix stammered a compliment and took her hand to dance. Blushing was practically the only color Bianca displayed, with her white-blonde hair and pale gray eyes and porcelain skin, and her tendency to dress in silver and white and icy blue and cream. She even favored white flowers and moonstones for decorations.

CHAPTER SEVEN

Arden had gone to bed after the welcoming festivities with the awful, aching surety that part of her dissatisfaction came from jealousy. Ambray would be a brilliant marriage alliance, and Alix would be very happy with Bianca, if first impressions meant anything. Arden wanted Derrien to look at her like Alix looked at Bianca, even as she recoiled from the image of him being so starstruck and somewhat silly. She wanted the freedom to let her heart relax and encourage him. She wanted Derrien to be free to feel whatever she dared to hope was growing between them, now that their friendship had been healed.

To stop tormenting herself with regrets and longings, she focused on the dilemma of Maddix's latest letter. While she found some pleasure in delaying her response for an entire week now, and frustrating Maddix's courier and the insistent maidservant, that couldn't last very long. She suspected that irritating Maddix wasn't wise.

Besides, what if he was right, and they would end up married for the sake of the alliance between their kingdoms? He had told her he paid strict attention to the diplomatic interactions of all the surrounding nations, and a wise king never forgot a slight, an insult, a dishonorable action, a broken promise, or an unprovoked attack. What if he was that way in his personal life, not just political?

Yes, Maddix needed to be dealt with soon, just to ward off future problems.

"I think you need to be a little more forceful in impressing on him the duties and requirements of a Gifting," Glynna said.

Today, she had come out without Derrien, because the farms were close enough together and enough foot traffic all around, no strangers could come near her without arousing suspicion. Arden had come to rest at a stream that served as the boundary line between two farms. While many local farmers knew Glynna accompanied Arden, not everyone they encountered even half a day's walk from Port'ham did. She and Glynna had made it a practice to carry on their conversations out of the hearing of most people. It wouldn't do for those who didn't know what a Gifting entailed to fear their princess was slowly losing her mind, talking to people who weren't there.

"A Gift or blessing hoarded, especially from selfish or bitter reasons or to cause harm, will turn to poison sooner or later. Those who profit the most from the hoarding will be harmed the most, as the poison spreads through the land."

"Yes, I did mention that to him, several years ago. Do you know what his response was?" Arden shuddered, disgusted with herself that she hadn't taken warning back then. "He said if I stayed in Westerland and kept my Gift for my father's kingdom alone, that was just as selfish and would eventually harm the kingdom. I had a royal duty to spread my Gift abroad."

"Oh, clever. That royal snot just sounds worse, the more I learn about him." She nodded and patted Arden's shoulder, as much as she was able. "Never you fear, dear, we'll find a way to free you of him, and if Yeshen blesses us, ensure all his schemes and nastiness fall back on him. But remember, never stoop to use the tactics he's been using on you. Such things have a way of rebounding and making the injustice even worse."

Arden nodded and murmured agreement and tried not to feel irritated. Glynna was right, and she knew she should be grateful for such warnings. At the same time, didn't she have a right to wallow, just for a little bit, in her irritation and bitterness? If she could find a way to expose Maddix's true face to the world, without humiliating herself and confessing yet against her silliness, she would do it.

She just needed to figure out how.

The question returned to her thoughts when she settled at a roadside well to have her lunch of bread and cheese, and record in her journal her observations of the soil and insects and the health of the fields she had walked through that morning. She would spend an hour before dinner discussing these things with her father's division ministers, to help them prepare for the approaching harvest.

She caught a glimpse of herself as she pulled up the bucket from the well to have a drink with her meal. Arden laughed at the smudges of dirt and sap on her face that she had picked up in her rambles, reaching through vines and digging in the soil. Further inspection of her roughspun clothes revealed more smears of dirt and sticky places from broken branches, and one sleeve was torn where it had caught on brambles. Her feet were especially dusty, in her sturdy wooden clogs made for tromping across fields and through forests. She slipped her shoes off and spilled the first bucket of water on them and laughed at the streaks of mud that resulted. The cool water on her hot, dusty feet felt incredibly delicious.

Derrien was supposed to come meet her for this afternoon's inspection of fields farther out from Port'ham. She missed his company this morning, and wondered if he would laugh when he saw her dirty and mussed, with wet, muddy feet.

Maddix wouldn't laugh, she knew, with a sudden dropping of her spirits. He would lecture her on the duty of royalty to always present a proper image and command the respect of everyone.

"Oh, why do you always have to show up and spoil my fun?" she whispered. Then it occurred to her that if he saw her right now, Maddix wouldn't recognize her. Wouldn't that be a delicious joke to play on him?

Not that she wanted to see Maddix any time soon. Or for the next twenty years, for that matter.

She smiled at the thought of sharing that observation with Glynna when her mentor returned and bent to raise another bucket of water from the well.

Lately, Glynna couldn't seem to stay in one place. She kept flitting away, vanishing for half an hour at a time and then floating back with that particularly distracted look on her face that always gave Arden a momentary thud of fear. Was Glynna losing herself? Would she someday fade away so even the one she Gifted would not be able to hear or see her? What would she do without Glynna?

"Grow up and stop acting like a selfish child who thinks the world revolves around her, that's what," she whispered. Arden knew Glynna needed to retire to that resting place regularly, to commune with Yeshen and other Gifted souls, and refresh herself. Common sense said the harvest combined with all the turmoil over Maddix had been especially draining on Glynna. Her teacher would return soon, and everything would be normal again.

Except for the dancing and socializing scheduled for this evening. Another evening of watching her brother stumble over himself in his growing infatuation with Bianca.

"Please, Yeshen, let her be kind to him. Please, let them be happy, if they end up together?" she whispered, and punctuated that prayer by tugging up her skirts and dumping the bucket of water on her legs from the knees down. Arden gasped, delighted with the chill, and bent to raise another bucket.

She was digging in her satchel for the little wooden cup she carried on her rambles, to dip up a drink from the bucket, when Glynna returned. She forgot about washing her face and neatening her hair, as she had intended, as she nibbled her bread and cheese and the two of them chatted about the notes she was making in her journal.

The muffled clopping of many horses' hooves and the rumble of wagon wheels on the dirt and gravel road caught Arden's attention as she was putting her journal away. Standing brought the road into her view, revealing the procession on the winding road that would eventually lead to the main gate of Port'ham.

Banners, scarlet and gold and black silk, displayed the castle tower crest of Stonemount. The horses were bright with silver tack, and tassels swayed on their saddle pads and bridles. The wagons gleamed with fresh paint, bright red that nearly matched the banners. Twenty horses all in deep, dark brown, all carrying Stonemount soldiers. Three wagons, their cargo covered with black tarpaulins.

At the head of the procession, sitting a glossy black horse two full hands taller than all the others, was Prince Maddix. Despite herself, Arden's heart skipped a few beats at the sight of that perfect profile and golden hair and the straight shoulders. He wore scarlet and black trimmed in gold and his scabbard had gold trim and his black boots gleamed in the afternoon sunlight. Next to him rode Lord Jaygo. Arden shuddered and stepped further back, as if the shadow of the roof over the well could hide her. She had never liked the way Jaygo looked her over, the few times she had seen him. She sensed that when Jaygo looked at her he didn't see a girl, or even a princess. She couldn't quite decide what the man saw, but it was something she represented.

Several serving men rode behind the prince and counselor. Despite their black livery trimmed in gold, immaculate hair and upright posture, there was something almost brutish about them. Like bears that had been drugged sleepy and obedient, dressed in clothes and trained to sit at table and eat daintily. As soon as the drugs wore off, they would tear free and batter anyone who happened to be close.

Jaygo gestured out across the road, to the fields on both sides. Arden held perfectly still, silently praying they wouldn't see her. To her dismay, the company slowed as they approached the tiny shelter that marked the well.

"All this will be yours someday," Jaygo said.

"A bunch of farmers should be easy to conquer," the man directly behind Maddix said. There was a hungry rumble in his voice. "I don't understand why your father didn't invade years ago."

"Common sense." Maddix smirked, an expression Arden had never seen him wear. It made him look sly, and arrogant. It made her feel as if he despised the rich fields ready for harvest. "A war to take over Westerland will destroy too much. This will be mine through my son. My first son will inherit Stonemount, and my second son will inherit Westerland when his uncle dies without an heir. Alix will die without an heir, won't he?"

Jaygo nodded, and the two brutes riding behind them chuckled.

Arden wanted to run. She needed to hear more. She had to protect her brother.

If she married Maddix, if she gave him a son, then Maddix would kill her brother.

"Never, never, never," she whispered, and caught her breath, afraid even that was too loud.

"It's all right, dearheart," Glynna murmured. "Consider this a gift from Yeshen. We are warned. We can prepare."

Arden wanted to cry out how they could be prepared, when she never would have considered such a selfish, cruel scheme in her entire life.

The man sitting behind Jaygo turned to look at her. She wondered if she would live to reach the palace, to warn her family.

"I'm thirsty," the man said. "You, girl." He gestured at Arden. "Bring us something to drink."

"Since when do you settle for water?" the other man said.

Maddix chuckled, a sneering kind of sound that Arden never would have expected him to produce. He leaned forward to see past Jaygo, who rode on the well side of the road. His gaze traveled over Arden and she fought not to cover her face. She prayed the dirt on her face, the smears on her clothes, the kerchief covering her tightly braided hair, wound around her head, changed her enough to hide her.

"Clancy, stop frightening the peasants," Jaygo said with a sigh that clearly said he thought this was amusing.

"I'm not the one who froze her," the second brute said.

"Yes, but Baethon is the pretty one of you two."

The man who had called out to Arden let out a guffaw. She couldn't tell the difference between them, both with heavy features and dark, thick hair, wide noses, and muscles straining at their livery.

"Water, you silly chit," Baethon said, and smiled. She doubted he was trying to be kind.

"Yeshen, help me," she whispered, and bent to fill the bucket.

"Not bad looking at all. What do you think?" Maddix said, clearly making no attempt to soften his voice. Arden turned around in time to see him studying her figure.

Jaygo sniffed loudly. "Typical of the peasants in this country, Highness. She's like a wild flower. Lovely today, but prone to fade quickly."

"Then I should pluck the flower immediately—though she'll need to be washed." A nasty chuckle escaped him.

"Yeshen hears," Glynna said. She rose up higher than the roof of the well shelter and gestured down the road.

Arden thought she heard hoofbeats. Would Maddix dare try anything if there were witnesses? How many hooves did she hear? She delayed a few seconds, bending to put on her shoes, and pretended the bucket was too heavy, holding it out awkwardly in front of herself with both hands. As she stepped across the little wooden bridge that covered the deep ditch between the road and the well, she saw a familiar roan horse come out from behind the cluster of trees that shielded the bend in the road.

Derrien. In uniform, meaning he had come directly from errands for her father. Riding alone but leading her mare. Arden nearly stumbled and dropped the bucket in her relief. She believed she could run and leap into the saddle, if need be, and they could race away if Maddix tried anything. She didn't want to learn what he considered "plucking."

Everyone's attention turned to Derrien, and the grins on the two serving men faded. Maddix looked slightly disgruntled, but she saw him smooth his features into that mask of benign, gracious royalty she had seen him wear every time he visited Westerland. It was indeed a mask, Arden realized now. He had fooled everyone, not just her.

"Welcome to Westerland, Prince Maddix," Derrien said, bowing in the saddle. His glance shifted just slightly to Arden. She took a chance that no one was looking at her and pressed a finger to her lips. "Have you had a pleasant journey?"

"And you are?" Maddix asked after a pause and sat up a little straighter.

Arden was close enough now, she thought perhaps he was surprised. Why? It wasn't like he didn't want to be recognized, with all the pomp surrounding him. Did he think he could reach Port'ham and the palace and surprise everyone? Or maybe he was just passing through, and hadn't intended to stop in at the palace at all?

That was rude of him.

Then again, he might have been planning on kidnapping her and convincing her they had eloped, and the soldiers were there to intimidate anyone who might try to rescue her.

Yes, after the little she had just heard, and the new interpretation of his letters, that was exactly what she expected from the real Maddix.

"I am Derrien Fitzcairn, captain of the guard. You have caught us unprepared, as all our energies are focused on the current visitors at the palace. And yes, we are preparing for harvest." He gestured at the fields heavy with grain, the orchards on the other side of the road. "What brings you to Westerland? We weren't expecting you for another six weeks, at Princess Arden's birthday celebration."

"Yes. True." Maddix's expression soured for just a moment. "Other visitors? Don't tell me his majesty is entertaining other royal envoys, perhaps thinking of changing his long-time alliance with Stonemount?"

"My duties are to protect Westerland, not advise the king." Derrien shrugged. "How can I be of service to you?"

"Oh, very well done," Glynna said. "You say you're not a diplomat, but you're knocking the pompous ass completely off balance."

Arden swallowed hard to keep from laughing. She knew she shouldn't laugh. Any moment now, Maddix would turn and recognize her and then they would be lost.

"Yes, well, this is not an official visit. We are traveling through to Ambray, to try to iron out some trade difficulties. We can only stay overnight—if it will not strain his majesty's resources to offer us hospitality, with other guests in the palace?"

"Westerland has been blessed by Yeshen, and hospitality is our greatest pleasure." He glanced at Arden and dropped the reins of her mare. "If you will excuse me, I must attend to an errand, and then I will go ahead to alert his majesty that you will be arriving soon."

"Give me that," Clancy snarled, and snapped his fingers and gestured at the bucket Arden had put on the ground, three steps away from his horse. When she didn't respond immediately, he raised his hand like he would slap at her.

"Rose," Derrien said, his voice louder. "There you are. Queen Elise sent me for you. Did you find those herbs she needs?"

Arden gaped for a heartbeat, then she fought not to laugh as she realized the trick he was playing on Maddix.

"Yes, mi'lord. I'll get it." She darted away, across the little bridge, and snatched up her satchel.

She whistled for her mare as she jammed her journal, the pen and inkpot back into the satchel, and hurried back to the side of the road. She shuddered a little, at the way Maddix, Clancy and Baethon all watched her legs as she climbed into the saddle. She refused to tug her skirts down below her knees. Derrien gestured with a tip of his head for her to go. She dug her heels into her mare's sides, nearly knocking one wooden shoe loose, and trotted down the road.

Derrien was her hero. As if he hadn't been one already, long before this?

And Maddix didn't recognize her.

How would she face him this evening? How could she look him in the eyes and smile at his flattery and not confront him with what she overheard? How could she resist him when he maneuvered her into a hidden corner or out into the darkness, for some privacy?

How had she not died from poisoning, all those times he had stolen kisses?

~~~~~
~~~~~

Arden's dress for tonight's festivities, so new it still had a few pins from the castle seamstress' hands, was a shimmering, elegantly simple gown in a shade of blue-green that matched her eyes and made her hair's red tones more pronounced. Just this morning, she had been impatient for tonight's dancing. Just to see Derrien's eyes light up when he saw her in it. Now, the thought of dancing with Maddix while he continued his game of seduction and courtship, made her hate the dress. His presence sullied it, and he would flatter himself that she wore it for his pleasure.

Derrien waited at the bottom of the staircase from the family's quarters when Arden came down to the formal dining hall. She sent up a silent prayer of thanks that he was always right where she needed him to be. He didn't even need to be told that she feared Maddix would try to intercept her and steal some private time.

"Please, Yeshen ..." she whispered, and couldn't complete the prayer, because there were so many things she wanted to ask, for herself and for Derrien and both of them together.

Uppermost in her thoughts was concern for Mistress Rose, Derrien's mother. She had fallen ill during the spring tour of Westerland, serving in her capacity as teacher-examiner. Her duties focused on ensuring that the schools paid for by the crown had all the supplies they needed and families were able to send their children to school without creating a hardship. Her traveling party had been attacked by troublemakers from over the southern border, and she had been injured. Five months later, she still hadn't fully recovered.

"Oh, now isn't that suspicious?" Glynna said, her tone sour as she faded into view.

Arden turned to look where her teacher looked. Her heart sank.

"Sweetheart." Maddix appeared from the shadows of the hallway off the other side of the staircase.

CHAPTER EIGHT

Maddix's glance was a palpable touch as he looked Arden over, head to foot, and his smile widened in a hunger that made her feel dizzy. His greedy, pleased glances had made her feel dizzy before, but not like this, sick and weak. She wished she had confronted him this afternoon when he thought she was just a dirty peasant girl, a "flower" to be "plucked" and enjoyed before she faded. What sort of lies would he have come up with? Would he have given her another lecture on the duties of royalty to be a shining example of graciousness and beauty and manners, and scold her for lowering herself?

Some of the chill and sickness inside her faded as fury took over. Fury with herself for enduring his lectures disguised as "loving" advice.

"You are a vision … and I am greedy enough not to want to have to share you with anyone." He held out a hand to her as he approached her at the top of the stairs.

"I don't care how it looks, how rude it is, you need to run," Glynna said.

If she didn't feel so sick and furious, Arden might have laughed. She took two steps downward rather than toward him. His eyes widened in surprise. Arden choked back a sound that probably was laughter trying to burst out. Not the right time for that. Movement caught her attention, and she looked down the stairs to see a girl in an apprentice healer's blue-trimmed apron run up to Derrien.

"Come, darling, don't play coy. Run away with me. Right now. We'll find a chapel and a priest and be married before nightfall. Then we'll ride all night and all day, until we're safely over the border in Stonemount. We have a right to snatch some happiness for ourselves, and hang all our royal duties and politics. Arden!" His voice cracked in shock when she took two more steps down the stairs, evading his outstretched hand.

She didn't hear him, all her attention focused on Derrien as his face paled and his shoulders hunched, as if he had taken a physical blow. She hurried down the stairs, aching for him, holding back tears even before her mind grasped what that apprentice's appearance had to mean.

"Derrien?" Arden reached out to grip his shoulder. "Mistress Rose? Is she worse?"

"Dying." The word, half-whispered, spoke a world of anguish.

"Go to her. You're not going to let this silly state dinner delay you, are you? Of course not. Your mother is far more important."

"I know you need me, but—"

"Your mother needs you more. You need to say goodbye."

"She would want you there." He choked. "She always considered you a daughter."

"But I—" She closed her eyes. A single shudder worked through her and she fought down a scream of fury at herself, for dithering when she knew what was the right thing to do.

"Is there a problem?" Maddix joined them at the bottom of the steps.

"Highness?" Lord Comyn appeared at the opening into the long hallway into the business wing of the palace. Arden could have flown across the open floor and kissed him.

"Please offer my regrets to my parents and to Princess Bianca and the delegation from Ambray." She turned to curtsey to Maddix. "And please accept my regrets, Prince Maddix. Mistress Rose was my teacher, and a cherished mentor, and she needs me now." She glanced up the stairs. Caitlin had appeared, and she nearly cried out in relief. "Caitlin, I need you to go to my workroom. Bring the herbal infusion I've been working on. The one in the blue crock. Follow us to Mistress Rose's cottage."

Comyn glanced at Derrien, the sympathy in his glance making clear he fully understood. He nodded to Arden.

"Well, Prince Maddix. It is a distinct honor to have you visiting, and such a surprise," Comyn said, as Derrien caught hold of Arden's hand and they ran for the main doors of the palace.

~~~~~

By the time the company had moved from the dining room to the ballroom, Maddix's face hurt from holding onto a pleasant expression when he wanted to snarl and sulk. His mouth tasted foul from praising Arden's devotion to the dying woman. He couldn't remember who she was supposed to be, but his impression was of yet another commoner who had been allowed to get too close to royal blood. The sour twisting in his stomach threatened to bring up his dinner, every time he glanced over at Alix and Princess Bianca. He didn't need to hear the delighted whispers and twittering of the court ladies to confirm his suspicions. The two were falling in love, and from the approving glances the Ambray ambassador and other officials gave their princess, the wedding and strengthened alliance between Westerland and Ambray were as good as done, set in stone.

How dare that idiotic farmer prince step in and snag Bianca for a bride when Maddix and Jaygo had plans for her? The idea of Alix having
~~~~~

any kind of dynastic plans and trying to snag a claim to Ambray's throne was ludicrous. Maddix would have laughed if he wasn't so disgusted with their starry-eyed silence and blushing smiles. While he was pleased with this proof that Bianca was just as much a simpleton as his spies had reported, having her fall in love with Alix would just complicate his plans for her. For them both. Maddix considered having to murder Alix, and make sure it was done before he could father a child on Bianca, and go through the tedious business of comforting the widow and winning her heart.

His seething disgust at Arden for abandoning him and delaying the final step in seducing her made his head hurt. Seeing the smug expression on Jaygo's face pushed Maddix to the breaking point. He couldn't give two rotten figs for the schedule and timing of their plan. He was going to go over there and start winning Bianca's heart now. She was enough of a trusting little ninny, he could easily convince her that he had been forced to marry Arden as a matter of state, that his heart had always belonged to her. He could use sympathy to trick her into marrying him long before it was appropriate. He could make it into a romantic story that would win sympathy from every surrounding kingdom. And he could dangle Bianca in front of Arden during their marriage, however long that misery lasted, making her jealous, making her fight to ensure herself he belonged only to her, that he loved only her. And stealing Bianca from Alix and breaking his simpleton farmer's heart would just be the sweet course in the feast.

He pulled his shoulders back and headed around the perimeter of the ballroom, focusing his predator's gaze on Bianca. She noticed him when he was directly across from her. Their gazes locked. She blushed and couldn't break free. Maddix's fury leaped into vicious delight. This was going to be great fun. Especially if by the end of the evening he could convince Bianca that he had long adored her from afar, and he had been suffering all these years in terror that someone would steal her heart before he could offer his in exchange.

~~~~~

Mistress Rose lay in her narrow bed, close to the fireplace that dwarfed her. If not for the chestnut hair she had given her son, her pallor would have made her vanish among the snowy sheets and pillows.

She had been shivering uncontrollably when Arden and Derrien reached her cottage two hours before. They moved her from her bedroom to the front room of the cottage, where the fireplace was larger, and built up the fire so it roared. She didn't shiver now, but lay peacefully, thin and small and smiling, one hand held in Derrien's and the other hand carefully clasped between Arden's.
~~~~~

Arden's herbal infusion had brought her some relief, easing the awful rasping of her breathing. Caitlin had gone back to the palace less than half an hour ago to retrieve the dry mixture, so Arden could make more. Rain had started falling just before she left, and Rose had insisted the girl shouldn't bother. She didn't want anyone fussing so much over her. She felt no pain. She was simply tired.

The little woman looked at her two companions and smiled, sighing. A little more of her life and energy left with that sigh. She was tired, from years and loneliness for her husband. They had found each other later in life than most sweethearts. Derrien was a complete surprise, for they both thought Rose too old to have children. Their son grew up with the heir to the throne as his closest friend and had taken over his father's title and duties as Captain of the Guard and leader of Westland's small army. He was a good man, as honorable and respected as his father.

What more could a woman want, other than to rest and be reunited with her love?

One thing, and that was out of her hands, though she prayed for Derrien and Arden to be allowed to spend the rest of their lives together, harder than she had prayed for anything since her husband died. They were so good together. Her son had loved the princess since she was a toddler, and Arden's eyes didn't shine for anyone as much as they did for Derrien. Rose could hope. Having lived her life close to the throne, she understood all the political and diplomatic necessities, but she could still pray that Yeshen would grant her son and the princess the same unity she and her own husband had enjoyed.

Rose sighed and a film of weary tears touched her eyes. She felt her life sliding gently away, like the raindrops rolling down the glass in the narrow cottage windows.

"Mother?" Derrien whispered and brought her hand to his lips.

"Take good care of our Arden. She needs you." Rose smiled at her breathy voice. She certainly hadn't meant to say that, but it needed saying.

"I will, Mother. I promise." He brushed a kiss across the tiny hand.

"Arden?" the little woman breathed after a few moments when even the fire seemed to soften its crackling.

"Yes, Mistress Rose?" the princess whispered, tears in her eyes.

"You'll take care of my boy?" Her words wrung a groan from Derrien.

"I promise. With all my heart."

"He needs someone to look after him." She smiled, closed her eyes and shrank a little further into her pillows. "All the big, strong soldiers are just little boys at heart. He needs someone to make his porridge and mend his socks."

Arden muffled a breathy giggle, which drew an answering smile from Mistress Rose.

"What is taking Caitlin so long?"

"Please," Rose whispered. "Don't fuss. I'm … just tired."

"It's all right, Rose. You'll be going home soon," a new voice whispered. "Darrick is waiting, and Yeshen is calling you home. I promise, I will watch over Derrien, and I will do everything in my power to make sure he and Arden can be together."

"Who?" she whispered. A golden-green light seeped through her eyelids that felt so unbelievably heavy.

Then she heard her husband calling, his voice young and strong and thick with joy.

~~~~~

"She's gone," Arden whispered. "Isn't she, Auntie?"

"Yes." Glynna frowned and looked away, as if she could see through the cottage walls. "I'm sorry, dear, but…something is very wrong. I'll be back as soon as I can."

She didn't so much fade out as pop out, her comforting glow of magic gone. Arden turned to Derrien as he went to his knees next to his mother's bed and put his head down on her crossed hands. His shoulders shook with silent tears.

Arden caught her breath, feeling as if something yanked her sideways off her stool. She clutched at the side of the bed and fought to catch her breath.

Glynna was right. Something was very wrong. An icy, gritty fog wrapped around her and was trying to pull her up into the air, severing the magical roots that bound her to Westerland. She fought not to cry out and held as still as she could until the aching sensation faded away. Then she bent forward, resting her head on top of Derrien's, and wept with him.

~~~~~

By the fourth dance with Bianca, Maddix had made up his mind. He was going to have his fun with Bianca and use her to blacken Alix's reputation and poison relations between Ambray and Westerland, with a bonus of punishing Arden for wasting his time and playing coy just as his plan was coming together. He had the entire plot clear in his head. Clancy and Baethon would steal Westerland livery before they left the palace and kidnap Bianca on her way home to Ambray. He would conveniently sweep down from out of nowhere, rescue her, and carry her off to Stonemount, with a quick, private little marriage ceremony.

He would paint himself as her hero while his agents spread ugly rumors that Alix had given the orders to kidnap her. Everything was perfect, a much better plan than the one Jaygo insisted he cling to. Why not marry Bianca, who was nineteen? Why wait for Arden who was suddenly lady bountiful instead of listening to all his careful training in what it meant to be a true royal?

He would continue his secret correspondence with Arden, stirring her sympathy for his disappointing marriage, encouraging her to doubt her brother's honor, pointing out all her father's failures as ruler of Westerland. And when Bianca died after giving him his son, Arden would be ready to race to his side to comfort him. The silly girl would probably consider herself quite noble, coming to help him raise his orphaned son.

Jaygo didn't know what he was doing. He was a fool, and Durmad would agree with Maddix when he finally shook himself free of the man.

"Highness." Jaygo seemed to rise up through the polished wood floor of the ballroom, as he had an ugly, inconvenient habit of doing.

"Not now." He forced his face to hold onto the besotted smile that had worked quite well to charm Bianca.

"Highness, I regret interrupting your dance with the lovely lady." Jaygo bowed deeply to Bianca.

Around them, the dozen or so other couples were slowing or stopping. Maddix nearly snarled at Jaygo, when he realized he had come to a stop. He should have kept Bianca swirling around the ballroom floor. Confound the man. This just showed what a tight rein he had wrapped around Maddix. Utter nonsense. He was the prince, he was the master, not the other way around. Jaygo was only a messenger, and a faulty one at that.

"A messenger has arrived from Stonemount. Your father has taken a turn for the worse. He could be dead before we return," Jaygo continued, raising his voice just enough to be heard by everyone, yet implying he was trying to speak privately, and fighting for composure.

For a moment, Maddix let himself hope this was the truth. The sooner he had his father off the throne and out of his way, the better for all his plans. Plans he had formed without Jaygo's now-questionable guidance. He closed his eyes and fought to control his expression. The struggle would make a good impression on everyone around him. Too bad that silly little Arden wasn't here to see it. Maddix opened his eyes and looked down at Bianca, who gazed up at him with tears filling her lovely, huge eyes. He nearly choked on the effort not to shout from the triumph spiraling up inside him. She was his, sitting daintily in the palm of his hand. How to play this moment correctly, so she would be compliant in the next stage of his plan?

"Please forgive me, lovely Bianca." He made his voice raspy and released his hold around her waist, kept hold of her hand as he bowed deeply to her, and kissed the front and back before standing upright. "Duty calls me away."

Her eyes were dazed and sparkling with more than tears, and an entirely becoming blush painted her cheeks.

"If I could, I would sweep you away and take you back with me to Stonemount, to comfort me in the dark days lying ahead of me," he added in a throaty whisper. Maddix could almost smell the sour tang of Jaygo's disapproval. He released Bianca's hand and backed away. She wobbled a little and her blush deepened even more. If he read her correctly, she found the idea quite attractive.

Making his farewells and expressing his regrets to King Alfred, Queen Elise, and Prince Alix took far too much time, when Maddix was aching to find out the truth. His mind raced through all the possibilities, all the dreams he had woven during these interminable years of waiting for Arden to be old enough to elope, and for his father to finally waste away enough to die.

Then a new thought hit him.

"What about Uncle Ambrose?" he asked, as he and Jaygo hurried down the long hallway to the guest wing and his quarters. The only thing keeping his father alive all these years, when the ridiculous, sentimental old fool should have curled up and faded away, was the presence of Ambrose. His healing gift had foiled numerous small, subtle attempts on the king's health, with slow-acting poisons and drugs to make him hallucinate and doubt his sanity. For the king to die with so little warning, something drastic would have happened to Ambrose, so he couldn't heal his nephew. And then there was always Dylon, with his inconvenient ability to show up at the worst possible time with the right herbal potion to counteract poisons or diagnose a new problem and treat it correctly. Maddix begrudged the time he spent keeping Ambrose ill enough that he couldn't leave the capitol city but not so ill he would die and give his healing Gifting to the wrong person. Why couldn't the idealistic idiot be more loyal to Stonemount and his own family's ambitions? Then there was the delicate balance he no longer could trust Jaygo to maintain. Clancy and Baethon were useful and loyal, but didn't have the necessary subtlety, so again, Maddix had to do all the work. He had to separate Dylon from his grandfather so he wouldn't be there when the stubborn old man died, to receive the Gifting. At the same time, he had to allow Dylon to return often enough to allay any suspicions and keep Ambrose alive and in good spirits. Pretending to care about the few remaining members of his family was exhausting.

"The last I knew," Jaygo said, his voice pitched so Maddix had to strain to hear him, "the healer is in decent enough health, and was working with the king on plans for the harvest festival."

"Meaning my father isn't dying. Yet." Maddix stomped through the door of his guest quarters and through the sitting room to his bedroom. He fumed quietly, his face heating, as three palace servants finished packing his luggage. They hurried away, to carry his bags to the horses being saddled. Finally, he was sure they were alone, but even then he couldn't raise his voice and roar. "Then what is this emergency that you interrupted a very entertaining—"

"Yes, I saw how you were entertaining yourself." Jaygo's cold tones and the slight sneer curling the right side of his mouth once could make Maddix sick with the certainty he had made a mistake.

Now, he just wanted to stick a knife between the infuriating old man's ribs and be rid of him, once and for all. In some ways, Jaygo was more of a nuisance and hindrance than his own father.

"Stick to the plan. I had thought at least you had the wit not to let a pretty face distract you," Jaygo continued. "We need to get away from Port'ham and across the border into Stonemount as swiftly as possible." He turned and stomped to the door out of the suite. "Before we're discovered."

A surge of glee nearly choked Maddix. He hurried after Jaygo. "What did you do?"

Jaygo merely glanced over his shoulder and continued down the hallway, through the reception area at the front of the palace, and down the pitifully short flight of steps. Clancy and Baethon were noticeably missing from the assembled horses and mounted soldiers. That meant they had carried out whatever nasty trick Jaygo had concocted. They would be waiting several miles outside of the city. Maddix turned to look back at the palace. To his delight, he caught sight of Bianca standing on the balcony over the entrance, looking down at him. Her face sparkled, and he knew those tears were for him. He bowed to her, then vaulted into his saddle.

"Homeward," he announced, pitching his voice so it bounced off the buildings on all sides. "To Stonemount. Pray Yeshen is merciful, and my father is still alive when we arrive," he called, and dug his spurs into his horse.

CHAPTER NINE

The priests had left, taking Rose's body with them to prepare for burial. Derrien moved stiffly, dousing the fire, while Arden stood in the doorway holding a lantern. The best thing for him was to take him back to his quarters at the palace, rather than leaving him in his mother's empty house to grieve alone. She would have preferred to stay here with him, but someone was always sneaking around, looking for fodder for gossip and scandal. She couldn't afford to let a whisper start now, when Maddix had likely come to Westerland to pressure her to elope with him. He might even use the threat of scandal to force her hand. She dreaded going home, to learn that while she was away Maddix had announced their betrothal. How far could he insist and push, until Alix confronted him with the truth? How long could her father hold out against the nobles who had been insisting on a marriage alliance since the day she was born?

If only creating a hint of scandal would ensure she married Derrien… But nothing was sure. Hadn't that been impressed on her over the last few days, with all her daydreams and silly romantic notions shredded before her eyes?

From the doorway, the city at near-midnight appeared to sleep. The rain that had vanished an hour ago threatened to return, churning in clouds across the sky and hiding the moon and stars. She wrapped a cloak scented with lavender tighter around her shoulders. Mistress Rose's cloak. Derrien hadn't been so fogged with grief that he hadn't noticed the chill in the air. He had insisted she use it, and keep it, that his mother would want her to have it as a remembrance.

"All right," Derrien sighed, and stepped back from the dark fireplace.

She reached for a second cloak hanging on the peg by the door. From the worn embroidery on the collar and the lack of any scent at all, Arden guessed this had been his father's cloak, and Rose had kept it by the door, a holder of memories.

Glynna flared into being in the doorway, the glow of her magic wavering.

"You have to come home. Quickly. It's Caitlin."

"What happened to her?" Arden's voice hurt from the need to shout her question, but the thick stillness of the darkened street restrained her. "Is she all right?"

"She will be." Glynna wrung her hands and flew two circles around Arden while Derrien came and snatched up his father's cloak. "She was attacked when she was fetching the herbs. She surprised someone in your workroom."

"Arden?" Derrien shouted her name and reached to catch her as her legs folded.

"The tree," Arden whispered. Now she understood that odd, detached feeling. "Someone killed my tree?"

"They took it," Glynna growled.

Arden thought she would be violently ill. She clung to Derrien, her mind racing, while all the implications battered at her. Somewhere in that dizzy spinning, she was aware that he gathered her up in his arms and yanked the door closed, to hurry down the wet streets to the palace.

All that magic she had poured into the tree. All the blessings, the protection she had woven into it, to guard and guide Westerland and nourish the crops and ward away pestilence and blight. Gone. Once the tree had been planted, nothing would ever be able to move it, with its roots spreading out far underground, spilling her stored magic throughout the entire kingdom. Why had she delayed planting it? Tying Westerland to her, no matter how far away she traveled.

Arden almost wished someone had destroyed the tree. Stealing it was far worse, because they could appropriate her magic, force it to bless another kingdom. How could she stand knowing her magic was forced to benefit a thief?

"It won't benefit them, will it?" she whispered, when the lights of the palace gates were visible.

"What was that?" Derrien paused and looked around, and found a bench tucked under an awning in front of a closed shop. He put her down and brushed damp hair out of her face. "What happened? You scared me half to death."

"Someone stole my tree." Arden nearly burst into tears when horror wrinkled his face, swiftly transformed into fury. Derrien understood, and his anger for her helped steady her spinning head and churning insides. "Auntie, they stole my magic, everything the tree is supposed to do for Westerland, but it won't do them any good in the end, will it?"

"Planting that tree with lies wrapped around it? Burdened with theft and selfishness?" Glynna shook her head. The glow of her magic darkened and she shuddered. "For a few years, they will believe they have triumphed, but then their stolen prosperity will turn bitter and poison them. Whoever took the tree likely understands enough to know what a treasure it is, but they don't understand enough to look ahead and see how they will slowly kill themselves, their family, and in the end, their kingdom."

~~~~~

"A tree." Maddix took a deep breath to release a stream of curses at having been yanked away from a thoroughly pleasant game of seducing Bianca and frustrating Alix. A flicker of green magic among the leaves on one side of the tree stopped him. Then he understood.

This was Arden's silly little magic apple tree she had been so proud of. He had been bored silly the first time she described to him what she hoped to do. Every time she had mentioned it in one of her letters, he had skimmed over it. Jaygo always managed to get his hands on her letters, so he knew all the details, which didn't seem so trivial now.

If he was lucky, all Arden's plantwise magic resided in that little potted sapling clutched tight in Clancy's hands, resting on the front of his saddle.

Which meant … no plantwise magic for Westerland.

"Oh, very well done," he said, nearly purring.

"You need to come up with a suitable response when Westerland comes looking for that tree," Jaygo said, after only a few seconds of gloating.

Maddix didn't miss that "I told you so" glance the man gave him. No doubt, Jaygo would hold that petty little theft over his head for months, maybe years to come. He might even try to take the tree with him, when Maddix dismissed him from his service and sent him packing. Best to get that tree planted, safely inside the private portion of the palace gardens, with guards around it. Guards who were loyal to Maddix and would only laugh if Jaygo threatened them.

"What makes you think anyone in Westerland will suspect me?" he said after only a few seconds of thinking.

"Let us hope they won't." Jaygo glanced over his shoulder at Clancy and Baethon, who had taken their accustomed spots right behind them. "Did you have any trouble getting in and out again?"

"We stole the palace livery and we used that darkness charm you gave us." Baethon's thick voice sounded bored. "Nobody came near the princess's rooms until we were leaving."

"Until?" His voice cracked.

"Some serving maid came in." Clancy chuckled. "Knocked her flat before she could make a sound. She probably didn't even know we were there."

"Did you hit her hard enough to kill her? We don't want the alarm raised until we're several hours closer to the border."

"Oh, she's out and gone." Baethon spat. "If she's not dead, then her brains are scrambled for the rest of her life. We know what we're doing."
~~~~~

Maddix muffled a chuckle. Especially when Jaygo gave both henchmen a caustic look before turning around in his saddle to face forward.

"As I was saying …" Jaygo heaved a longsuffering sigh that made Maddix want to tell Baethon to hit him right then and there, and preferably leave him on the side of the road. "Westerland might not suspect us, but we need several responses ready, depending on the tone of the message when they come looking. They may ask if we've heard any news. I can't imagine any of them having the wit or courage to accuse us outright. Still, best to be prepared."

"Best to attack, instead of waiting for them to get into position," Clancy grumbled.

"True." Maddix grinned and cast a sideways glance at Jaygo, lit with flickering light from the lanterns carried on tall poles by the soldiers in front of and behind them.

This was turning out even better than he could have hoped. He wouldn't even be disappointed to reach Stonemount and find out his father wasn't anywhere closer to death. He had Arden's magic apple tree. What did he need her for at all? Likely no other prince in any of the surrounding kingdoms would want her, once they learned she had so foolishly poured all her plantwise magic into the tree, and then let it get stolen.

Maddix didn't know as much as he would like to about the rules of magic, but common sense said Arden wouldn't be drained forever. He would leave her alone, rejected by other princes and kingdoms, and follow the plan he had come up with while dancing with Bianca. Let her believe the marriage with Bianca was a matter of state, leave her in silence for months, to eat herself up with jealousy and a broken heart, and impress on her the golden opportunity she had missed. Then, by the time her magic returned and she was a desirable bride again, he would have sired a son, preferably two on Bianca, arranged for her death, and could turn to Arden, playing the part of broken-hearted, grieving widower.

This was perfect. This was better than the original plan. Not that he was going to compliment Jaygo on his decision. When was the man going to learn that he had stopped being the teacher and master long ago? Certainly Durmad was ready to discard him, the moment he made too many mistakes.

"If we're careful, Arden will suspect nothing for months. When her magic returns, if it does, she'll be weak and desperate to be reunited with her tree. We'll draw her to Stonemount and if she doesn't comply with our plans, we'll simply take her prisoner until she's learned her lesson,"

Jaygo said.

Maddix said nothing. He could already think of a dozen ways that plan would fail. It was up to him to make sure nothing went wrong.

~~~~~

The gardens of the royal palace of Stonemount were half the size of the city that surrounded it, stretching out for acres across rolling meadows broken by sweeping stands of trees and exquisitely maintained flowerbeds. Dylon supported his grandfather as he and Ambrose headed into the sheltered corner of the garden where Maddix had asked them to join him. His message had simply stated that he had been gifted with a tree imbued with magic, and he needed Ambrose's approval of the spot where he wanted to plant it.

They walked in silence, with Maddix's muscle-bound assistants, Clancy and Baethon, carrying the potted sapling. The chosen spot stood close to a narrow, silvery stream that meandered through the royal gardens, where several ancient trees had stood for years even after they had been killed by lightning. No other plants had tried to encroach into the area after the master gardener and his servants chopped down the trees. There was plenty of sunlight all day long and few shadows, and the remaining trees provided an appropriate frame to display the treasure.

Dylon wasn't surprised when Maddix left it to them to plant the tree and hurried away with his two assistants. He claimed he wanted Ambrose's healing magic to be woven into the soil and water, to protect the tree. Dylon didn't believe for a moment the story he had given them, about attempts along the way home to Stonemount to waylay his traveling party and steal the tree. However Maddix had obtained the tree, it was through twisted enough means that he wanted them to keep silent about its presence. To protect Ambrose and stay on Maddix's good side, Dylon would comply.

The two healers planted the tree with all the care due the tender sapling and dipped up water from the stream in their own hands, taking many trips to water it. Dylon felt it only appropriate, and fitting. His sensitivity to magic at work had grown slowly over the years, and he was awed at the potential for blessing and healing and prosperity shining softly in the leaves of the little tree. He said a silent prayer that Yeshen would use the tree to guard Stonemount against Maddix's arrogance and selfishness. Could a little tree like that have the power to neutralize the harm his cousin would do?

"Look at that," Ambrose murmured, as they stepped back to look at the little tree. The green-gold glow edging the leaves grew a little brighter. Then with faint popping sounds, five more leaves sprang from
~~~~~

the main trunk and uncurled. The little tree shook slightly and stretched, adding another inch to its height before their eyes.

"I think it likes its new home," Dylon murmured, his mouth dropping open in wonder, despite his own experiences with magic since childhood.

"That is very good for us. I don't want to think what could happen to Stonemount if the tree was not happy here. Arden is a talented girl, but I doubt she realizes what she put into this amazing little creation of hers."

"Arden?" He shivered, sensing this was at the core of what wasn't right about Maddix's story. "Princess Arden? Of Westerland? Oh, no …"

"Exactly."

"Why would she be stupid — sorry — why would she be so foolish as to give something so full of magic to Maddix?" He thought he would spew the remains of his dinner right there on the disturbed soil of the planting.

"I don't think she did. Such a massive working and weaving of magic was likely intended to stay in Westerland, when she left to marry." Ambrose sighed. "The taint of deception is already nipping at the roots of this innocent little tree."

"Maddix stole it?" He kept his voice down, shuddering at a sudden fear that one of Maddix's bully boys would descend on them if they heard.

"He seems to prefer taking and threatening, rather than asking. If a gift isn't given in fear, he doesn't value it." Ambrose sighed. "We need to make a very good excuse for you to leave, some vital errand for me, so you can deliver a letter to Arden, warning her. And watch what you say about the tree. If Maddix even suspects that I identified Arden's magic woven into this tree … well, I already know he reads my letters to and from Arden. He could stop them altogether, or substitute his own letters for mine, to turn her against me."

"Or make her think you despise her." Dylon studied the little apple tree, seeing it in a new light. Some of that light was pity for her loss, mixed with wonder at what the girl had wrought.

~~~~~

Arden held hands with Derrien during Mistress Rose's funeral and didn't care what the gossips and rumor-mongers said or thought, or what news reached Maddix. Let him get jealous and rage and threaten her and finally show his true colors. She would welcome it. Nothing was right inside her. She sensed when her little tree was dry, she sensed when it was shaken on the thieves' long journey. She fought tears of fury when that was all she knew. Certainly not a sense of direction, a sense of
~~~~~

distance. Something to give her hope of retrieving her tree before it was planted and lost to Westerland forever.

She wondered sometimes if she would fall ill or faint or even die if the tree was harmed.

So she clung to Derrien as much as he clung to her, both of them comforting each other. She put on a brave face and had her temporary maid servant, Lily, paint her face to hide her pallor. Derrien needed her, and she refused to distract him in his grief to worry about her. Certainly the loss of his mother was a greater tragedy than the loss of her tree. So she smiled for Derrien and teased him to eat and get rest, and held his hand and straightened his hair and his clothes. And when he seemed most dazed and lost in grief, and fighting not to show it, she kissed him. That certainly shocked him back to alertness.

The kiss shocked her, too, because it was so utterly sweet and right. Magic throbbed through her, from her lips to her toes and the ends of her hair. Derrien's eyes lost that aching, shadowy look for a few moments, and he smiled for her. So after that, they stole kisses whenever possible. Which wasn't nearly as often as she would have liked. Never before had she realized so clearly what a public life she led.

She vowed she would never kiss any other man. How could she, when this first kiss was so utterly perfect? Derrien belonged to her. And when he was healed enough, she would make sure he understood.

Arden told no one about the kisses except Caitlin. She visited her maid and best friend several times a day, in the dark, quiet, cool room where she lay, recovering from her injury. The blow to her head was so grievous, she needed to lay perfectly still. Light hurt her eyes and sounds louder than a whisper made her head want to split open. The two girls whispered together, and Caitlin smiled for the first time and her coloring looked better, when Arden confided in her about the kisses.

Caitlin was the only one Arden told, when she sensed that the apple tree had crossed the border of Westerland, taken into another kingdom. The two wept together, though Arden was quick to scold her friend not to cry, she would only hurt her head more.

At the funeral, Arden held tight to Derrien's hand and was comforted by the returning warmth and strength in his grip. He was healing. She promised herself she would kiss him at the graveside and hoped devoutly that Mistress Rose would see and know and be happy.

If Maddix had any spies intruding on Mistress Rose's funeral, she hoped they would see her kiss Derrien, and report that to their master. She wanted him to know that he would never persuade her to leave her family and kingdom for him, no matter how he flattered and lectured and drowned her in poetic words.

She and Derrien led the procession from the palace chapel, heading for the garden gate, to walk down to the river and the burial grounds. On the second step of the chapel, she felt as if her feet were sinking through the stones, turning into roots reaching for soil. Arden clutched at Derrien's hand, but her own hands wouldn't cooperate. She sank down into soil, into darkness.

When she opened her eyes, Derrien held her on his lap, clutched tight against him. Her mother knelt on the steps, holding her hand and cupping her cheek. Her father stood over Derrien's shoulder, gazing at her with such concern she nearly burst into tears. Glynna hovered just past Queen Elise's shoulder.

"Stonemount," Arden whispered, in answer to the question on Glynna's face. "My tree was just planted ... in Stonemount."

Derrien wanted her to go back to the palace and rest, but she insisted on finishing the funeral, seeing Mistress Rose safely buried next to her husband. Arden tried until her head ached to focus on the words of the priest, quoting holy writ, and the singing of the children's choir. Mistress Rose had been choir mistress for nearly thirty years, and their sweet song, pure and steady despite the tears making so many faces glisten, was a tribute to her devotion and their love for her. Arden's throat was too tight to sing along, as a final gift to Mistress Rose.

Her mind raced through the implications, the possibilities, the problems. She wanted to write a short, stark letter, demanding Maddix return her tree. Even if he agreed, he wouldn't be able to. Once her tree entered the soil of Stonemount, nothing but the strongest, fiercest magic could uproot it. She knew enough statecraft from discussions over family dinners and sitting in on her father's council meetings, she couldn't just accuse Maddix of theft. He would deny the tree was there, or claim he knew nothing about it, and take offense, maybe use it as an excuse to attack Westerland.

What could they do?

She prayed, clutching tightly to Derrien's hand, and asked Yeshen to guide her father and the council in the proper course of action. Part of her feared that the smartest tactic would be to pretend she didn't know where the tree was. What kind of weapon could she put into Maddix's hand, into the hands of any enemy of Westerland, if she revealed the tight bond she had with her tree?

CHAPTER TEN

King Doyne accidentally intercepted a letter for Maddix from Princess Bianca of Ambray. What he read first shocked, then infuriated him. Even as he sought out his erring son to confront him, Doyne wondered if he were being ridiculous. It was nothing more than a silly little love letter. He had seen for himself, the girl had little under her white-blonde curls but a childlike delight in everything. But the last he had heard, King Berston of Ambray was depending on a marriage alliance with Westerland, and Bianca was intended for Alix. Bianca had a good heart and a soul of honor woven through her sweetness. She would never survive as Maddix's bride. Which was the plan, according to the letter. Doyne had hoped for years, and had certainly encouraged Maddix, in pursuing Arden as his bride. His son had indicated some impatience for her eighteenth birthday, when he could offer marriage. Arden was a smart girl, with enough common sense and humor to stand up against Maddix's too-high sense of his own importance. She would make him a good king for Stonemount, and not be injured or wearied in the struggle.

Doyne felt his years more than ever as he approached Maddix in the garden, only a short distance from that magic tree Maddix claimed Arden had given him as a token of her love. He couldn't find the words to confront his son, just shoved the letter into his hands and stood back and crossed his arms, waiting for a response. Sickness churned through his middle when he realized he expected yet another ridiculous, complicated lie from his son that he would have to untangle while badgering him to tell the truth.

Maddix glanced over the letter. Instead of being upset his father had read a letter meant for him, he merely shrugged and shoved it into his pocket.

Doyne choked on another burst of fury and frustration. It was a love letter, evidence of Bianca's heart freely given. Didn't his son value it at all? Didn't he feel any guilt over the deception and dishonor he practiced? Or was he acting as if he didn't care because those two brutes who were his shadows were somewhere nearby? Doyne thought he had seen their hulking forms move away among the older trees.

"Well?" he growled. "What do you have to say about this? Or have you conveniently forgotten that you've been courting Arden of Westerland? With her father's approval and mine."

"It's not a marriage of my choosing, Father." Maddix shrugged again and glowered at the tree, two feet taller than when Doyne had seen it just a week ago. "If you approve of that milk-and-water courtliness and diplomacy, why don't you marry the silly girl?"

"We have been allies with Westerland for two hundred years."

"An alliance with Ambray will profit us more. We could beat Westerland in a war in a month."

"Destroy our friends?" Doyne's voice shuddered at the stupidity of it. "The people who feed us? All so you can marry a silly bit of fluff? What is wrong with Arden? She's a beautiful girl. Intelligent. She cares about the common people."

"Too much," his son snapped, his mouth twisting as if he had tasted something foul. "She's a filthy little peasant who grubs in the dirt."

"She's a far better queen than you'll ever deserve!"

Clancy and Baethon stepped out of the shadows only a few steps behind the king. They wore fierce, feral grins that would have prompted Doyne to banish them if he saw them. Baethon cocked an eyebrow in question, then held up the thin wire of a garrote, strung between his hands.

Maddix's eyes widened for a moment, then he glanced at his father and nodded. Doyne turned to see what his son had looked at behind him. The garrote whipped down before his face and wrapped around his throat.

"Stonemount deserves a better king," Maddix said, and turned his back as his father twisted and kicked and held out a hand, mutely begging for help.

He clenched his fists and walked away quickly, until the sounds of choking and struggling vanished into the peaceful quiet of rustling leaves.

Unseen, the apple tree shuddered as if trying to twist itself free from its roots. The golden-green glow of magic paled.

By the time the two brutes dragged King Doyne's body to the other side of the extensive palace gardens and hurried to catch up with Maddix, all appeared normal with the tree. In the falling shadows of evening, the magic glow did not seem quite as bright as before.

"No one saw you?" Maddix said under his breath as they turned their leisurely steps toward the palace. He barely glanced over his shoulder to get two identical nods. "When my father doesn't appear for dinner, I want you two to lead the search."

"What are you going to do in the meantime?" Clancy grumbled.

"I have orders to write. I'm king now. Stonemount has to be looked after, you know." He sighed. "There is so much that my father left neglected. I've become king just barely in time to save our country."

~~~~~

Ambrose avoided the hue and cry, the clatter and fuss and wailing as the news of his nephew's death spread through the palace. He went to the garden, concerned how this sudden death would affect the tree. Trying to comfort Maddix would be a waste of time. He didn't feel like exhausting himself trying to get through the many layers of toadies and henchmen and opportunists who surrounded the new king. Ambrose had avoided such people even before he renounced the crown in favor of being a healer. Sometimes he suspected most of the inhabitants of the palace didn't even know who he was, other than a weary old man who the late King Doyne looked after and visited regularly. His prolonged illness had made him a shadowy figure on the edges of palace life. Besides, Ambrose doubted Maddix felt any grief over his father. The strongest emotion the new king of Stonemount had showed his father in years was impatience.

Unexpected activity filled the quiet corner of the garden when Ambrose reached it. Jason, the head gardener, headed a team of men building a wall of raw stone around the apple tree. The stream that flowed past the spot had already been dammed up, half the flow diverted elsewhere and the rest filling a depression in the ground. Ambrose felt ill. The trapped water would grow stagnant and fallen leaves would collect in it and rot and breed insects. Could the magic of the tree fight off the disease that would try to breed there?

Ambrose came closer to look past the activity to the tree. The disturbance of the ground, the stoppage in the flow of the water already affected it. The magic in his blood helped him sense the dimming of the tree's magic. Soon, it would produce only ordinary apples. Even that wouldn't last long, as the contained magic turned backward on itself, and the fruit became poisoned. Ambrose pitied anyone who would make the mistake of eating those apples.

Soon, no one but the new king's sycophants would be allowed to even look at the tree, much less take an apple. Perhaps he was being self-righteous and vindictive, but he firmly believed anyone harmed by the apples would deserve it.

~~~~~

The day after Doyne's funeral, Dylon was sent away on an errand for King Maddix, barely given enough time to jam clothes into a pack and say goodbye to his grandfather. Ambrose fought to calm his mixture of outrage and fear as he stomped down far too many hallways, to the new wing where Maddix had established himself, to demand an explanation. The new king's too-rapid actions were just proof that he had been preparing for this moment for some time now. Ambrose feared all sorts of vicious plans, changes Doyne would never have approved. He had to wonder how many members of Doyne's council had already been sent packing, not just out of the palace, but out of the city.

"What are you up to, Maddix?" he whispered, and prayed Doyne had no idea what his selfish snot of a son was about to do to the kingdom he had so lovingly, faithfully served.

Maddix and his two hulking shadows were alone when Ambrose reached the massive office suite. They wore those smiles that made Ambrose send up a prayer of thanks that he was an inviolable healer every time he saw them. No one appeared at all surprised when he glared at them. Their smiles grew a little wider, the sparkles of nasty mischief in their eyes a little brighter.

"Uncle Ambrose, what a pleasant surprise." Maddix gestured at the chair pulled up before his massive desk piled high with papers.

"No, I don't think so. Where did you send Dylon?" He planted himself behind the chair and rested his clenched fists on the back of it. Nothing in the world would convince him, even for politeness' sake, to take on the position of a petitioner.

"On an errand of such vital importance, I can only trust someone of the royal bloodline. Something he seems to forget far too often. As do you, Uncle Ambrose."

"Meaning?"

"You two are all that remains of my family. Your health has been precarious ever since your brush with death. I have heard of a miraculous plant with healing properties equivalent to the phoenix, and I have sent Dylon in search of it. And ... I have established orders that you will never be allowed out the doors of the palace without an escort. I can't take the risk of you being harmed. If my own father can be killed within the palace walls, what could happen to you out where I can't protect you?"

"I am a healer, you young fool! Ageless tradition makes me safe from all harm."

"Really? Those scars you wear say otherwise." Maddix stood, resting his fists on the table and leaning over it, almost mocking Ambrose's pose. "My duty is to protect Stonemount's treasures."

"Are you going to build a wall around me, like you're building around Arden's tree?"

Maddix blanched and leaned back. Ambrose felt a flicker of triumph, then knew he had made a serious mistake.

"You are mistaken," he said, his voice momentarily soft.

"The Gifted know the touch of each other's magic. I knew Arden made that tree the moment I touched it."

"What of it? She gave me that tree. Begged me to take it. To strengthen the alliance between our kingdoms. She wove her magic into it to protect Stonemount."

At least Maddix hadn't stooped so low he would claim Arden had given him that tree out of love.

Or perhaps he had such a low opinion of love, he would never consider it a valid reason to do anything?

"The tree is mine," Maddix continued. "I can do with it what I please. And it does not please me for the rabble to steal apples that should help my valued advisers."

"You've forgotten everything I ever taught you about Gifted magic," he said, feeling unutterably tired.

"On the contrary, Uncle Ambrose. I remember every word, and I am grateful, because I will use all you taught me for the good of Stonemount, and Stonemount alone."

Ambrose shuddered and fought not to show his revulsion and the chill that settled into his bones.

~~~~~

Maddix's courier was a hearty, chunky man named Rilling. He had served King Doyne, carrying messages between Stonemount and Westerland and enjoying the time he spent in the country of farmers. He had made many friends there, and sometimes pushed himself to arrive a few hours early so he could visit them before delivering his messages to King Alfred.

This time, he went straight to the palace. Between the rumors of what he carried and his uncomfortable new uniform and the still-painful, mysterious circumstances of King Doyne's death, he had no taste for gossip with friends.

Rilling stood before King Alfred's council table, hands clasped behind his back, studiously concentrating on the patterns in the stone paving while the king and queen and prince and chief counselor read through the packet of papers he had brought. He knew they wouldn't blame him, and he was grateful. He just prayed they wouldn't ask his opinion. Spreading rumors said those who argued with King Maddix and humiliated him when he was a prince had vanished. What was to say that someone wouldn't hear what he told the leaders of Westerland, and it wouldn't eventually reach the throne of Stonemount?

Maybe it was time to retire — in Westerland.

The door opened and Rilling gratefully turned to the distraction. The girl who swept through the door wore a simple, homespun gown of deep blue, riding just above her ankles like peasant girls did to keep their
~~~~~

skirts out of the way while they worked in the fields. Her long, red-gold hair hung loose down her back, kept off her forehead with braids, and flowers sprinkled through her hair. Her golden skin showed her outdoor life, but there was a sweetness and softness that no peasant girl could achieve even with the most expensive cosmetics. No wrinkles. No stains. No lines of harshness from years of hard work behind and before her. She moved with the grace of a dancer.

Rilling watched her cross the room to the table, expecting her to take away the tray that held the luncheon the king and queen had been sharing when he arrived. Instead, she settled down in a chair next to Comyn and folded her hands in her lap.

She glowed. Golden-green magic surrounded her in a soft corona like mist, there and gone again and returning so gently it was barely noticeable after a moment. That fact penetrated Rilling's thoughts and he realized that this beautiful young woman was Princess Arden.

But Maddix had been saying for days that she was ugly and shriveled and unpleasant, every time one of the older nobles mentioned the hoped-for alliance with Westerland. Maddix claimed it was his royal duty to marry better, such as Princess Bianca of Ambray. He insisted he would only harm Stonemount, foisting such a miserable creature on his kingdom. Didn't the king know what she looked like?

Rilling swallowed hard before he choked on a burst of slightly hysterical laughter.

If Maddix didn't know ... who would he punish when he found out the truth? Not the ones who lied to him, because they were likely long gone. No, Maddix would punish the one who told him the truth.

"Ah, Arden." King Alfred summoned a flat smile. "My dear, some news has come from Stonemount."

"Does Maddix explain or just excuse, or outright lie?" Arden said, her voice trembling strangely.

"The king—" Rilling choked. The news was in the letters. Why should he take the responsibility of breaking the news to them?

"You may go." Comyn turned to him. "You've done your duty."

Rilling scurried out of the room as fast as his dignity and the stiffness of his uniform would allow. He couldn't resist one more wondering look at Arden. How could anyone say she was ugly and shriveled and unpleasant? He choked on laughter as he tugged the door closed behind himself, but the laughter had a brittle edge, touched with terror. What if King Maddix didn't know what he had lost? What if he had been advised wrongly? What if he found out, and lashed out against the courier who had carried the fateful documents?

It was time to find his favorite inn and get as drunk as he could, as quickly as he could.

~~~~~

"Father?" Arden hid her hands in her lap and squeezed them to keep them still. There was something in the air of the room she didn't like. Her parents had never looked so somber when a courier from Stonemount arrived. And why did the man wear a new uniform? She didn't like all that scarlet and black. It made her think of war.

Her head hurt all the time lately. Glynna tried not to show it, but she was worried, and that just made Arden more fearful. What had she done to herself, creating the apple tree to protect Westerland? And more important, perhaps more grim, what had Maddix done to her, by stealing her tree? Arden knew she hadn't drained herself completely dry of her magic. She had been able to do small things, limited in focus, healing a few plants at a time after the massive effort of infusing the apple seed. Glynna had assured her that her magic would replenish. Yet in the weeks since the theft of the tree, she felt even weaker, as if the magic that had begun to grow within her again had been drained away. Or perhaps not drained away, but dried up, blocked, turned to dust.

She needed to create another apple tree for Westerland. The efforts to gather up and purify her magic and begin the long process of infusing the seed exhausted her, and made her head hurt. What if this time, she hurt herself, so she could never work plantwise magic again?

How had her effort to protect her kingdom, such a proud, lovely, loving goal, turned so bitter and painful? What had she done wrong?

And now, with her parents and Comyn looking so somber, Arden felt again that she had failed Westerland, and those she loved.

Her father shuffled a few papers around and cleared his throat several times. Arden read his reluctance there without seeing his eyes. Elise touched her husband's hand, steadying him, and a look of compassion passed between them. Alfred nodded, cleared his throat once more, and held up the paper as he read.

"By decree of his Majesty, King Maddix of Stonemount—"

"King Doyne is dead?" Arden's heart leaped in her chest.

This was the worst possible news. Would that courier she had seen even now be leaving a private message for her, with Maddix demanding an immediate wedding? As king, could he change the terms of the alliance between their kingdoms, and demand she be given to him, when his father had always advocated a love match? Would he be so busy establishing himself in his father's throne that he would leave her alone until she was eighteen? Or maybe the year after that?

She would have time to create that apple tree for Westerland.

What did her stolen apple tree have to do with Maddix's letter?
~~~~~

Then she knew: Maddix would demand that she be given to him in exchange for the tree. Or perhaps he would claim that he had caught the thieves, and he would make a grand show of returning it to Westerland, and likely use her gratitude to force her to submit to his plans.

The problem was that Arden could feel how her tree put down roots a little deeper every day into the soil of Stonemount. Tainted soil. Even if she wanted, she couldn't uproot it and bring it home to Westerland now. Much as she ached to do so, to heal the tree before it turned poisonous.

"That's not good news, no matter how you slice it," Glynna said, floating through the wall opposite the door. She came to hover next to Alfred's chair and read over his shoulder as he continued.

"Because of the great value we place upon our magical apple tree, given to us by the wizards of the Swordtop Mountains—"

"The nerve of him!" Glynna blurted.

"We hereby serve notice that anyone who tries to lay claim to our tree or threatens its well-being shall be considered an enemy of Stonemount and give us cause to declare war." Alfred set down the paper, as if it were about to burst into flame.

"I think that tells us quite a lot, and answers most of our questions," Alix said between gritted teeth.

"That boy is more of an arrogant booby than I ever dreamed," Glynna said, only sorrow in her voice. "He's slicing his own throat."

"You're right, Auntie." Arden took a deep breath and considered the implications of what her father had just read.

"What did Glynna say?" Elise asked.

"Mother, one of the first laws of Gifting magic is that its creations cannot be used for evil. If you mix a lie with such magic, or steal it, that magic turns to poison. And now Maddix has done both."

"I told you, child. Give him enough time and his wickedness would turn and hurt him," Glynna said, nodding.

"Meaning, Highness?" Comyn asked.

"When the tree produces apples, they will not heal, and they will not bless. If Maddix continues to deny the tree was stolen from me, the apples will only cause sickness, even death. What makes him think he could get away with such a lie? Surely he can't still be planning to trick me into marrying him."

"My dear child," Alfred began, his voice cracking with his years, "there is something more I must tell you."

CHAPTER ELEVEN

Derrien considered Rilling, the Stonemount courier, to be a friend. He knew something was very wrong when the gate guard at the palace told him the man had come and gone and had not sought him out. Derrien felt a moment of irritation, mostly because he depended on the unofficial news that Rilling brought him to accurately judge the state of things in Stonemount.

He stood in the doorway of the Rooster and Steer tavern and studied Rilling through narrowed eyes. He didn't like the man's new uniform. It spoke of big, grim changes in Stonemount. Even more, he disliked the way the man bubbled in his beer one moment and then looked ready to break into tears the next.

Something was very wrong. Why was Rilling here, drinking in a corner instead of visiting the baker around the corner with the lovely little brunette daughter who giggled only for him?

Finally, Derrien couldn't stand it any longer. He nodded to the barman and crossed the sparsely populated floor to settle on the bench opposite the sodden courier.

"It's been a long time, friend. I just heard the news about King Doyne's death. How do things stand in Stonemount?"

"Tight and quiet." Rilling's voice was a little too steady for someone who looked half-gone in his cups. Did something else shake him besides the beer? "Nobody knows quite what to say or even where to look. King Maddix is not going to be very happy when I get back."

"Any reason?" Derrien asked after several seconds of trying to find a more delicate way of asking.

"He's been making it very clear that your king has been pressuring him to marry Princess Arden, and what a distasteful proposition it's been. Enough to threaten the friendship between our countries."

"Distasteful?" His brain seemed to stick on that word, and he couldn't move past it, like oxen mired up to their knees in drying mud.

"Yep," Rilling continued, his voice trembling. "He says she's no better than a peasant. Filthy. No manners. And a fat, ugly sow." He bubbled sick chuckles into his beer as he took a hasty sip. "When I tell him she's the most beautiful woman —" His voice shrilled and broke. His hand shook when he wiped his mouth. "He went off and came near to kidnapping Bianca of Ambray and brought her home as his queen. She's pretty, but she's this feathery, whispery little thing. The difference between her and your princess … The king made a bad bargain. He won't like finding out how bad. He likes to share his pain when he's angry, I've heard."

"Then don't tell him. Stay here. Let me help you."

Derrien dug into his belt pouch with a hand that trembled, pulled out a handful of coins and put them into Rilling's lax hand. Most of the coins were silver, a few gold. King Alfred paid his people well and provided them housing and clothes beyond their uniforms and food from the royal kitchens. There was very little Derrien ever needed to buy. Except in celebration.

And he suspected very soon, he would want to celebrate.

The question was how soon Arden would share that celebration with him.

"That's … a great deal of money. For what?" the other man asked, slowly closing his fingers around the glittering pile.

"You've made me a very happy man, my friend. And I like to share my joy. Go get sobered up and tell Melisia you're settling in Westerland. Maybe you should become a baker."

The astonished grin Rilling gave him was no match for the one Derrien now wore.

~~~~~

Derrien knew Arden would be in the gardens, taking comfort from the plants there. He hurried through the gates and saw her stumbling blindly across the grass, one arm outstretched as if reaching for the chapel door another dozen steps away. He felt sick. What arrogance made him think that she would be glad at this news? She had laughed at herself when she confessed the secrecy Maddix had tricked her into. Derrien had hoped that any affection she had for the new king of Stonemount had died. He had hoped that the smiles she gave him, the kisses they shared, had been full of promises. If she was hurt at this final blow to the dreams she had carried since childhood, Derrien wasn't sure what he would do. He adored Arden, but a man had his pride, and being second choice was a bitter cup to drink.

Still, how could he stand there, watching her stumble in pain at this final shredding of her heart? He hurried across the grass to her.

She shuddered and pressed both hands against her face just as he reached her. Derrien enfolded her in his arms. The trembling all through her body sent a hot flash of angry pain through him and he wished he could face Maddix of Stonemount so he could strangle the man.

"It's all right," he murmured into her hair. "He's not worth it. Everything's going to be—" Derrien turned her to face him, and nearly dropped her when he realized she was red-faced and tear-streaked and
~~~~~

shuddering from silent laughter.

Laughter so deep she could hardly breathe or walk. Arden clung to him, gasping, drunk with laughter. She shuddered so hard she nearly twisted free of his arms and finally caught her breath.

"Of course it's going to be all right! We're free!"

She pulled free of him and executed a giddy pirouette. Laughter finally squeaked out as she took his hand and led him in a stumbling dance over the grass. Derrien took a deep breath and sent a silent shout of thanks heavenward, then took a firmer grip on her hands and eagerly joined in.

"What are you going to do now?" he couldn't help asking.

"Oh, dear ... " She paused for a few seconds and made a face at him, but the laughter wouldn't retreat. "Don't make me think about the future. The present moment is too wonderful to ignore!"

"How wonderful?" His voice cracked.

Arden froze for three long heartbeats, so he feared he had hurt her. Then her face flushed and she smiled with a new shyness that made him catch his breath, and slowly twined her arms around his neck.

"If I kiss you now ..." He swallowed hard, and his arms ached as he wrapped them around her, trying not to crush her with the jubilation surging through him. "I can't in all honor let you marry someone else. Not if you feel even a little bit—"

Arden kissed him, long and softly, sweetly, until he saw sparks of green magic behind his eyelids.

When they both had to stop to catch their breaths, she stayed pressed tight against him, and tucked her head under his chin.

"You did just ask me to marry you, didn't you?" she whispered.

"Begged. Pleaded. Vowed all my honor." His voice cracked. Then he stared, as a thin, elderly woman, all green and gold light, faded into view behind Arden, and smiled at him. She spoke, but he couldn't hear what she said.

"Auntie?" Arden leaned back enough she could turn to look at the woman, then at Derrien, then back to the woman. "You can see Auntie Glynna?" When he nodded, she clung to him again. "Then everything is perfect. That's proof. Yeshen blesses us."

"More important, does Auntie Glynna approve?"

Arden laughed and kissed him again.

~~~~~

Spring always arrived slowly, reluctantly in Stonemount, as if the warmth and fertility and greenness had become lost in the winding, cobblestone streets and couldn't find a way across the city. Yet centered on the apple tree and radiating outward a little more each day, spring
~~~~~

came early in the royal gardens. Royal tradition opened the palace gardens to all the citizens of Stonemount. In celebration of the news that Bianca was carrying their first child, Maddix played indulgent father-to-be, and gave in to her pleading to follow that tradition.

For ten days, even at twilight, when most hard-working artisans and merchants and crafters were settling in for a well-deserved night of rest, there were people in the gardens, enjoying the unexpected bounty of life and a touch of magic.

Maddix found the whole process, the very concept of sharing his private retreat with the general population, disgusting. He sometimes wondered if he would ever again be able to enjoy a walk in the gardens, even after the gates were closed again, simply because the memory would pollute the environs for him. Like everyone else, he came often to visit the green-golden glowing apple tree, but watching the marvelous young tree brought him no comfort or pleasure. Even the reports from his spies that Princess Arden had done no visible plantwise magic since the disappearance of her tree didn't give him pleasure.

Ambrose found him one evening scowling at the gate in the wall around the tree. He lurked in the shadows of the older, larger trees surrounding the cleared area, as if some invisible wall held him back. This was one of those golden evenings, the sky streaked with purple and rose, the clouds promising a blessing of nighttime rain and fair weather the next day. Ambrose walked through the gardens breathing deeply and wishing joy on everyone he met. Maddix's scowl was like the slap of an icy rag across his face. Ambrose honestly couldn't tell if the dark threads of grit and decay weaving through the garden came from the tainted, imprisoned tree, or from Maddix himself.

Despite the sickness Ambrose sensed at its core, the apple tree was taller than the tallest soldier now, gleaming softly with golden-green magic. The tree was so thick with leaves it was almost impossible to see the tiny apples that peered out between them. And that was the greatest marvel of all. A tree less than two years old bearing apples, in many different colors. Pale pink and golden and deep wine colored and streaked gold and green and red. The air within fifty yards of the tree smelled warm and sweet like harvest time. What could possibly make Maddix scowl like that?

Ambrose seriously doubted that his great-nephew had taken to heart any of the warnings he had given him. So what troubled him?

"It's a crime," Maddix snarled under his breath, and finally turned his head to glare at Ambrose. Before the elderly healer could ask what he meant, Maddix pointed with a jerky swing of his stiff arm.

A peasant couple stood barefoot in the thick moss that carpeted the ground around the apple tree, looking up at the branches. They were examining the apples, visibly trying to decide which one to pick. He looked around, and finally found a child sitting just within the wide-open gates. Even in the shadows, the child was pale, with dark patches under his eyes. Clearly, the couple was trying to find an apple to heal their child.

Ambrose shivered and sent up a silent, swift prayer that the blessing Arden had woven into the tree still dominated, and the apples now on the tree would give blessing and healing. He couldn't bring himself to warn them and incur Maddix's fury. Dylon still had freedom to come and go, although he was certainly gone from Stonemount more often than he was present. Ambrose knew Maddix wouldn't dare touch him, but he could find ways to use Dylon to punish his grandfather.

Please, Yeshen, protect your innocent people, he prayed.

Asking why the couple hadn't come to find Ambrose and ask him to heal their child was a waste of time. While many of the guards knew they were to fetch him if someone needed healing, no matter what time of the day or night, few did so. Maddix made sure everyone knew Ambrose was one of the greatest treasures of Stonemount, and he had a royal duty to protect his aging great-uncle's strength. Ambrose felt Maddix used the excuse of "royal duty" far too often to justify things his father and grandfather never would have condoned.

Too much had changed in the months since the death of King Doyne. More and more, the stamp of royalty and the idea of facing the palace gates and guards intimidated most people. Too many nobles supported the elevated attitude Maddix had toward royalty. The ones who disagreed either kept quiet, or they stayed at their country estates and rarely came into the capitol.

"Those apples belong to the nobility," Maddix continued, "not to filthy peasants."

"It is never a crime to heal a child, no matter who his parents are," Ambrose replied, trying to put a little humor into his voice. The longer Maddix believed that he complied with his beliefs and orders, the longer Dylon would be safe.

Ambrose saw the parents take the apple they had selected to their child. All the apples were small, little more than a few bites even for a child. Ambrose prayed again, for protection even more than healing.

In moments, the child struggled to his feet, then wriggled free of grasping arms as his parents tried to hug and hold him.

Maddix gave a disgusted sigh, part growl, and stalked away.

Ambrose waited until the joyful family was gone. Then he went through the gates and walked up to the tree and pressed his hands against the unnaturally smooth bark.

"Be strong. Be clean," he whispered. "Somehow, Arden will find a way to heal you, and free you. I promise."

He wasn't sure how he would keep that promise, when he was a prisoner, and Arden's letters no longer reached him. For all he knew, Maddix had told the world he was dead.

Perhaps that was for the best. The worst, most dangerous thing Arden could do was come here to Stonemount. Not even for the sake of the magic apple tree should she ever put herself in Maddix's hands.

~~~~~

King Maddix of Stonemount did not want to come to Princess Arden's wedding that fall. Despite his best efforts, he couldn't come up with excuses. He refused to admit that he might have made some miscalculations. Especially when Jaygo was present, always giving him those looks that made clear he was disappointed in him. How dare he? Jaygo had long ago passed from master and teacher to an advisor whose wisdom and value faded every day.

Bianca wanted to go to the wedding. He couldn't tell her no, because she had fully recovered from birthing their son, his heir, Maxin. Until his agents were secure enough in Ambray to begin eliminating members of the royal family, Maddix needed to play adoring husband. Besides, all the healers and nursemaids said Maxin would start growing soon. He was just delicately built like his mother, and he would prove a healthy, strong active child, now that the heat of summer had passed. Maddix chafed at the traditions and advice of the healers that he and Bianca not have another child for at least two years. If she had recovered from birthing Maxin, then why couldn't she get pregnant again? It was a conspiracy to deny him all the success he had certainly earned.

The wedding invitation coincided with the regular convocation of kings to meet and share news about the activities of magic wielders and threats from overseas, the harvests in different kingdoms, and to renew alliances and friendships. Maddix needed to present himself as the more-than-worthy successor to his father's throne. The route to this year's convocation went straight through Westerland. Most of the kings coming from the eastern side of the continent had been invited to attend the wedding, to stop and refresh themselves on their journey, before continuing west to the coast for the convocation. Maddix sneered outwardly, but inwardly trembled in loathing and fury at the image he would present to his peers if he absented himself.

Sending Jaygo in his place simply would not do. Maddix didn't trust him. He seriously considered arranging for a convenient accident to befall Jaygo and stop his judgmental glances, his constant murmurs
~~~~~

meant to be correction, but served only to irritate.

The most galling part of anticipating the wedding festivities was seeing Arden herself. His spies reported she continued to bloom in beauty. He tried to tell himself that her rustic charms would begin to fade soon, that her skin touched by the sun would toughen, and all that dirt she wallowed in for her plantwise duties would dull and dry her skin. Every time he slandered her vibrant coloring in his mind, Bianca's delicate pallor grew less appealing, like cold, plain rice.

Like any peasant, her hips would spread and her backside enlarge with each child she gave her common-born groom. And that was the most galling part. She was marrying the captain of the guard. How dare she sully herself, tainting her royal blood, making herself even less appealing? She had a duty to be at least endurable during the short time Maddix would be forced to marry her and impregnate her, so their son could take over his uncle's throne. Someday. How dare Arden add another name to the list of people Maddix had to kill to fulfill his long-range plans?

He considered the invitation to the wedding an insult, a slap in the face. They were mocking him. Even though he knew no one in Westerland had the wit to guess at the plans he had made, he still felt as if someone were mocking him, challenging him to act, insisting that he had failed. Somehow.

Yet he went, playing at joyful ally and friend and adoring husband and proud new father.

Before he left Stonemount, he left instructions for the healer in the palace staff to reduce the daily dose of herbs in Ambrose's meals that dulled his alertness and stunted his healing Gift. If the stubborn old fool insisted on continuing to live, then he could at least make himself useful and employ his healing Gift to making sure the heir to the throne grew stronger and healthier.

Maddix fought to be pleasant on the journey to Port'ham. Bianca was so excited, far more lively than usual, that he found some actual pleasure in the journey. She was a sweet thing and adored him and he did enjoy pleasing her. Yet even that had its limits. He contented himself with knowing that his bride was the most beautiful woman in the surrounding ten kingdoms.

Until Arden emerged from the palace gates into the garden where the wedding took place.

She glowed. She shimmered. Light flooded from her face and green-gold magic radiated from her so brightly her elegantly simple white gown and her bouquet and crown of white roses almost vanished. Every man attending the wedding sat up a little straighter or stood a little taller.

Maddix ground his teeth and his stomach knotted. Arden would have looked at him that way on this very day, if he had stuck to Jaygo's plan. He looked at white-blonde Bianca and for a moment his sparkling, pale wife was a washed-out little thing compared to golden, glowing Arden with her red-gold hair hanging past her knees and her green-blue eyes shining and huge and bright with dreams.

Her lips were soft pink and pursed in a smile she couldn't repress even in the most solemn moments of the ceremony. Maddix knew with stomach-turning certainty those lips would have been sweet and eager, and until a year ago, reserved for his pleasure alone. Bianca had giggled and twitched away nervously the first few times he took her into his arms. Bridal nerves had been charming, but not for long, and he grew weary of being tender and patient long before he had any satisfaction. Arden, Maddix suddenly knew, would have been eager from the first kiss. No ridiculous coaxing. No swallowing of angry scolding. No tears to endure. Laughter and eagerness and passion.

And now Derrien would have it all. Maddix hated the man now as much as he hated Alix since they were boys, wrestling in these very gardens. He tried to tell himself the man was only picking up his throwaways, and Arden was too flawed to make a proper queen. He tried to tell himself Derrien didn't have the wit to realize he wasn't marrying a proper princess.

Derrien had stolen her love away from Maddix. Derrien had tricked that filthy, simpleton princess into betraying Maddix. She was even duller and more simple than he had first thought. How else could she be so happy right this moment with her simple wedding and common-born bridegroom? She was a silly child and would have adored him, done everything he asked, used her plantwise gift solely for his service. And he had thrown it away.

For two agonizing seconds, Maddix considered the idea that he might have been a fool.

CHAPTER TWELVE

No. He was not the fool. Fools were those who thought the adoration would last, who looked at their brides with bedazzled eyes, vowing themselves to slavery through their hearts. Bianca looked at him the same way, he knew, but that was different. Wives were supposed to worship their husbands.

Maddix looked at Bianca sitting beside him under the canopied pavilion for the noble guests and smiled. The healers were fools. High time for Bianca to give him another son. If she died giving birth, so be it. Common sense said to kill Derrien before Arden got herself pregnant and ruined her admittedly stunning beauty. Yes, the timing would work out quite well. She would believe herself heartbroken, and he could convince her that she would find healing and shelter in his arms. He would appeal to their shared heartbreak, both of them bereaved, if necessary.

With such thoughts in his head, Maddix was able to smile and cheer with everyone else when Arden and Derrien sealed their vows with a kiss.

~~~~~

The enclosed pavilion for the royal family and their special guests was mercifully empty when Derrien escorted Arden to it, late on the afternoon of their wedding. She protested that she was fine when he insisted she rest. In truth, her feet did hurt a little. She wasn't used to so many hours straight in shoes, cut off from contact with the soil. Arden kicked off her crystal-beaded wedding slippers the moment they stepped through the cloth flap of the door. Her new husband only laughed at her. He kissed her as he guided her to the couch, lingering for many delightful seconds, quite stealing her breath away. She gasped a little when he started to draw away and Derrien laughed again.

"Don't—" Arden caught her breath as he pressed her hand to his lips and a thrill shot through her body at the simple touch. His eyes spoke promises to her, mixed with his laughter and his concern for her. She couldn't speak for a moment, and in that moment, he took his leave. She sank back against the thick cushions of one of the many couches filling the long pavilion and chuckled a little.

Several times as she prepared for their wedding, Arden had wondered about Maddix's reaction when he came to the ceremony—if he came at all. Thoughts of him had put a bitter note in her joy, and she
~~~~~

had pushed his image resolutely away. Still, he kept sneaking back and she wondered what his face would show when he realized she was in love with Derrien.

To be honest, she wanted him to be jealous, to be furious, to be stricken with the realization of what he had lost. She wanted him to confess that he had stolen her tree and beg for her help in stemming the slowly growing seepage of poison throughout Stonemount, as a result of his lies and theft.

Arden hadn't seen Maddix and Bianca when she stepped up to the altar to make her vows, and she was too happily nervous to look for them. Derrien filled her vision, her heart, her world.

A few leaves sprouted in the roses twined in her hair and a new bud appeared among the thornless stems with a faint popping noise. Arden sputtered laughter and wondered if anyone would notice. If she kept this up, her rose crown would be three times bigger at the end of the day than when it had started. It was a good thing she had put aside her bouquet at the end of the ceremony. It had started trailing roots and some of the white roses were turning pink and red. Accurate reflections of her feelings for Derrien, she admitted with a sigh that tended toward a giggle.

Pitchers of wine and cider and fruit-flavored water filled the sideboard, among bowls of fruit and sweets and pastries for the enjoyment of guests who came to escape the crowds in the gardens. As King Alfred had done for her christening, the palace gardens were open for the common people to share the celebration. Arden supposed there were three storerooms' worth of little gifts already piled up at the garden gates, left by guests on their way to the many celebrations scattered throughout Port'ham.

She teetered between laughter and tears when she considered the gifts she had seen. Dainty lace shawls and thick socks. Jars of preserved fruits. Braids of onions. Jars of dried spices and sweets. And baby clothes. Dozens of little blankets and caps and shirts in all sizes and colors. She lost her breath just seeing all the nappies and rattles and decorations for the crib. She wouldn't have to make anything when she and Derrien had their first child. Or their fourth or fifth.

She wanted children. Lots of children. Arden shivered and wrapped her arms tight around herself to still the quivering sensation that came every time she considered that making love with Derrien would eventually put a baby in her belly. Besides, every time she did that--

Four pops answered her unfinished thought and she burst out laughing as her crown felt noticeably heavier.

"Oh!" a delicate, breathy voice exclaimed, effectively announcing Queen Bianca's entrance into the royal pavilion. "I thought I was imagining things..."

"Have they changed color yet?" Arden smothered laughter and turned to face the newcomer.

Bianca was a confection—as always—in pale blue, trimmed in lace and silver and diamonds, all fluff and feathers and sweetness. It was hard to be angry with her, even knowing Alix nursed a wounded heart. Arden knew her brother was much better off without the good-hearted but flighty girl. He would not have resented protecting and guiding Bianca for the rest of his life, but it would have drained him.

"Well, the tiniest ones are rather pink." Bianca giggled and rustled loudly as she crossed the carpet and settled down on the couch opposite Arden. "Why do you do that?"

"I don't do it on purpose, believe me."

She wished she could be friends with Bianca, but knew Maddix would never allow it. Arden had heard enough rumors of the changes in Stonemount and the things his supporters said about her, she could guess what Maddix would do with any overtures of friendship to his wife. He would likely say Arden was jealous and angling to destroy his marriage, at the very least.

While it riled her to refrain from striking back every time another report of Maddix's ridiculous, cruel statements reached her, Arden tried to act as if she didn't care. That his words, his lies didn't matter. That grew harder as she felt the apple tree shrivel and its inner core of magic darken as a result of his lies and false accusations. Glynna and her parents and other older, wiser souls maintained that if they fought Maddix's poison, they would only muddy the waters and make things worse. If they left him alone, eventually his poison would turn around and bite him.

"How are you?" she asked, shaking herself free of her thoughts. She had to attend to her guest, after all. "I *am* glad you could come to the wedding."

"Despite how Alix feels?" A flash of guilt wrinkled Bianca's pretty little face for a moment.

"My brother never had a broken heart before. He'll recover." She bit her tongue to keep from adding: *I did, and very quickly.* "But how are you? Tell me about your son!"

Like any new mother, mention of her baby turned Bianca into a chatterbox. And effectively saved Arden from having to make polite, safe conversation. She cringed and hoped it didn't show, when Bianca begged her to have a daughter first, so their children could marry and seal the union between their kingdoms. Was Maddix starting that particular scheme already? Arden vowed she would never step foot in Stonemount, and neither would any child of hers, as long as Maddix ruled. Not until the land had been cleansed and her apple tree's magic was healed.

"Oh, I almost forgot!" Bianca blushed daintily. "I wanted to ask you about the apple tree."

"Apple tree?" Arden would have thought Bianca would never know about the tree. What sort of lies had Maddix told her about it?

"The apple tree you gave Maddix. I know he says some high and mighty wizards gave it to him, but that's just male pride. Uncle Ambrose told me you made it, so I know you can help it, even if nobody else can."

"How is Ambrose? I haven't heard from him in months," she said, rather than the truth, that she hadn't heard from Ambrose since before King Doyne died. Better to talk about him, however, than inform Bianca that Maddix had stolen the tree.

"He hasn't heard from you, either."

"But I write to him every three months."

"Well, someone steals your letters, then, because he never hears from you." Bianca shrugged. "But the tree—I'm worried about the tree. It droops. I don't know anything about trees, but none of the other trees in the garden have started turning colors yet. The apple tree is brown, and it won't let go of its leaves. Do you know what's wrong with it?"

What sort of trick was Maddix playing? Had he sent Bianca to trick Arden into revealing information that he could use against her?

She shuddered at a brief image of Maddix chopping down the tree if he ever learned that she could feel the tree's condition, its suffering. He would kill the tree to hurt her. That was just the kind of man he had revealed himself to be.

"Bianca, this is important. Magic turns deadly if one person hoards it. If he surrounds it with lies. The tree was created to be shared. Don't eat the apples. Don't give them to anyone you care about. They'll be poison until Maddix tells the truth about how he obtained the tree, and then shares them with the entire kingdom."

As if her words had been a summons, Glynna floated through the wall of the tent and hovered between the two young women.

"But … they're magical healing apples. How can they turn to poison?" Bianca bleated.

"I know they will. Don't eat the apples, I beg you."

"But you wouldn't hurt me, would you? I thought we were friends!"

"We are." Arden choked on the need to laugh at such a ridiculous statement. What kind of an idiot was Bianca?

Just the kind of idiot I would have been, if I had continued to believe Maddix's lies and eloped with him when he asked me. Arden felt sick, and a moment later, she felt light enough to fly. She was free of him, and married to Derrien, just as she had dreamed for years.

"No. That can't be true." Where other women would turn red, Bianca only went more pale. "You're jealous!"

"Jealous? On my wedding day? Don't be a greater fool than you already are."

With a squeak, Bianca jumped to her feet and fled the pavilion in tears.

"Well, at least you tried," Glynna said, and floated down to perch on the couch next to Arden. "Sometimes the truth isn't pretty, or tactful."

~~~~~

It was a perfect late fall day, warm and bright, the fields green with the first sprouting of the winter wheat, the trees crimson and gold. The crops this harvest had been four times more abundant than last year. The people all attributed their blessings to Princess Arden, as they had attributed the harvest to her the year she was born. The young bride was blissfully unaware of the adoration of her people, enrapt in adoring her handsome, adoring husband.

That afternoon, she stood at her worktable by the window, looking out over the gardens. As had become habit, she didn't see the trees or the late-flowering vines. She only saw her husband and brother, slowly strolling through the gardens as they talked. As always when they had a serious discussion, the two gestured with their hands, or sometimes stopped and punctuated their words with a stomp or shook their heads—or when they laughed, slapped each other on the back or pushed the other away. She smiled, hearing their laughter float up to her window.

She completely ignored the seedling in its small pot in her cupped hands, until Glynna grew tired of hovering and waiting.

"You have to concentrate, dear." She smiled, completely understanding the ways of young love.

"I know, Auntie, but…" Arden sighed. "I didn't drain myself of all magic with my first tree, but maybe I started trying too soon with this one?"

The apple seedling was only eight inches tall. It had a good number of leaves, but nothing like the amazing growth of the first tree. Still, the leaves were bright and thick and darkly green, visibly quivering with life, and glowed a soft, sparkling golden-green.

"Like your attention, maybe your strength is divided," Glynna suggested after a moment of thought. Her eyes brightened and her
~~~~~

sympathetic smile suddenly widened.

"I don't think so."

"Silly girl. How long have you been married?"

"Not nearly long enough!"

"That's not what I meant. It's not my place to teach you about your body since I don't have one of my own but ... did you ever consider you could be pregnant?"

Arden stared for five long, stuttering heartbeats. She nearly dropped the pot as she fumbled blindly to put it down on her worktable. Her feet kicked up the rugs as she ran for the door of her workroom.

Glynna stayed where she was, her smile growing wider as she saw the princess scurry down the stairs much as she had done as a child. She heard the thud as the door slammed open at the bottom of the tower and turned to float to the window in time to see Arden fly out the door and across the leaf-strewn grass to meet up with her husband and brother. From so far away, Glynna couldn't hear their words, but she didn't need to. Arden grabbed Derrien's hands and started dancing him around the garden.

Glynna chuckled when Derrien stopped short, nearly yanking Arden off her feet and stared down at her. Then he gave out a shout and wrapped his arms tight around her, lifting her off the ground and spinning her wildly around as he kissed her. Alix stepped back, his grin wide enough for Glynna to see at the top of the tower.

A soft humming filled the air, like a chord strummed on a tiny harp. The apple seedling trembled violently and abruptly geysered eight more branches, dozens of leaves, and grew more than a foot taller. For several seconds, the glow of golden-green magic was nearly blinding.

"You really should learn more control, child," Glynna said, shaking her head even as she smiled. She glanced out the window again, where the happy dance was just starting to slow. "But later."

~~~~~

Alix was alone in the gardens the early summer day Arden went into labor. He could have sat with Comyn and the other noblemen of the court in his father's study while they waited for the news and supported the nervous king, soon to be a grandfather. He could have gone into the chapel where the ladies of the court were praying and chattering with excitement. He could have stayed in the outer rooms of Arden and Derrien's suite, listening to the bustle of activity, supporting his closest friend through this nervous time when all a man could do was worry. Derrien was too busy holding Arden's hand and too excited to need any support.

Though Alix could face enemies with bloodlust in their eyes, and
~~~~~

had while on border patrol, the idea of standing idly by while his little sister suffered through labor made him feel nauseous. And, he admitted only to himself, he felt some measure of jealousy that she could smile through her pain. When would he ever find his true love?

"If the wizards were still roaming the land, I would ask one of them to make a maiden for me out of flowers," he told the apple tree that towered eight feet over his head, lush with leaves and the perfume of white blossoms.

The tree swayed a little, lithe on its slim trunk, untouched by any wind. Did it respond to his words, or what Arden went through this moment?

"Maybe I should ask for a maiden made from one of your apples, hmm?" He stroked the trunk and sank down on the grass under the wide-spreading limbs. "You're a part of her. Would an apple maiden look like her? Is it wrong to think my sister is the most beautiful woman in the world?"

The tree shuddered, then seemed to twist and reach for the window of Arden's room. From where he sat, Alix couldn't hear anything, but he saw faint flickers of movement beyond the gauzy curtains.

"You're worried about her too, hmm? There's nothing I can do in there. I came out here because I know as long as you're all right, so is she." He flinched when the tree bent away from him, so the top leaves almost touched the ground.

Alix leaped to his feet as a cry cut through the balmy air. He stared, breathless, at the window of his sister's room. Pink flowers burst out among the white apple blossoms and golden apples appeared at the ends of ten branches. He staggered backward, grinning, his legs trying to fold underneath him. Alix put out a hand and leaned against the trunk as he sank to his knees.

"Yes, I'm very happy for her, too," he whispered.

~~~~~

The fuss finally quieted. The ladies of the court witnessed the child's first kicks and cries, and left in happy tears, to spread the joyful news. When the new mother had been washed and dressed in clean clothes, Queen Elise put her granddaughter into the new father's arms. Derrien sat down gingerly on the edge of Arden's bed, cradling the tiny, pink-wrapped bundle.

He had ridden at a mad gallop through raiding parties and across mud and rocks, holding a bow in his hands, arrows in his teeth, guiding his mount with his knees, and felt far more unsure of himself now than any other time in his life. He thought his chest would burst from the multitude of feelings spinning around inside. He wanted to laugh and
~~~~~

cry and hug Arden and kiss her breathless. But then, kissing her breathless had ultimately led to this moment, hadn't it? And he most certainly didn't want her going through this day again, despite the reassurances of a dozen ladies that Arden's labor had been easy and quick.

"She has your mother's eyes," Arden whispered, tugging back the blanket to see their daughter's tiny, wrinkled face. "The most incredible shade of violet."

"My father used to tease her she should have been named Violet, not Rose." Derrien's voice was rough, as if he had spent the last three hours shouting instead of holding Arden's hand, whispering encouragement and love, and willing her every ounce of his strength.

"I approve of the name," Elise said with a chuckle, "if my opinion has any value."

"Mother!" Arden laughed, which made the sleeping baby open her violet eyes and give out a sound like a hiccup.

"I think she likes it." Derrien gently touched the pale curls sitting on his tiny daughter's forehead.

"Very well, then. Violet you shall be." She smiled up at her husband and he couldn't resist the happiness in her eyes.

They kissed and the moment prolonged, engulfing their whole world as it had done at their wedding. Elise wisely stepped in and retrieved her new granddaughter from the young father's arms before he started to relax, or forgot she was there.

CHAPTER THIRTEEN

News did not travel well from Westerland to Stonemount, usually taking twice as long as new coming from three times as much distance. The news of the birth of Princess Violet took three months to reach the palace. Spies and messengers hesitated to report on happy events in their long-time ally. Either they had adopted King Maddix's attitude toward Westerland, that anything happening there wasn't worth his attention, or they did not want to incur the wrath of their superiors.

The royal family of Westerland, especially Princess Arden and her flourishing magic apple tree, were unwelcome topics in the palace. Rumors said Queen Bianca was failing, after having given birth to a still-born daughter. This despite reserving every shriveled apple the ailing tree produced exclusively for her use.

Few people dared to ask why the wizards who had gifted Maddix with the magic apple tree couldn't come and make it healthy again. Those who wanted to cause trouble asked instead why Ambrose the healer, the king's own great-uncle couldn't heal the queen. Only a few knew he urged Bianca to stop eating the apples, but she was a stubborn little bit of fluff and insisted the apples would not harm her, the apples weren't the problem.

When the news reached Maddix of the birth of Arden's daughter and the celebration throughout Westerland, he sneered and told himself to be grateful he had not married her. He would settle for nothing but sons. At least Bianca had given him one son, who was finally thriving. He refused to admit, even to himself, that was because Ambrose was no longer being slowly poisoned, which allowed him more healing energy to use on Prince Maxin.

Maddix crumpled the parchment with the details of Violet's birth and silently cursed her for adding yet another name to the list of people he had to kill to attain his goals. Meaning more delays. Did the stupid little farmer princess think he enjoyed having people killed? Yes, Clancy and Baethon enjoyed the task, and he was relieved to hand the work to them, but Arden was being totally unreasonable, first refusing to let him do her thinking for her, and now adding first a husband and now a daughter to the barrier between him and taking the throne of Westerland.

Violet was third in line for the throne, and wouldn't be allowed to leave Westerland when Maddix married her widowed mother. While

Maddix considered using Arden's grief over Derrien's inevitable and necessary death to make her pliable, he couldn't wrap his mind around how to turn a mother's bereavement into a tool. Perhaps that was a weakness in him. He blamed Bianca's screaming fit when he told her not to fret, when she had regained her strength, they would work on having another child. Women in her condition were known to be unreasonable, so he hadn't tried to cheer her with the new realization that he did regret their stillborn daughter, because daughters were just as useful for taking over other countries.

He usually avoided Bianca until her maids dressed and painted her into a semblance of her former beauty, so she could come to dinner. Now, though, Maddix stormed down the hallway to her rooms. The parchment with the news of Violet's birth crinkled in his tightening grip.

Bianca was asleep when he stormed through the door, her delicate beauty shriveled like the half-eaten apple clutched in her claw-like hand. Her pale luster had turned to the white of melting snow, less a color than an impression of draining weakness that made him feel sick and tired himself, just looking at her. He used to enjoy cuddling up next to her in the enormous royal bed, waking often in the night to look at her and revel that she belonged to him and no one else. Now, Maddix could barely force himself to greet her when she tottered into the dining room. He was relieved when she tottered out an hour later, to return to her bed.

Maddix stood over the tiny shape huddled under inches of blankets, shivering slightly in the warm night air. She was only the faintest reminder of the woman he had married and that sickened him. He felt he had been robbed, but who could he blame?

His gaze landed on the apple in her hand. A surge of nausea worked through him, turning into rage, and he snatched the apple up and flung it out the open window.

"Maddix?" Bianca whispered, her eyes flickering open. She got only a grunt for an answer as he unfolded the crumpled parchment and read through the message again, torturing himself. "I had the most amazing dream."

He remembered a time when he loved listening to her silly dreams. Even when he laughed at her, she continued telling him. He liked seeing the amazement and wonder and puzzlement that flickered across her once-lovely face when she recited her totally meaningless dreams.

When had he stopped finding enjoyment in her silliness?

"Another one?" he snarled. "Don't waste your energy telling me."

"You're angry with me."

"Me? Angry?" Something snapped inside, like a fragile twig that let an entire log jam slide through a narrow spot in a swollen river, thundering toward a dam already shaking from the pressure of the water. "Why? Because you talk all day long and say nothing? You're good for nothing. You're lucky that farmer princess only produced a girl. If she had a son, you would be even more hopeless."

"Arden had a daughter? How wonderful." Bianca struggled to sit up. "We must send her a gift."

"I'll send her my curse."

"Why?" Wonder of wonders, a bit of color touched her face. Or was that just a shadow from her frown of utter and characteristic confusion?

"She cursed me with that tree."

"No, Arden would never hurt anyone. Not even you." Tears touched her eyes and Bianca's voice grew stronger even as it trembled.

"Not *even* me? What reason would she have for wanting to hurt me?" His voice cracked, breaking the tone that so perfectly conveyed wounded innocence struggling for dignity.

"Is she right, Maddix? Have you been lying, turning the tree's magic to poison?"

"Lying about what?" he growled and crumped the parchment into a hard ball that he flung to the floor. He leaned over the bed, and Bianca cowered away, terror bringing color into her face for the first time since the birth of their daughter. "What lies does she claim I've told?" His voice dropped to a chill whisper.

Bianca whimpered, then her eyes rolled back in her head. Her body stiffened, convulsing twice, before she went limp.

Maddix stared, his heart thudding so loudly he nearly missed the whisper of breath escaping her body. His mind raced and he swallowed down a howl of fury. How could she do this to him? The timing was all wrong. None of his players were in the right place for the next step of conquest.

Voices in the hallway, beyond the closed bedroom door, broke him out of the racing of his thoughts. Too many plans, too many calculations, had to be redone, backed up and revised. His head would burst before he knew what to do.

Infuriated, the voice clearest in his head was Jaygo's, advising him that when the pieces did not fall into place, when someone failed in their assigned task, he should continue in his role, his task, until a better opportunity presented itself.

Maddix released the breath that had begun to ache in his chest. Yes, continue in his role. He had garnered so much sympathy, so many more people willing to anticipate his every need, as he played the role of bereaved father.

"Bianca?" He made his voice cracked. "Bianca, please, darling!" He went to his knees on the bed and leaned over her still form, shaking her, just as the bedroom door opened. "Bianca, wake up!"

In the shadows of the bedroom, it didn't matter that he couldn't conjure up tears. The pain in his voice and the shaking of his body served more than adequately. He fought the maidservants just a little, when they tried to hurry him from the room, and covered his face with one hand as he staggered down the hallway, out from this place that already smelled of death. He went to his office and closed the door, and filled the waiting time with plans and calculations, until the palace healer knocked timidly on his door and regretfully informed him that Queen Bianca was dead.

~~~~~

Arden was surprised when Maddix asked if he would be welcome at the Harvest Festival that fall. His father had not been able to attend since Maddix was a child, and the king now wanted to rectify that neglect and move toward rebuilding the ancient friendship between Westerland and Stonemount. She thought about what she had overheard the day her tree was stolen, the lies Maddix had told, the poison seeping ever outward from the heart of Stonemount, and the rumors that Bianca had not died of a lingering fever after childbirth. She found it highly unlikely that Maddix cared about the friendship with Westerland, unless it profited him. And harmed Westerland.

Yet what could she do? What could she say? She had told her parents all she had heard and seen and felt, and they were just as wary of any overtures of renewed friendship. The king's entire council was in agreement. Yet to respond inhospitably to Maddix's request would just give him reason for further cruelties and lies. That might just be what he hoped for. King Alfred and his advisors agreed to proceed with caution and give him no excuses to strike at Westerland.

~~~~~

Maddix appeared perfectly at ease, as if he had been coming to the Harvest Festival every year since childhood. The boyhood pretense of friendship between him and Alix had been little more than politeness, mixed with the eagerness of one boy to explore a different place and the eagerness of the other boy to show off his home. There were few words exchanged between the two men now, beyond what was expected by courtesy, but they didn't look daggers at each other as they had at Arden's wedding. Maddix clapped for the mummers and minstrels and praised the cider, tossed coppers to the children who came to sing for the nobles, and gorged on sweets and toffee-coated apples.

When Derrien joined in the fun and games between the palace guards and the city guards, Maddix showed none of the disdain Arden had expected. Rilling had passed along many reports of what Maddix said about the royal family of Westerland, thanks to friends he maintained in Stonemount. King Maddix despised a man who would descend from, as he termed it, "the lofty position granted by his marriage" to socialize, and especially to engage in games and contests with the commoners he had left behind. Arden scolded herself to ignore Maddix and let herself enjoy the silliness as her husband and his loyal troops battled with feather dusters for swords and cushions for armor, more liable to get hurt tripping over each other than from the blows and bumps.

<div align="center">~~~~~</div>

Mid-afternoon on the second day of the festival, Caitlin brought baby Violet out to join the family after her nap. Maddix stayed seated and held his practiced expression of polite amusement, while the royal family gathered around the baby. He flinched several times when Violet giggled and squealed and made jabbering noises for her grandfather and uncle.

He watched, alert and braced to head off trouble, when two men in dark clothes slunk through the shadows between the surrounding pavilions of other noble families. The problem with hired thugs, he reflected, was that they cared more about money than doing a job properly. They had no loyalty to anyone, so they were likely to speak what little they knew to save their own necks if they were captured.

Finally, Clancy and Baethon returned from their gluttonous wanderings, clutching turkey legs and tankards of hard cider. Clancy sauntered up to the royal pavilion and leaned against the support pole, not looking at his king but close enough to take a softly spoken instruction. Baethon sauntered into the shadows where the two strangers had gone.

Minutes later, he stepped from the shadows and nodded to Clancy, who in turn glanced at his king and nodded to him. Maddix allowed himself only the faintest of smiles and turned to watch the royal family as they finished their ritual of adoring baby Violet. Alix gestured across the gardens toward the dancing square set up outside the garden gates and offered his arm to Caitlin. The girl blushed prettily, tucked a few loose strands of raven hair back into her crown of flowers, and curtseyed to her prince.

Alfred and Elise smiled at each other and linked arms and wandered away, down the narrow lanes between the pavilions, leaving Arden and Derrien alone with their daughter. Maddix smiled for the first time in hours and slouched a little in his chair. He was waiting for it, but still twitched slightly when two dark shadows leaped from

101

between the pavilions and flung the king and queen of Westerland to the ground.

There was little time for outcry from the victims. Less time for anyone to realize what had happened. A single shriek went up from a woman who saw blood on the knife cruelly yanked from King Alfred's throat. Maddix flicked a glance at Clancy, who nodded to Baethon.

"Murder!" Baethon roared and dashed straight at the dark-clothed men. "Guards! Guards! They've murdered the king and queen!"

The two strangers stood frozen for a mere heartbeat, stunned at the accusation coming from the man who had given them gold coins just a few moments before. Terror folded their faces and they fled.

Derrien raced after them, shouting for the palace guards. Clancy and Baethon reached the two assassins several crucial moments before Derrien. Both strangers were writhing in the torn grass, blood bubbling from slit throats before he could shout for the men to be taken alive.

Behind them, Arden dropped to her knees next to her parents' bloody, too-still bodies. She clutched her daughter close, hiding the baby's eyes from the sight. Her mouth worked in a silent cry. All color left her face and she swayed as if she would fall.

Across the garden, Arden's apple tree shuddered, the branches waving as if in a human seizure. The glow of magic winked out with the abruptness of a thunderclap.

~~~~~

The two assassins carried gold coins with the boar's head crest of the treasury of Ambray. Under their clothes, stained with blood, the palace guards found papers with the seal of Ambray, ordering the men to kill every member of the royal family they could reach. They had specific instructions to kill Arden, because the king of Ambray blamed her for the death of his daughter. Wizards had investigated and determined that she used her plantwise magic to turn the apple tree's magic to poison. Likely out of jealousy, because everyone knew, according to the investigators, that she expected to become queen of Stonemount. Witnesses insisted they had overheard her on her wedding day, encouraging Bianca to eat an apple every day, to help her conceive and birth another child.

Many hours later, Arden, Derrien, Alix, Comyn and Maddix stared at the coins and papers spread out on the table in what was now King Alix's study.

"My friends," Maddix said in a soothing voice that no one was willing or able to appreciate, "there can be no doubt. I have seen that handwriting many times over the years. That is the handwriting of Prime Minister Gregory. Ambray has turned against you. Against us,
~~~~~

actually. They also blame me for Bianca's death. They are threatening to take my son from me."

"Letters can be forged. Handwriting can be copied. I don't believe Ambray had anything to do with it." Alix shook his head and clenched his fists, raising them for a moment as if to crash them down on the table. He dropped them into his lap instead.

"The time for swallowing our private hurts for the sake of peace is over. It is time to go to war. Before Ambray strikes again. Before they follow through on their threats."

"Something about this feels very wrong," Derrien said, his voice steely quiet.

"Treachery is always a sour note." Maddix glanced around at his tiny audience and stood to emphasize his words. "We can't give them time to prepare. We must attack immediately."

"What good can we do against Ambray?" Alix asked. "Even our two countries combined could only match them. We have no advantage."

"Alix," Arden blurted, "you can't be serious! War? Without confronting them, without giving them a chance to prove their innocence?"

"My dear Arden, all I can offer is what I have heard and seen, and the evidence sitting here before us. I want to give you justice. Give us all justice." Maddix held out his hand in a gesture that reminded her all too much of that first dance when she was a silly child full of dreams. The memory made her shudder.

"Mark my words, no good will come of this war. We will destroy ourselves, and innocent people."

"We will not destroy ourselves." The slightest smirk caught up one corner of his mouth. "The king of Brentonwald has expressed his interest in allying with us."

"Brentonwald?" Alix sat back farther in his chair. "They could swallow us and Ambray and have room for dessert."

"Alix—don't joke at such a time." Arden buried her face in her hands, struggling against tears.

~~~~~

Despite her arguments, Arden stood at the gates of Port'ham less than three weeks later to bid farewell to her brother and husband as they led the soldiers of Westerland to join forces with Maddix and Stonemount's army. They would meet at the common border with Ambray and move up into the enemy country. Arden's only consolation, as she held her baby daughter up and helped her wave good-bye, was that Alix had sent secret envoys to the king of Ambray, pleading for a chance to speak and find the truth and wrest peace from the jaws of war.
~~~~~

Winter would come quickly, and she prayed that their family would be together again before the first snows fell.

"Stand up straight and hold your head high, my dear," Glynna whispered, as if all the people waiting in the gates of the city to bid farewell to the departing soldiers could see or hear her. "You are the light of your kingdom. You must set an example your parents would approve. No tears. You must be confident, or your people will have no hope."

"Oh, Auntie ... if only I could be with them."

"War is no place for the plantwise, child. Except in the aftermath, to help the healers," Glynna admitted after a moment's pause. "It's no place for your menfolk, either, and if your brother's plan works, they'll be home in only a few weeks, excited and tired and grateful for the adventure they missed. Let's go inside where no one can see us, shall we?" She brushed her ghostly fingers across the princess's cheek, managing to dislodge a single tear.

Violet chuckled and flapped her little hands, trying to grasp the transparent ones over her head. Arden smiled at her daughter's antics, then caught her breath at a return of that trembling aching deep inside. That tiny crack in her iron control would turn into a flood in another moment if she didn't take her teacher's advice. With Comyn's hand resting on her elbow for guidance and support, she hurried down the cobblestone streets to the sanctuary of the palace.

Late into the night, she sat at the base of her apple tree, cradling her sleeping daughter, wrapped in blankets against the fall chill, and prayed, staring up at the stars with eyes swollen and misty with tears.

CHAPTER FOURTEEN

War wasn't quite what Alix or Derrien imagined. They knew well enough how to make camp, how to blend into the landscape and spend most of their time spying on the enemy, laying ambushes and using the landscape to cause the enemy soldiers hardships, and very little time in actual fighting. They knew about wounds and filth and the aloneness. What they hadn't imagined was how some people treated war like a festival. What they hadn't expected was how Maddix acted as if he were the injured party, and he was being gracious by allowing them to participate in his "righteous campaign," as he called it.

Then there was the involvement of Brentonwald. What stake did they have in all this? Alix didn't like Lord Anselm, the ambassador from Brentonwald, who was also a warlord and led a full third of Brentonwald's army. There was something a little too cool and cynical about the man. Alix wondered if he would be angered or amused that the secret attempts at talking peace gave signs of succeeding.

On the night before they were to meet Ambray's forces on the battlefield, Alix and Derrien sat by the fire ring in front of Maddix's tent, studying maps. They could have been inside the massive tent, but there was something about the thick carpets and leather folding camp furniture, the numerous skins of wine and other delicacies spread about for the allies to enjoy that made both men shudder.

They rather enjoyed sitting on logs next to the fire, occupying themselves with what King Alfred had always said was the true business of war: making peace as quickly as possible, with whatever came to hand. They had their backs to Maddix's open tent door. He emerged from his tent and paused a moment to observe them hard at work. His chuckle startled them. He stepped over a third log to reach his folding chair, draped with a crimson blanket, and set down yet another of those sloshing skins of wine he was always offering to his allies.

"Hard at work planning strategy, my friends? Why bother? The landscape favors us. What is the use of paying soldiers good silver if they can't manage war without going about on leading strings?" Maddix stretched out so his glossy black boots rested on the log that should have been his seat. His black uniform made him blend into the darkness beyond the fire, so his ruddy face and golden hair seemed to float disembodied in the darkness.

"True," Derrien said with that calmness that Alix envied, as if he could put aside all his animosity toward the man, "but it's foreign to our soldiers. That reduces our advantage."

"We are in the right. Avenging your murdered loved ones and protecting my innocent son."

"And much profit for all, when we win." Lord Anselm emerged into the firelight from the darkness beyond Maddix's tent.

He was a tall, gaunt, cold man, this commander of the Brentonwald army. A cynical twist to his upper lip and amused gleam in his eye as he bowed to Maddix made Alix wonder, hope, that perhaps the man didn't like Maddix or respect him. The hope grew stronger when his nod of respect for Alix and Derrien lacked that cynical touch. If Brentonwald could be persuaded to stand with them when they talked peace with Ambray, this whole adventure would be turned into nothing more strenuous than a camping trip.

"Lord Anselm." Maddix stood quickly. "Will you join us?"

"Only for a short time. I must prepare for tomorrow's battle. If there is a battle." Again that gleam, and a flick of his gaze toward Alix that made the young king wonder what the man knew. Rumors and old tales said there were more wizards in Brentonwald than anywhere else across the continent. They were active, moving among the people rather than retiring to study and vanish into their quiet, magically shielded valleys, as most higher magic wielders did in the rest of the civilized world. What if Anselm were a wizard, hundreds of years old, and he could read their every thought?

For a moment, Alix wished Arden were with them. As a Gifted one, she could see magic in other people. She could tell him if a flicker of dark purple magic hovered around Anselm's fingers and hair and gleamed in that sparkle in his eyes.

"Is there something I don't know about?" Maddix asked with a chuckle.

"King Alix is a true statesman," the gaunt man said with a bow toward Alix. There was nothing amused now in his voice and face, and that was a comfort. "He tries to bring peace through talk and avoid killing the peasants who make us rich."

"You're working behind my back?" His voice cracked and his hand clutched at his belt knife. "What kind of treachery —"

"I have told you everything I've done, Maddix." Alix stood but kept his hands clasped behind his back. He was quietly proud of himself that he kept his voice calm and even and low. Why let the common soldiers around them know their leaders argued? "If you won't listen, that isn't my fault. I don't like the idea of corpses filling fields that should be full of crops."

A page boy dressed in Stonemount's livery hurried up through the darkness, sweating and flushed, with dark smears under his eyes. Alix felt a moment of irritation. The boy couldn't be more than twelve and expected to work as hard as a grown man. The boy held out a scroll as he approached the fire. Maddix stepped forward, reaching for it. A flash of fury touched his face when the boy handed it to Alix instead.

"An envoy from Ambray asks to speak with you, Majesty," the boy rasped. He stepped back on trembling legs. Whether from exhaustion or fear, Alix couldn't tell.

"Well done, brother!" Derrien exclaimed. He held out his belt flask to the boy, who took it with a grin and nod of thanks.

"How wonderful," Maddix murmured through gritted teeth, pasting a grin on his face.

"Where is he, lad?" Alix remembered he had some bread and cheese left over from his supper, which he had taken walking while inspecting the troops a few hours ago. He found the sack and dug in it, giving the generous remaining hunks to the page. "Lead the way. You've done a good job."

The boy flashed him a trembling smile, conspicuously avoiding looking at his own king.

"Coming, Maddix?" he asked, as he and Derrien turned to follow the boy back out into the darkness.

"In a moment. I have to put the wine away. We should save it for celebrating, later." Maddix stooped and scooped up the sack of wine.

Lord Anselm gave Maddix a mocking bow, the cynical curve of his mouth stronger than ever, and vanished into the darkness after the other two men. Maddix let out a sigh that turned into a snarl. He hefted the wine sack and contemplated smashing it to the ground for a moment.

"What's the fuss about?" Clancy asked, sauntering up to the tent from where he had been dicing with some of the elite Guardsmen.

"Alix the peacemaker," he growled, and dropped the wine sack in his chair. "He's ruining my war!"

"That's not very friendly. Did you at least get some poisoned wine into him? Finally?"

"It was the perfect plan. Get both those virtuous idiots too sick to fight and then have them conveniently killed in battle."

"The best way to hide a dead body," his friend offered in a slow, sly voice, "is in a pile of dead bodies. It can still happen that way. You can't tell *all* your soldiers there will be peace, can you?"

Maddix's pouting snarl turned into a grin, then a chuckle, then a roar as he turned and stepped into the darkness to follow the others, with Clancy at his heels.

~~~~~

The preliminary peace accords between Ambray, Westerland and Stonemount lasted only until noon of the following day. Little actually needed to be said. Maddix couldn't seem to bluster or hold onto his righteous anger while Lord Anselm watched him with those dark, penetrating eyes. Alix was rather glad the man sat at their table, though he only listened and offered no advice or objections. Bianca's two eldest brothers had been with their father on the battlefield, preparing to defend their country, righteously infuriated at being accused of murder, insisting that they had never blamed Arden or Maddix. And certainly no wizards had consulted with them over Bianca's death. They seemed to be more in favor of continuing into battle than seeking peace, but their father overruled them.

The kings and counselors agreed all the armies would return to their countries and would maintain peace over the winter while investigators from all four countries examined the evidence and followed all the stories and rumors and accusations to their sources. Alix was in a somber mood as they shook hands and gave the command for the four armies to return home. He wondered if the trails the hunters followed would evaporate into thin air before they led anywhere, or if there would be a sudden rash of destroyed reputations and dead bodies to take all the blame, and no one to defend them.

Such thinking did them all little good. Alix tried to pray and put the outcome into the hands of Yeshen and the advisors he trusted. Then he turned his focus to returning to Westerland to prepare for the winter.

His thoughts were on a sled he wanted to make for little Violet as the army of Brentonwald separated from those of Westerland and Stonemount. He was trying to decide which horses to give Derrien and Arden for Solstice gifts when he and Maddix led the way into a stony valley only a few miles from the place where their two armies would separate and head for home.

~~~~~

Maddix leaned forward in his saddle, unable to put aside his anticipation. He managed to hide his sneer as he saw the distracted, eager expressions on Alix and Derrien's faces. From comments both men made during the last few hours of their journey, both were thinking only of home and seeing Arden and her brat again.

Their combined armies stretched out behind them in a long line as the valley around them narrowed into a pass where only ten horses could ride abreast. Maddix grinned and nodded in anticipation. The rocky, steep slopes ahead of them were the perfect hiding place for the mercenaries Clancy always had on hand.

The setting sun shone in the eyes of the two armies as they came around a bend in the ever-narrowing valley. Maddix used the brightness as an excuse to turn his horse aside. Shielding his eyes, he looked for the dark spot that would be Clancy, preparing to emerge and give the signal. Neither Alix nor Derrien noticed when Maddix dropped back in the line. The Stonemount soldiers at the front of the line had been warned what would happen. They too slowed their horses so only Westerland soldiers rode behind their king and commander.

A horn ripped apart the quiet of the valley. A horse screamed. Rocks clattered. Hooves thundered against stone. From hiding places among the rocks, mercenaries streamed down on the startled Westerland forces. Maddix laughed, hiding his face behind his hand in case someone saw him and managed to survive.

It was rather like the mock battles at the Harvest Festival, he mused as he pulled his horse further from the lines of battle and rode up the slope for a better view. Only this time the blood and the weapons were real. He found Alix and Derrien in the confusion and shouting and rising dust and waited impatiently for Clancy to follow his plan. Nothing could be left to chance. It had to be done today, soon, or not at all. There were too many Stonemount soldiers who didn't know his plans and were even now rushing forward to join the battle. The tide would turn and Clancy's forces would have to retreat if they wanted to save their skins.

There. He saw Clancy, faithful Clancy with his wonderfully devious schemes pulling back from the battle and climbing up on a massive boulder to get a perfect view of the battle. He glanced around once, met Maddix's gaze, and looked away. They couldn't pretend to see each other, even for a moment. The wrong person might notice and remember later at an awkward time. Maddix saw nothing wrong with slitting throats to silence wagging tongues, but he preferred to do as little slitting as possible. Excess of any good thing soured the pleasure, he had discovered.

He had also learned that as much as he might enjoy seeing his enemies suffer, sometimes it was better to be sure than to be entertained. Clancy's entire quiver of arrows were tipped in poison. All it would take to kill Alix and remove one more obstacle to the throne of Westerland, was one arrow securely lodged in his flesh. Two arrows, to be sure. And enough confusion in the battle to delay drawing the arrowhead out until it was too late to fight the poison.

Maddix kept his attention divided between Alix and Clancy, willing the tide of the battle to push the farmer king closer to where Clancy had a vantage point. The shouts of battle rang in Maddix's ears, but he ignored the din. From where he stood, he could barely smell the sweat of the horses, the blood and churned ground and the metal-acid stink of pain and anger and fear in the sweat of the men; the sour salt smell of sweaty leathers and the death released bowels of fallen and trampled bodies.

Alix wheeled his horse and let the animal struggle up above the tide of the battle at an angle from the boulder where Clancy perched half-hidden. Maddix barely restrained a cheer. He urged his horse forward, as if that would push Alix more clearly into the bowman's line of sight. A curse exploded from his lips as several mercenaries flung themselves at Alix's legs from both sides, battering at the king with clubs and knives and trying to yank him from the saddle in both directions. The horse shrieked and reared and lashed out at the men with its hooves. Three fell and Maddix hoped the men died for their stupidity in interfering with Clancy's mission. He cursed again when he saw Alix struggle to stay on his horse's back, one foot loosed from the stirrup and his leg waving foolishly in the air as he fought for balance.

A shape leaped from the writhing battle that started to pull back from Alix like ebbing tide. Maddix barely noticed, caught up in the poetry of Clancy's leisurely raising of the bow. From the corner of his eye, Maddix saw only a Westerland uniform. Alix fell between his horse and Clancy's position. Derrien dashed under the horse's legs and flung himself over Alix, just as the first arrow launched. It nicked his leg, missed Alix, and skittered out into the melee like a stone skipping water.

Maddix cursed and urged his horse down into the dying battle as more Stonemount soldiers surged up through the narrow valley. He had to be seen trying to save Alix's life or he would have no chance at winning grief-stricken Arden's compliance. He even considered the trouble that might result if some of his loyal soldiers thought he had run from the battle, but that was a minor consideration.

Another arrow arched up into the air as Derrien caught hold of Alix by his bleeding shoulders and dragged him upright. The horse stayed close by, for some reason Maddix couldn't comprehend. The stupid animal should have run as soon as it lost its rider.

The second arrow missed completely. Derrien had Alix up on his feet. The man collapsed. Even from thirty yards away, Maddix heard Alix's bellow of pain and it was sweet music. A third arrow flew, hitting Derrien between the shoulder blades. The man arched in a spasm, nearly losing his grip on his brother-in-law, but Alix caught at his horse's stirrups and stayed upright long enough for Derrien to grasp the arrow and pull it from his back. A fourth arrow flew, but where it landed was hard to see.

Soldiers poured into the gap between Clancy's boulder and where the two men struggled to get Alix back onto his horse. Clancy flipped a salute to Maddix and jumped down into the shadows to race to safety. Maddix dug his spurs into his stallion's flanks and fought through the dying battle to reach Alix's side.

There was little satisfaction in watching Derrien go pale and struggle to keep on his feet and finally crumple into a breathless heap. Maddix declined to play at the sympathetic role he had prepared. It was hard enough to concentrate on pretending concern for Alix and knowing the man would live despite his shattered leg and many bleeding wounds. He couldn't play at worry for Derrien or grief for Arden's sake.

After all, Jaygo had raised him never to forget anything, never to let an opportunity for power and profit to pass him by.

"Odd, isn't it?" he murmured to Alix hours later, when the wounded had been made ready to travel and the dead had been wrapped for travel or buried, and the two armies were ready to leave this unexpected battlefield behind. He smiled bitterly at Alix's pain-filled grunt of non-interest, then schooled his face to innocent curiosity as he turned to face his ally. "I'm a widower, and Arden is a widow. Perhaps it would have been best after all if we had obeyed our fathers' wishes."

"You and I both know that our fathers wanted a love match, not a marriage of state," Alix said with that icy calm that barely masked his fevered agony.

"Yes—well—it could have been a love match. In time. I believed it was a love match."

"You have a strange way of showing love, by bullying my sister into keeping secrets, and then running off with Bianca with no warning. Then you slandered my sister's beauty and her chastity, in writing and from your own lips, witnessed by your courtiers. There is no love, and there will be no match." He raised his hand, signaling for the soldiers who carried the sedan chair he rode in now. His splinted and bound leg made it impossible to ride in a saddle.

"But it would be best for both our countries." Maddix struggled for calm, when what he wanted to do was leap at Alix, knock him from the chair, and beat him unconscious.

"Find yourself another bride, Maddix. My sister loved Derrien with all her heart and she will grieve for him. You'll be an old man before she's desperate enough to consider your suit."

"I'm not talking romance and silly lovers' talk," Maddix ground out, and surprised himself by following the chair as it moved away, toward the wagon Alix would ride in on the journey home to Westerland. "I'm talking politics."

"Politics? Violet, my niece is my heir. I would never keep her from her mother, yet I'd be a fool to let my heir leave Westerland to live in another country, where accidents could happen to her. I've learned too much to be a fool, old friend," Alix said in a cold voice that rooted Maddix's feet to the ground.

For a moment, he felt an incredible, paralyzing terror that Alix knew everything. Someone had been listening, had passed on all the plans for vengeance and conquest that Maddix and Jaygo and their supporters had made all these long years.

Cursing silently, Maddix tried to put on a polite face, bowing as if Alix had won the argument. He turned and walked back to his own waiting wagons and horses and soldiers, trying to move as if everything were right in the world and he had not lost a major battle of wits and strategy.

Maddix nearly laughed aloud, bitter laughter, when he caught himself wishing Jaygo had ridden with him to battle. The irritating old man was, unfortunately, the only one he could trust right now to keep tight control on Stonemount while its king and the best of its soldiers were gone. Jaygo would have known how to broach the subject of marrying Arden without upsetting anyone.

He needed her, he hated to admit. He needed her plantwise magic to rouse the failing crops all through Stonemount. He needed Arden's child in his power, to use against Alix. He needed to get Arden pregnant and have sons with her, so he could claim the throne of Westerland someday.

He needed her to heal that cursed tree that seemed to suck all the life and color out of Stonemount and yet gave nothing back. Maddix had ordered the tree cut down, but no axes could bite into the trunk. Fire refused to catch hold on the branches.

CHAPTER FIFTEEN

If he couldn't trick her into marriage, perhaps he should try to make her feel guilty enough to come to Stonemount to heal the tree? While she was there, he would have unlimited opportunity to fuddle her simple woman's mind and bend her to his will. That could be entertaining.

But he would have to admit there was something wrong with the tree. And admit she had made the tree, rather than the mysterious, seldom-seen wizards. He could always claim that he had just recently discovered where the tree came from, that his soldiers had liberated it from a band of brigands and he had recognized its magic and planted it to protect it. She would believe his story, because hadn't she believed all his other stories and twisting of facts for his convenience?

Yet in the end, he would have to admit that she had made the tree, and only she could heal it.

"No," he growled. "I won't give her that victory." Maddix swallowed a curse and forced his face back into a pleasant expression as his escort soldiers glanced at him in fear-tinged curiosity.

He wouldn't give Arden the satisfaction of knowing he needed her meager magical talents. He would prove that anyone with a modest amount of magic could serve him. And wouldn't that shame her? Wouldn't that teach her not to defy his plans and goals? He would find someone else to heal the tree. Even if he had to promise half his kingdom to do it.

Maddix nearly laughed aloud when he realized the silent vow he had made. Wasn't that how it always happened in the old stories? The king promised half his kingdom or the hand of his prettiest daughter in marriage, and then wonderful things happened. Heroes arrived, magic occurred, and everything was set right again. Well, he would do it. There had to be someone, somewhere, who had more magic than Arden and could cure the apple tree. Then, bolstered by the magic he had taken from her, he would settle accounts with Arden and Westerland.

~~~~~

Arden met the returning soldiers at the gates of Port'ham, in the same spot where she had stood watching her brother and husband ride away. She wore all black and her long hair was braided with black ribbons and covered with a black veil. The entire city seemed wrapped in black mourning and though there wasn't a cloud in the sky the sun's light was dimmed. She expected cold wind and rain at any moment, all
~~~~~

too appropriate for the late fall, yet with special significance. Alix and Derrien returned to her at the head of the troops, but her brother rode in a wagon instead of astride his horse, pale and wrapped with bandages. Her husband rode in the second wagon, invisible under the black cloth draping his hastily made coffin.

Even then, seeing the physical proof of the nightmares that had plagued her dreams since the storm that sliced branches off the apple tree, she still couldn't cry. Arden stared with reddened, swollen eyes and the ice inside grew a little more solid. She was aware of Glynna hovering protectively around her, but for the first time in her life the woman's ghostly presence brought no comfort. Her parents killed by assassins, her husband murdered in an ambush when peace was within their grasp, and her brother likely to be a cripple for the rest of his life.

"This is all Maddix's fault," she murmured as the wagons carrying her brother and husband rode past her, though the gates into Port'ham.

"Careful, child," Glynna crooned, as always trying to touch and give her comfort. "You must rise above this, or Maddix will win."

"He already has won." She didn't care that Comyn gave her one askance glance, then looked through the empty air around her as if he could see Glynna after all this time.

"No. As long as you can love, as long as you can hope, you are the victor. Remember: Give him enough time and his crimes will always turn around to punish him."

"Time." Arden choked on what could have been a sob or a bark of bitter laughter. "See what our patience has done to us. Look what Maddix has done to us." She looked at Comyn as she spoke and the faithful old counselor nodded, sympathy as well as understanding.

"You are the soul and heart of this kingdom, Arden. Do not let the poison into your heart, or the entire kingdom falls! Look what Maddix's poison has done to his own land," her teacher continued.

"Look what it has done to us! I curse Maddix. He has taken my husband and nearly killed my brother, all for his pride. All he has now is his pride, and may he choke on it!"

Her voice rose as she spoke, until it rang off the gates and wall around the city. Those who stood at the gates nodded and murmured among themselves, echoing her words and approving. And on the final word, a thunderclap rang through the air though not a cloud could be seen in the sky.

In the Westerland palace gardens, the apple tree shivered, twisting slightly as if it tried to wrest itself from the soil. One bright burst of golden-green light erupted from it, then vanished, leaving the tree looking rather shrunken and wrinkled and ordinary. A single apple fell and rolled across the matted grass.

~~~~~

Ambrose sat in his usual spot with his back against the wall, watching the ailing tree in the Stonemount royal garden. It shivered and hundreds of half-dead leaves fled its branches. Just as the whispering rustle of the shedding began to die away, a loud crack reverberated through the garden, bouncing off the stone wall and echoing out until it hit the palace walls. Three branches split off the main trunk, falling to the ground with a clatter.

"Oh, my dear Arden," the tired old healer whispered. "What have you done now? Maddix deserves it, but can you pay the price?" He pushed himself to his feet and tottered on aching legs to the battered, lightless tree. He leaned against it for nearly an hour, comforting them both. Now, even he doubted there was anything but the faintest touch of magic left in the shriveled, poor trunk.

~~~~~

Maddix paced the confines of his study, growling under his breath, wanting to smash something, anything. Preferably, smash someone in particular. Several someones. But Alix was far out of his reach, hidden behind hordes of healers and loyal palace guards. Arden was sending back all his letters without even opening them. How could he seduce her simple, stupid woman's mind and heart if she wouldn't even read his letters?

He would have found some satisfaction in swinging the brat, Violet by her heels and throwing her against the wall, but Maddix knew better than to hope he would ever get the chance.

And now this final blow to his carefully crafted plans, taking a major weapon out of his grasp. Word had come that Dylon was dead. How could he control Ambrose without a threat constantly hanging over Dylon's head? The truly frustrating part was that he couldn't bring his wretched distant cousin's body home to Stonemount and have a grand state funeral, and impress everyone with his grief. Dylon had been his usual self-sacrificing idiotic self and had gone into a copper mine to help rescue some trapped miners. The cave-in had been caused by flooding, and there was no hope of retrieving the bodies that had been washed away. While Maddix had always loathed Dylon, he did value him as a hostage.

Now, he had a new task: ensure Ambrose became even more isolated and immured in his rooms, so people forgot he was there, and when the time came, he would have no one to receive his Gifting but the one Maddix chose. For a time, Maddix had intended to take his great-uncle's Gifting himself, but possessing any kind of magic required that he use it once in a while. He loathed the thought of having to look at, much less touch anyone who was ill. According to Ambrose's idealistic lectures, using the healing Gift required some sympathy on his part.

Maddix firmly believed whoever had made up the rules for Giftings had been insane and needed to be violently punished with a lingering, painful death. Feeling sympathy and being forced to use the magic rather than save it for profitable purposes was disgustingly inconvenient.

He flung himself into his chair to finally do what he dreaded most: send a letter to Durmad, asking for guidance. How could he do it without sounding like a whining brat, as Durmad had accused him of several times, and without actually admitting he needed help? It was aggravating. Humiliating. He might need to finally order Jaygo's execution just to raise his spirits. Of course, removing the arrogant, self-righteous old smirker might clear the air and make it easier to think. Maddix was constantly on the alert for the old man to saunter into his office at the worst possible time and start lecturing him.

Clancy and Baethon stepped into the room. From their sour expressions, they didn't have any good news for him. He played with the idea of executing them, too. On the other hand, it might be amusing to set each one against the other, with some story of treachery. Then again, he would have to go to the trouble of finding some other brutes so loyal, who enjoyed the dirty aspects of the jobs he gave them.

"Well?" he snarled. He wouldn't like the news, but he had to hear it to find a remedy. Perhaps.

"The whole kingdom knows the tree is dying," Clancy said with that bored tone that used to amuse Maddix. He had a gift for sounding bored about the most delightfully bloodthirsty details. The trick didn't work now, though, and that just made Maddix angrier. "Far too many people credited it with the bounty right after it was planted, so now the shortages are blamed on the tree. Plus, news over the border is that Princess Arden cursed you."

"Then close the border!"

"If we do," Baethon said, sounding only faintly regretful about reminding him, "we can't get any food from Westerland."

"Then tell the people Alix closed the border." Maddix cheered up a little at that. He always liked making someone else the villain when his people suffered.

"Westerland will say otherwise."

"I'll keep them too busy to care what we say."

"How?" Clancy said.

Maddix clenched his fists, when he would have dearly loved to punch that glimmer of doubt off the man's face. No, that was too direct. He wanted the realization that he was being punished to sneak up on his victim, and the knowledge that a cure would come too late.

A cure? As in a sickness? Or better … poison?

Maddix had his answer. A slow grin lit his face. Now, where was that precious little treasure? He yanked a tiny key from the chain around his neck and stomped over to a cupboard kept locked even from his closest friends.

He found a box he had filled years ago, when all his schemes were nothing more than smoky dreams and too many people stood between him and success. Always best to be prepared for any difficulty, to destroy any obstacle. The box was coated in gold, inside and out, to prevent the contents from escaping. It was a fine black dust, so dark it absorbed the light that hit it. One of his earliest letters of guidance from Durmad had told him about the dust, how to obtain it, how he could use it, and how he should save it for the perfect opportunity, when stealth and patience were vital to his triumph.

"Make a tiny hole in the lid and drop it in the main well of Westerland's palace." He handed it to Baethon as he spoke, his voice rich with gloating anticipation.

"The last time you tried to use poison—" Baethon began.

"This will dissolve slowly. It needs to build up over time before it has any effect. Before anyone realizes that anything is wrong ... all the children in the palace will be dead."

His smile widened more as he contemplated the consternation and growing panic and the inability of anyone in Westerland to determine the cause. Not without a powerful healer like Ambrose to sense the poison at work. And no one would have access to Ambrose and his Gift unless they came to Maddix first.

"Starting with Arden's daughter?" Clancy asked with a rumbling chuckle. He relaxed, slouching a little in his chair. "It's about time you solved that problem."

"Then, you sweep her off her feet and finally make progress in taking over Westerland," Baethon said. "Seems to me it'd be easier making her come to you. Make her marry you to save her brat's life. Too bad everyone knows the apples are bad."

"She has her own apple tree, idiot," Clancy said, with a tiny glitter of some amusement in his eyes that chilled Maddix.

Those two weren't plotting against him, were they?

Definitely, he needed to sow some seeds of jealousy between them. Maybe Jaygo was working against him? Encouraging doubt in his two loyal henchmen? Definitely, he would have to deal with Jaygo soon.

"Plant some of the dust around the roots of the tree while you're there," Maddix said, and shrugged, as if it was a ridiculously simple solution and they should have thought of it for themselves.

"In the winter?"

"Just get it done!" He swung his arm wide, gesturing toward Westerland, and nearly swept the troubling pile of papers off his desk. Maddix shuddered at the thought of touching them.

And that was another dilemma to deal with, one he hadn't anticipated. How had his neat, clever, entirely logical plans gone so utterly wrong?

He braced his arms on the desk on either side of the small pile of papers he had read with the fascination of someone facing his own possible death. They were marked with the dark green wax seal and rampant lion of the royal court of Brentonwald. They had been delivered by Lord Anselm, now Brentonwald's ambassador to Stonemount. The dark, gaunt man had made several pointed remarks to back up the politely worded messages in all the papers. Only a fool would ignore the implications.

"No." He shook his head. "Let Arden suffer for a while. I have a larger problem to deal with. Brentonwald wishes to arrange a marriage alliance, with their Princess Fiera."

"She's beautiful," Clancy said with a leer that told exactly what kind of beauty he appreciated.

"And Brentonwald is dangerous. She has too many brothers for me to kill on my way to the throne." Taking that massive kingdom was too long-term a plan to consider ever wearing the crown, and even for a son of his to wear. But a grandson, yes. He needed a royal-blooded, compliant, conveniently dead-in-childbirth wife for that scheme to work. According to all reports, and his own few encounters with Fiera, she only fit the first criteria. For now. She was too strong-willed for his tastes, and too intelligent for him to seduce her into supporting his plans. She could see through him, perhaps warn her father and brothers if she guessed anything.

And even worse, what if this marriage alliance was a strike against him? If he could gain a foothold in multiple kingdoms through marriage, what was to stop others from using the same tactic?

"What's to stop them from killing you after she gives you a son?" Baethon said after a few seconds of too-deep silence.

"Exactly. I don't trust Brentonwald. And they've never trusted me."

~~~~~

Spring was still weeks away when the illness took hold in Violet. One day the little girl had been crawling around on her hands and knees,
~~~~~

delighting her pale, chair-bound uncle. The next day, she was just as pale and unable to rise from her little bed. Arden's first thought was to run to her apple tree, which had borne apples last winter despite the snow. This year, nothing clung to it but ice-coated brown leaves. The only glimmer of green came from the faint whispers of magic still humming through its trunk.

Arden stood for hours at a time in windows and doorways, looking down on the palace gardens at her tree, begging it to thrive, to glow brightly again, to sprout new leaves and apples and give her child back her health. She wondered sometimes if she were being punished for not begging months earlier for apples to heal her ailing brother. Derrien's death had left her in a gray fog where she hadn't cared about life. She thought sometimes she might have curled up and let herself fade away, except Alix and Violet needed her.

The snow finally began to melt, the only real sign that spring was approaching. If there was green spreading through the land under the mud and dirty white that blanketed it, Arden had no sense of it. She had not walked barefoot to feel the heartbeat of the land since the day Derrien and Alix rode off to war.

Violet was dying, and nothing else mattered.

One day, the only snow remaining in the palace gardens lay in the deepest shadows. Arden noted that detail and forgot it a moment later. She stood in the window of her bedroom, watching her tree, willing every last bit of life and strength remaining inside herself to the tree and begging silently for it to return to life and bloom and full magic. She knew she should go to the tree, take off her shoes and wade through the icy mud and throw her arms around the trunk—but she couldn't. Violet lay in her bed, weak and chill and suffering bad dreams as she slept her life away. Arden couldn't take her child out in the chill air and wouldn't leave Violet alone for the time it would take to go downstairs to the gardens and return. What if her child died in the short time she was gone?

"Ambrose—" Glynna began, as she floated over to Arden from Violet's beside.

Faithful Caitlin was in attendance as well. She was nobly born and deserved a better life than to wear herself out caring for someone else's child, but she willingly gave everything she had to either caring for Alix or Violet and trying to ease some of Arden's pain. A better, more faithful friend the royal family could never have found.

"My letters have not reached Ambrose in years. We know who is at fault." Arden's lips curled as if she would spit. A foul taste filled her mouth just from thinking about Maddix.

"There are a dozen remedies to try."

"And we shall try them all. If only I had apples."

"I don't think magic apples can heal this sickness," Glynna whispered.

"They must. There is nothing else to do."

"Except ask Maddix to let you go to Ambrose."

"I would rather die than ask for anything from Maddix!" Arden glanced at Caitlin and Violet, neither of whom reacted to her raised voice.

"Yes, you would. But what about Violet?"

Arden had no answer, except to break into tears. There was something amusing about it, she mused even as her ribs ached with the force of her sobs. She had thought herself cried dry weeks ago.

Glynna gasped, startling her. Arden caught her breath and hurried over to the window where her teacher hovered. A man sat on the wet grass underneath the pitiful, drooping, brown tree. She didn't recognize him, in his sandy brown roughspun clothes. Fury shot through her belly. Who was that? How had he gotten into the gardens? The gates were closed, simply to keep the people from seeing the tree and starting ugly rumors that it was dying.

"How did he get in here?"

"Oh, you can't keep him out of anywhere he truly wants to be." Then Glynna surprised her by chuckling.

"Auntie?"

"He's here for you, dear."

"Who?"

"Who are you talking about?" Caitlin joined her at the window and looked down into the garden. She frowned. That doubt and worry Arden hated to see dimmed her friend's eyes. Too many people had been looking at her with that expression, as if they feared she would break in a messy way.

"She can't see him," Glynna said. "He's here for you. Best to be polite and hurry down."

CHAPTER SIXTEEN

"Who?" Arden repeated.

"Steward."

She wanted to protest that no, that young man couldn't be Steward. Then she wondered how she could doubt. She hadn't doubted when he visited just a few years ago and told her how to create her tree.

Maybe she had been fooled back then? Yet that would mean Glynna had been fooled, too, and how could someone who dwelt in the spirit realm after being Gifted be fooled by an imposter?

Yet Arden doubted, because truthfully, no one had seen Steward in decades. Most people believed he had faded away, if they believed he had ever existed. He wasn't truly needed, because all the land on this continent had been tamed and settled, the magic harnessed, tied up in Giftings, and put to good use. Steward was responsible for taming wild magic, teaching new wielders in the craft, standing in judgment over those who would misuse their magical talents. Many tales of Steward described the battles he fought to hold back evil magicians and wizards, He had worked in Yeshen's power to raise the barrier of the Cascade Mountains, to keep Durmad from spilling his poisoned magic across the continent. Other tales said the duties and power of the Steward passed from father to son, mother to daughter, from generation to generation, so no one knew exactly what Steward looked like when he or she appeared. And other tales said Steward was dead, worn out and wounded in the last battle with Durmad, He had crawled away to die somewhere, without an heir to receive the Gifting and continue the duty.

But if Glynna said that was Steward, sitting in the garden under her sickly, dying apple tree ... was it possible a cure had come at long last, in answer to her desperate, aching prayers?

Arden darted to the bed where Violet lay, sleeping fitfully, wrapped a blanket around her daughter, tucked a corner of her skirt into her belt to pull it up out of the way, and ran down hallways and stairs, to the garden.

"She isn't sick," the young man said, when Arden got close enough to see the amazing green of his eyes, like fresh grass after the rain. "Stop using the water from the palace well. Violet is the only child, and because she is so small, she has succumbed to the poison first, but eventually everyone who drinks from the well or eats food made with water from the well, and even washes with that water will sicken."

"Poison?" Arden turned to Glynna. "How?"

"Something is in the well itself, isn't it?" Glynna said. When Steward nodded, her expression grew grim and she darted away, heading toward the courtyard that held the main palace well.

He got up and turned to rest one hand against the trunk of the apple tree. "The two apple trees are linked. What touches the heart of one touches the heart of the other."

"Then Maddix is killing my tree, too?"

"He started it, but your bitterness is adding to the poison."

"My—" Arden couldn't breathe for several moments. She clutched Violet closer.

"You need to learn to forgive."

Arden choked on the words she knew better than to speak. Demanding to know why she should forgive when Maddix would never repent, never admit he was in the wrong, never confess his crimes. The list was too long. If he had done all the things she silently accused him of, just to her, what crimes had he committed against others, against his kingdom? What evil was he doing, to counteract the blessing she had woven into her apple tree?

"You need to make him act, to go too far, to reveal what he has done."

"How?" Now she could breathe a little easier. Yes, she thought she could do anything necessary to save Violet, and as an added reward, expose Maddix's true nature and his cruelty and lies to the world.

"Ask him for what you need to heal your child."

"I can't!" She nearly laughed at how the words burst out of her, when she had just vowed in her heart she would do whatever was necessary. "He will demand I marry him."

"No, he won't. He doesn't dare. Brentonwald is maneuvering him into a corner, to force him to marry Fiera. She is still unfinished, untested, but coming up against Maddix will refine her. She will be good for him, slap him awake, make him see the evil influences in his life. Durmad is trying to move past the barrier of the Cascade Mountains, established by Yeshen. He needs kingdoms that will welcome him, and open doors not of the physical world. To stop him moving through the mountains, Stonemount needs to be strong again. Westerland needs to be stronger."

"How?"

Steward patted the tree trunk. "You have already done a great thing with your tree. With both trees. The sad thing is that if Maddix had simply asked, you would have given him your first tree, wouldn't you?"

Arden choked, caught between a sob and laughter. "Yes. I was that much a fool."

"To love is never foolish. But Yeshen was protecting you, even though your heart was broken. If you had given Maddix that tree, even when you were still blinded by his lies, it would have put its roots down in Stonemount in blessing and purity, because your heart protected it. That might have been enough to counteract the slow, steady drip of poison into the kingdom over the years. Your anger, the pain of your broken heart ..." He sighed and offered her a sad smile. "It accelerated the poisoning. You need to heal both trees, Arden, princess of Westerland, heart and healer."

"How?" Her voice cracked. "What about Violet?"

"Using water from outside the palace will halt the decline."

"But not heal her?" She gestured with her chin at the tree. "Apples could heal her. The tree should be bearing year-round, not just in the summer, but ..." She caught her breath, a sudden pain wrapping around her ribs. "Please tell me I didn't do that to her, to the tree."

"Many things." Steward looked past her, and Arden turned to see Glynna skimming back to them through the garden. Her usual bright spring green glow had dimmed, her face wrinkled in worry. "You need to rescue Ambrose. Maddix is holding him prisoner, to control his Gifting. Hoarding that Gifting, denying Ambrose the freedom to fulfill his duty to Yeshen, sickens Ambrose and sickens the land."

"How can I go into Stonemount and free him? I don't even know what he looks like."

"I do," Glynna said.

"You don't need to go to Ambrose. Sent to Maddix, make it clear you know Ambrose is one of Stonemount's treasures, and you would never ask him to travel so far or to leave the safety of the kingdom. Ask to meet at the border. Beg for the sake of the friendship and alliance between your countries. Hint that you would be open to a marriage alliance between his son and heir, and Violet."

"Send my daughter to Stonemount?" Her arms tightened around Violet so strongly the child whimpered.

"You will never need to do that. The hope, the offer is only bait." Steward sighed. "If all goes well. The first step is to free Ambrose. He will finish the healing of your child. Releasing the bitterness you hold against Maddix will start the healing of your tree, and Stonemount's tree."

"I don't know if ..." She sighed, aching, trembling deep inside. "Auntie? What did you find?"

"There is a gold box in the bottom of the well. A tiny hole releases something black into the water ..." Glynna shook her head. "Steward, what do we do? Can you heal the well?"

"Remove the box and the well will heal on its own. Do not let anyone use the water until summer solstice." He stepped away from the tree and dug in a depression in the soil with the heel of his boot. "Under here is more of that poison Maddix's men buried. Cover your face and hands, do not breathe the air around it when you dig it up. Put it in a jar sealed with wax inside and out, and inside another jar sealed with wax, inside and out. Include all the soil around it for more than a yard in diameter. Cut away the roots of the tree within that area. This will help the tree, not hurt it. Like cutting away rotting flesh from a wound, so it stops poisoning the rest of the body. Give the jar to Ambrose when you meet him. He is the nearest healer who has the strength to counteract the poison, and then destroy it. Do the same with the box in the well. The men who go into the well to dredge up the box need to be strengthened with every antidote to poison your healers can find. They need to use hooks and nets, and not touch the box itself, and need to wash thoroughly after coming out of the well. When that poison is removed, the healing can begin, for well and for tree."

"But not soon enough for Violet," Arden said, her voice cracking. "That's why we need Ambrose."

"Yeshen asks for obedience and a soft heart. He doesn't require success, just effort. You need to take the first step. Trust, Arden. The fates of two kingdoms rest on you."

<div align="center">~~~~~</div>

Maddix stared when Jaygo finished reading him the letter from Arden. He thought at first the man had fabricated the entire thing, just to amuse him. There had been precious little amusement lately, with the wheels of state grinding inexorably toward submitting to the marriage alliance with Princess Fiera of Brentonwald. Still, after a moment of thought, Maddix couldn't imagine Jaygo going to that much trouble just to lift his spirits. The man had never flattered him unless he wanted something. Lately, the only expression he had seen in his counselor's eyes was disappointment and even disdain. Jaygo had given up his muttering about how Maddix needed to learn patience, and how he had ruined their carefully crafted plans. Somehow, that silence was more irritating than the muttering.

The letter from Westerland, in Arden's own handwriting, had to be real. He started to laugh. It made his ribs ache, despite the weakness of his laughter, because it had been so long since he laughed at anything. Maddix and Jaygo were alone in his study, but right that moment he wished Clancy and Baethon were there so he could share the delicious joke with them. They understood him as Jaygo never had.

"Arden and Westerland want my help? Oh, this is too funny."

"Now is your chance to counteract the influence of the tree. After all, she poisoned Stonemount through the tree, she should remedy the problem," Jaygo said, leaning forward against Maddix's desk. "Get Arden and her child to cross the border, make her come within the walls of the palace, and then don't let her leave. Convince her she needs to heal your tree before her child can be healed. It will be a simple matter to kill off her escort and then blame marauders on the border. You can feed King Alix lies for several months, about how you're tracking down the ones who captured his sister, and all the while, you can work your influence on her, charm her, threaten her, bring in those pet wizards you think I don't know about to influence her mind. In the end, you convince her and her brother that you rescued her and she is grateful, in love with you even more than when she was a child. And marry her. Everyone already thinks you have a silly romantic core, after how you carried off that elopement with Bianca."

For half a second, Maddix seriously considered the suggestion. Then he pushed it aside. Agreeing would give Alix and Arden a few days of hope, and he would never allow that. Not even to see the look of horror and anguish on Arden's face when he closed the trap around her.

Besides, following that plan would encourage Jaygo and make him think he was still clever and useful. The only reason Maddix kept him around was to keep him the face and voice that people remembered when they were angered with pronouncements and bad news.

"I will consider your plan. No need to respond right away," he said, and offered the old sly smile he had worn as a boy, when he and Jaygo first started scheming to rule the world. "Let them stew and fret for a few days."

Jaygo laughed. Maddix laughed inside as he thought about how frustrated the old man would be, when he had to carry out Maddix's true plan.

~~~~~

By the time the ground was dry enough for walking in the Westerland palace gardens, Alix could get around on crutches. That was, he reflected sadly, the only bit of good news in a long, long time. Involuntarily, he glanced over his shoulder at the window of Arden's bedroom, half-expecting to see his sister there, watching her pitiful little tree. He remembered how he had stood here with the tree just a year ago, waiting for little Violet to be born. He remembered how the tree had burst out with new flowers and leaves and fruit when the little girl uttered her first cry.

Now, the tree had leaves, but they were tiny and dull. There were
~~~~~

no flowers, and no hope of apples in the summer. Alix shivered, hating the feeling of hopelessness. Arden depended on this tree, yet it reflected her aching, bitter spirit and gave her nothing. That ate at her pitiful shreds of hope, and only made the tree worse than before.

The news that Maddix's tree in Stonemount was even worse off than this one did nothing to encourage Alix. If anything, it made him worry more. Arden was tied to both trees. What happened to her if one died? What if Maddix chopped down his tree, hoping to strike at Arden?

Something had to be done. Soon. Alix felt foolish for trying, but he had always sensed the tree was alert and aware and he had to try something. Besides, there was no one in the gardens at this time of the afternoon but him. He reached out a hand and rested it against the trunk, which felt cold as stone under his palm, It had always before felt warm, like there was living flesh under the smooth bark.

"Well, and what are we going to do, hmm? Arden needs you, and she needs me. The way we are now, what good are we to her?"

"Majesty," Caitlin blurted, dashing into the gardens. "The envoy from Stonemount is here." Her face held the first bit of color he had seen in weeks, and Alix liked that. She was a pretty girl when she smiled.

"Finally." He forced a smile, if only to encourage her. "Let's hope he has good news." He thanked her with a nod as she offered her shoulder for him to lean on, and they hobbled into the palace to meet the envoy.

<center>~~~~~</center>

The envoy from Stonemount was Ambassador Jaygo. Alix wondered why the man had bestirred himself to come to Westerland, when he had always expressed such distaste for their country. He remembered being awed by the dark-robed man as a boy, even then sensing the cold and disdain and feeling sorry for Maddix for having to work with him. Now, Alix knew the two deserved each other.

Why would Jaygo come to Westerland, except to bring important news? Alix let himself hope, despite his dislike for the man. Soon, Violet would be well, then Arden would smile again and life would flow through the apple tree, and from there through all Westerland. They would prosper again. He had to believe it.

Arden and Comyn stood on either side of the wide, deep chair that their father had always used for meetings of state. Alix was grateful for Caitlin's help as the girl helped him hobble to his seat. She smiled at him, blushing a little when he winked, and took his crutches away, out of his sight and yet near enough to be retrieved without trouble. Alix appreciated that. He appreciated so many things about her, now that he thought about it.

"Welcome, Lord Jaygo." Alix dragged his thoughts back to the

126

present moment. "Do you bring an answer to my sister's request?"

Jaygo glanced at the four in the room, then glanced over his shoulder, raising an eyebrow at the lack of counselors and nobles. One eyebrow cocked up in disdain, then he shrugged. Alix heard echoes of condemnation from the man from years ago, when he wore the same expression. *What can you expect from such a poor, backward kingdom?* Alix restrained his anger. Any price, even Jaygo's disdain, was small compared to restoring Violet's health and Arden's happiness.

"King Maddix," Jaygo began in that cool, disdainful drawl of his, "says you strain his generosity when you demand that the Healer Ambrose, an elderly man, face danger and the rigors of the journey to the border, simply because a child has a passing illness."

"A passing illness?" Comyn blurted in his cracked voice. "Princess Violet is dying, you pompous ass!"

"So now the world sees Maddix's true character," Arden said with a calmness that made Alix shiver, despite the burning anger stirred by Jaygo's words. "Because he will not share his uncle's gift of healing, he lies and says we make demands."

"Lies?" For once, Jaygo's disdain broke and a flush touched his cheeks. "You have gone too far—"

"No, you and Stonemount have gone too far!" Bitter laughter touched Arden's voice. "Maddix does whatever he wishes and lies to cover his crimes. We all suffer for it. He hoards treasures that belong to the entire world, and now they turn bitter and poison his kingdom. How are the spring crops, Lord Jaygo? Even this far away, I can tell Stonemount will go hungry this winter. It is Maddix's fault."

"The delusions of a woman scorned," the aging ambassador sneered.

"Scorned?" Now Alix understood what put that tone in Arden's voice. He pushed himself to his feet, though leaning heavily against the table. "As I recall, King Doyne wanted the marriage alliance, not my father. We have dozens of letters from Maddix, sent secretly to my sister over the years, urging her to run away with him, increasingly upset with her when she refused time and again, wanting to wait until our parents gave their approval. How can you say my sister was scorned when Maddix pursued her, and she never pursued him?"

"Letters can be forged. Someone played a nasty joke on all of you, pretending to be King Maddix," Jaygo said after a telling pause. His sniff of disdain wasn't anywhere near convincing.

"My sister laughed and danced until dawn the day we learned of Bianca and Maddix's elopement. Tell me, Lord Jaygo," he hurried on, cutting the man off when he opened his mouth to retort, "when will

Maddix marry Princess Fiera?"

"Who says such a marriage is even being considered?"

"Steward has told us much of what diplomats and power-brokers wish to keep hidden," Arden said.

"Steward? Such a man is a fable." Another of Jaygo's unconvincing sniffs of disdain. "Bring him to me, and I will prove he is a liar, a dreamer." He paused, eyes widening slightly in very evident discomfort. "What other lies has he been telling you about Stonemount's business?"

Arden smiled, settled into her chair and folded her hands in her lap. Alix had never adored his little sister as much as he did in that moment. Even if she had lied, she had slapped Jaygo hard and given him something uncomfortable to think about.

"Steward told me Brentonwald is unwilling to send their princess to a kingdom with an ailing magic apple tree. How strange that the wizards who gifted Maddix with that tree are unable to cure it. He must produce three apples with blessing magic in them, the day she enters the palace. Disappointing Brentonwald is unwise. Maddix makes promises he cannot keep, because he is afraid for the first time in his life. He will have no apples because the tree refuses to bloom."

"You should ignore your sister and the silly stories she imagines someone has told her, King Alix." Jaygo's voice cracked.

Alix scowled to keep from laughing aloud. The man's frosty reaction proved the truth of his sister's words. Arden had told him nothing of this, and he shuddered in wonder at the thought that Steward had spoken to her. She had merely told him that an old friend of Glynna's had come with a message, revealing the existence of the box in the well and the poison buried among the roots of the apple tree, and how to remove them and begin the healing. She hadn't mentioned anything about speaking with Steward.

Yet if Yeshen's voice and the hand that carried the Maker's magic throughout the land had come here to Westerland, why hadn't he healed Violet? Why hadn't he healed Arden's tree?

Alix needed to have a long talk with his sister about what she knew and kept secret from him.

CHAPTER SEVENTEEN

"I hesitate to impugn a woman who is clearly living in great distress. Unwarranted distress, over a passing childhood illness," Jaygo added with a sniff. "Yet I must state for the record that the stories of a marriage with Brentonwald, and all the accompanying details, are lies."

"You are the expert, aren't you?" Arden's voice was crackling ice. "We *asked* permission to come to Stonemount to ask Lord Ambrose's help. We made no demands, as you claim."

"So you say." Jaygo sneered.

"I think we should end this discussion before things turn unpleasant," Comyn cut in smoothly. "There is the long tradition of friendship and partnership between our kingdoms. We don't want to harm it any further, do we?"

"Hmph, no." He glanced at the chair at the end of the table, which had been pulled out and waiting for him, but he had yet to take. Now he reached to put one hand on the arm, preparing to sit down.

"Forgive us for wasting your time, Lord Jaygo." Comyn gestured toward the door. "If you leave now, you will be halfway to the border before dusk. I know you are uncomfortable in our rustic little kingdom full of farmers. The sooner you are home where you are comfortable, the better. Don't you agree?"

"But we have important business to discuss." Jaygo gaped for a moment, almost prompting a chuckle from Alix. "There is a food shortage in Stonemount and —"

"The hunger in Stonemount is a passing, minor affliction. Just like the illness plaguing my niece," Alix couldn't resist saying. He waited for Jaygo to recover from that setback and retort the hunger was real, as pervasive as Rilling's many old friends and other spies reported.

Jaygo must have sensed their anger, ready to burst the tight restraints they held. If he realized that they wouldn't give him what he wanted no matter what he said, or if he was afraid, it didn't matter. Swallowing loudly, visibly, the man backed out of the room, bowing just barely deep enough to be politically correct. Comyn hurried to slam the door closed before anyone could react and ruin their minor victory.

"We must act before they accuse us of trying to starve Stonemount," the old counselor said.

"I know." Alix's leg ached just like it did when the winter storms got worse. He sighed and rubbed at his face and wished he could go to bed, but it wasn't even noon yet. "Send patrols along the borders and tell the people anyone who wants food may come to Westerland. But no nobles, no soldiers. Let Maddix feed his loyal followers." He thought he saw a flicker of satisfaction on the old man's grave face. Comyn bowed to them both and hurried to obey this new order. Alix watched his sister a few seconds, wondering when she would break. "Well, little sister? What will you do now?" he had to ask.

"Did you hear," she said in a soft, detached voice, "that Maddix is offering a reward to anyone who can heal his tree? He needs those apples to placate Brentonwald, at the very least."

"No." He caught his breath as sudden understanding slammed him harder than the blow that had broken his leg. "You can't."

"Maddix has taken everything else I love. He won't take Violet." She glared at her brother with all of Derrien's fierceness.

~~~~~

Several minor healers had come in to inspect the water and guide the removal of the golden box, and they examined everyone who lived or worked in the palace and had either eaten food prepared with water from the poisoned well or washed in that water. Everyone had showed faint signs of being poisoned, but the healers were able to reverse the damage. However, Violet, the only child in the palace, remained ill. The healers tried to be encouraging, but they had never dealt with this particular poison, so they could not predict when she would begin to heal. Or if she would heal at all. Drastic measures were needed.

Such as the apples that had grown on Arden's tree last year.

There was no promise of apples returning to the tree, although new leaves had started to appear. Once the poison had been removed from the roots and the tainted soil taken away, the magic of the tree had begun the healing.

The only question was how long the tree needed to heal before it could produce the apples Violet needed.

Fresh air seemed to do the ailing child some good, along with water drawn from other wells. Arden walked circles around her tree in the garden, holding Violet and making sure she got all the spring sunshine and fresh air she could take. Glynna found them there a few hours after Ambassador Jaygo left Port'ham in such a hurry. Violet clung to her mother's dress and watched the sunlight filtering through the half-bare branches and didn't smile when Glynna sparkled into view.

"Your own apple tree will heal her," the woman said, after watching Arden complete two more circuits of the tree. "Be patient. Trust Yeshen. You don't need Ambrose."

"The blight of Maddix's evil has spread from Stonemount to
~~~~~

Westerland," Arden said with a sigh.

"Are you telling me your magic isn't strong enough to overcome Maddix? Even this far away?"

"It couldn't protect my tree from the poison, could it? Every day I come out here and I beg and I cry and I scrape my hands raw trying to make it grow. What more can I do?" A sob broke her voice.

"It's the bitterness in your soul, child. You're slowing the healing. If you don't give it up, learn to do as Steward advised, the tree will fail utterly, and the poison will spread throughout Westerland. Just like Maddix poisons Stonemount. While you are here, you still have hope, and some safety from Maddix's poison. Don't go into the heart of it."

"I need to try to find Ambrose. At least in Stonemount I have hope!"

"Don't put yourself into Maddix's hands."

"Who says I will? Who says he will even know I'm there?"

Glynna paused several heartbeats, studying Arden's expression. Then she nodded that she understood but didn't relax. If anything, her frown of concern deepened.

"Don't use Maddix's tricks. They'll destroy you instead of him. If you lie, even to Maddix, you will suffer for it. Mark my words."

"You can come with me, Auntie, or you can stay behind. It doesn't matter to me." She glanced once at the woman and started across the patchy grass to the palace doors.

"Oh, no, I'm going with you. You need someone to think clearly." Glynna vanished with a sparkle of light.

~~~~~

Glynna winced at the first crunching snick of the scissors as Arden cut off her luxurious, knee-length spill of red-gold hair. Caitlin cried, though she muffled her sobs so she wouldn't wake Violet, who lay sleeping on her lap. Arden sat before her dressing table mirror, wearing borrowed black widow's clothing, fitting for a peasant. After three strands of hair were cut off just past her shoulders and tossed aside, she could tell a difference. She looked smaller and felt lighter, without the frame of red-gold outlining and defining everything she wore. Unwillingly, she thought of Derrien and how he loved to play with her hair or bury his face in the fragrant silken strands when they were alone.

Derrien would approve of her disguise and subterfuge, Arden knew. Even if no one else precious to her approved, she knew Derrien would. It would be justice, stealing the healing right from under Maddix's nose. With the entire world looking on, the day Princess Fiera of Brentonwald arrived in Stonemount to claim her magic apples, Arden would claim her reward. She would tell them the truth behind Maddix's stories and machinations, and she would watch his power and pride
~~~~~

vanish, eroded like bones touched by lime or rotten leaves thrown into a fire. She would be patient. She would play at being a lowly, filthy peasant, to match Maddix's opinion of everyone in Westerland, and she would have her justice. And Violet's life. If Yeshen blessed them, she would help Ambrose escape Maddix's control. If no one believed her testimony, with the healed tree and her healed child, they would believe Ambrose.

Alix came quietly into the room when she was halfway done. He stared for several seconds as she clipped another long strand and tossed onto the already high pile of shimmering red-gold silk. He swallowed hard and leaned a little deeper into his crutch. It creaked and no one jumped.

"Well, at least no one will recognize you with your hair cut short," he said, trying to smile as Arden met his eyes in her mirror. "There's nothing I can do to stop you, nothing I can do to help. I'll check your tree every day, and I'll know if you're all right. The moment you're in trouble, I'll come with every soldier in Westerland."

His eyes were bright with the threat of tears, wide with pleading, begging her not to need his help. Arden nodded and tried to smile. She swallowed hard and blinked to fight the tears trying to betray her and turned back to her mirror.

~~~~~

In the years since King Doyne's death, the main border gate between Westerland and Stonemount had changed in unpleasant ways. The wall running along the border between the two countries had been expanded a mile in both directions, so that those standing at the gate couldn't see the ends, where they vanished into steep ravines and cliffs. Finding more friendly terrain meant walking days in either direction, sometimes crossing into other bordering kingdoms, first. The fierce terrain had been Stonemount's best defense. Now it was augmented with regular patrols, to keep people from crossing over unseen. And increasing rumors said the patrols were more to keep valuable artisans and merchants and scholars from leaving Stonemount without the throne's permission.

The guards at the gate were the same men, but there was no lazy, cheerful gossip, no more stepping casually across the line in the dirt to share a mug of ale or fresh bread brought by a wife or mother, or to teach games to the children who lived nearby. The gate had been built up taller and wider, the wood replaced with iron. The guards didn't even look across the wide bars of the gate, much less talk to each other. Trees had been cut down to make way for the wall, and cut back so far there was no shade, and no chance for people to climb up unseen and drop over.
~~~~~

The stream that meandered back and forth over the border had been dammed up, leaving stagnant little pools on either side of the wall, which bred flies and stank.

The people no longer smiled as they waited to pass from one country to the other, and they had never waited before. They were all dusty and footsore and refused to look at the guards who had once gossiped easily with them.

The day Arden arrived at the gate, all the traffic went from Stonemount to Westerland, every traveler burdened with their worldly goods. The sound of approaching hooves caused every head to turn, eyes wide in fear, expecting pursuit. Each time, it turned out to be a donkey, often pulling a cart, not a soldier or courier on one of the massive, death-black stallions King Maddix favored.

Arden went on foot, carrying Violet in a basket on her back, sitting on top of their spare clothes, a few coppers, and enough food for the journey. She had considered taking a donkey to make the journey a little faster and smoother but decided against it. A soldier's widow desperate enough to go to Stonemount to seek her fortune wouldn't have a donkey. Glynna, who floated several yards behind them, hadn't said a word since they left the palace two mornings ago before dawn, slipping out among the shadows. She drew no closer as they reached the border gate and a Westerland guard saw them and blinked in surprise. He stepped away from the gate and waited until Arden came to a stop just out of the flow of incoming traffic.

"Where are you going?" He looked a little abashed at his gruff tone, mostly from surprise. Arden didn't trust her voice, but simply gestured at the open gate. "I know that." He tried to smile. "But a pretty little thing like you shouldn't be traveling alone, and certainly not there."

He hooked a thumb over his shoulder in the general direction of Stonemount. The guards on the opposite side ignored him, while the people who had just crossed over laughed, wearily, some of them bitterly.

"I don't know what idiot told you it would be better," a gray-haired woman among the travelers said, "but take my advice and stay home in Westerland."

"I can't." Arden nearly smiled when her voice came out a whispery rasp. "My husband died in King Maddix's war. My only chance is in Stonemount."

"Relatives?" the gate guard said. He sounded a little relieved at his own suggestion, and Arden's heart warmed to him for his concern. "They must be nobles. They're the only ones who still have a good life in Stonemount."

"Your child?" The woman had stepped around to Arden's side and looked into the basket. She smiled at pale little sleeping Violet and tsked. "Poor thing. How long has she been sick?"

"Since her father died. Everything has been wrong since her father died." Arden set the basket down so she could see Violet and check her.

"If you're thinking of the king's magic apples, forget them. The tree is dying, and even if it weren't, King Maddix won't share even for the sake of a child." The weariness in the woman's voice couldn't mask her anger, and that encouraged Arden. There were people in Stonemount who didn't believe Maddix's lies.

"I heard the king will give anything to the one who heals his tree."

"If anyone can. He's earned every misfortune, but why do the rest of us have to suffer?"

"Because," her balding, red-faced husband said as he joined them, "we were stupid enough to believe him. If you have no one else, little one, come stay with us. No one should be so desperate they put their hope in King Maddix. We'll take care of you."

"Thank you." Arden's voice broke, aching for tears. "You have no idea how much your words mean to me, but I must go on."

She nodded thanks to them, then slung her basket over her shoulder and stepped up to the gate. A few travelers murmured and shook their heads as the guard opened the gate to let her through.

"Good luck," the guard muttered. He tried to smile as she started down the long trade road heading for the capital. "The Fates bless you."

"That was very kind," Glynna said. "I was ready to believe everyone in Stonemount was a fool and utterly selfish."

That prompted a sad smile from Arden. She said nothing but kept her face turned toward the capital, the palace, her tree.

And Ambrose.

~~~~~

Two days later, a courier raced past Arden when she halted by the side of the road to rest and drink and wash her face at a stream that was little more than a trickle. She was so caught up in the hint of color returning to Violet's pale cheeks that she barely noticed the straining black horse, coated in dusty lather and the panicking courier clinging to the saddle. If she had, she would have wondered what terrifying news the man carried.

If she could have stood in Maddix's study that evening when the king heard the report, she would have laughed at the man's consternation and then been very afraid. She was the cause of the hasty message. By slipping away so early in the morning, dressed as a peasant, Arden had avoided the notice of the spies set to watch the palace.
~~~~~

Maddix wanted every detail of Violet's lingering illness and Arden's torment as she watched her child die. Arden spent so much time indoors with her ill child, they didn't realize she had vanished until two days later.

The page boy who stood before the king quaked in his boots as he finished reading the message aloud.

Maddix, Jaygo, Clancy and Baethon sat frozen for several seconds after the boy spoke. Maddix grew alternately white then red in reaction to the words. The four had been playing their favorite game, moving markers across a vast map of the surrounding dozen countries, planning invasions and how the power would be divided once Maddix took over Westerland, then Ambray, then someday moved one of his sons or grandsons onto the throne of Brentonwald. The goals never changed, but as obstacles arose or fell, their strategy and timing altered to fit.

"What did you say?" Maddix said, his voice almost too quiet. The page's face grew so white it seemed to leach color from his midnight hair.

"Princess Arden and her daughter have vanished from the palace, Sire. No one knows where they have gone."

"She's coming here. To see Ambrose. That's the only answer." He stared unseeing at the army markers in front of him.

"Then that solves your problem," Clancy offered with a grin. "No one would be surprised if the journey killed the brat."

"And if her poor, distraught mother died of grief," Baethon added, his voice dripping with false concern.

"Watch the borders. I want her the minute she touches Stonemount soil." Maddix slammed a clenched fist down onto the map, making all the markers jump and fall. He grinned, baring his teeth like a hyena about to feast.

"Kill her?" He nearly drooled as he asked.

"Idiot. I need her to heal my tree."

"Then we kill her?" Clancy asked.

"That is a foolish waste of resources." Jaygo very carefully didn't look at any of them as he spoke. "You need her to give you a legitimate claim—"

"I know that!" Maddix leaped to his feet and pounded both fists on the table, so the markers jumped and toppled over. "Just how am I to marry and breed sons on two princesses at the same time?"

Clancy chuckled and slouched back in his chair, while Baethon waggled his eyebrows suggestively. For once, their filthy thoughts didn't amuse Maddix.

"Just consider that her presence will protect you from having to marry Fiera and worry about being poisoned the moment she gives birth to your heir," Jaygo said. Now he looked up at Maddix and the irritation and growing disdain hinted in his voice were clear in his eyes, if not the rest of his expression. "Send your special troops in disguise to hunt for her, capture her, treat her badly to ensure her child dies and she is ill and confused by the time she arrives here. Convince her you have rescued her. Then treat her far better than she deserves. Sweep her off her feet with passion and marry her before she can think clearly." He spread his hands, palms up, as if he were presenting a gift to his king. "Just think what good will you will gain from your own people. Everyone loves a love story. Regularly dose Arden with those nasty little potions and powders your pet alchemists have been creating for you all these years, to keep her confused and compliant."

He snorted, a glint of amusement in his eyes, when Maddix flinched at that statement.

"Oh, you thought I didn't know about your little hobbies?" Jaygo shrugged. "All that matters is gaining control of her mind, her will, her heart. When she is devoted to you, then the poison coming out of that dratted tree will end, and healing will begin. It can't help turning to a blessing, once the silly girl is reunited with her tree, and she agrees that she gave it to you as a love gift. Get her pregnant as soon as you can. And gain yourself at least two years of freedom and time to protect yourself against Brentonwald's schemes. If you're clever, you can blame Brentonwald for Arden's death, in retribution for interfering with their plans for your throne."

Maddix could almost forgive Jaygo for his disdain and irritation and that glimmer of self-satisfaction. The man had proven useful, after all. That didn't mean he wouldn't hesitate when the timing was right to have Clancy kill him. He had promised Clancy he could do it, after all, and a wise man never broke the promises made to useful, loyal allies.

CHAPTER EIGHTEEN

Morning gilded the roofs and streets and walls of Stonemount's capital, so the entire city seemed to be part of the gold and scarlet and purple of the sky. Arden blinked bleary eyes, sore from the smoke of her tiny campfire, and smiled at the glorious sight in the low, sprawling valley below her. She had stopped for the night at the top of a hill, with the lights of the city twinkling in the distance. She took the glorious vision of the city as an omen.

Then, as she finished washing with the chill water from a stream that raced down the hillside, she wished she had not claimed the omen. As the dawn crept into full morning the gold vanished. Shadows trickled through the city, turning it black as if an illness ravaged it. Arden hugged Violet closer and tried not to see the illness doing the same to her child. She busied herself with her hair, fed Violet, and neatly packed their few belongings away. By noon, they would be at the palace gates and though the journey was over the work had just begun.

"Not as beautiful as you expected?" Glynna murmured, fading into view as Arden paused to look down at the increasingly blighted city.

"I had silly, romantic dreams when I was a child." She tried not to sigh as she put the last of her journey bread into the basket.

"The city only reflects the heart of its king. Once, it was a beautiful, happy place. When the king was a good man who cared about his people. Westerland will become just as ugly."

"Never!" Arden flinched as her sharp word startled Violet. The little girl looked wide-eyed at her mother, who cuddled her close and murmured nonsense words to soothe her.

"When the bitterness grows stronger in your heart, it will affect the entire country. Your plan is wrong!"

"Am I evil to want my daughter to live?"

"You want to shame Maddix," her teacher said, with tears in her eyes. "You want to put the apples into his hands in front of his entire court and tell everyone only you could heal the tree because you created the tree."

"It's the truth, isn't it?" She kissed Violet once on her nose, prompting a giggle from the child, then settled her into the basket for this final journey.

"Truth is a flame that warms or destroys. It all depends on what is in your heart."

~~~~~

Dylon nearly forgot to stop at the alchemist's shop on the outskirts of the city to dye his hair and beard mousy brown. He hid his sable roots under a cap while traveling and gathering information for his grandfather, but he couldn't wear his hat inside the palace. It didn't go with the livery he wore as part of his disguise. He had established himself as a low-level servant, assigned to the groundskeeping staff and the stables before he faked his death, with the help of several allies of Ambrose. His position was lowly enough that few of the higher-ranked servants noticed when he was gone for months at a time. Those who did notice were friends and delighted in keeping secrets from Maddix and the nobles who supported him. They thought he was working for the day when Ambrose would be strong enough to flee to freedom. Ambrose's plan, using Dylon as his messenger to kingdoms all across the continent, reached much farther than that, and would take years.

Dylon wasn't surprised, but still worried, when he found his grandfather's imprisonment had been made even more restrictive. Bad enough that Ambrose couldn't leave the palace grounds, and everywhere he went he had two very visible bodyguards, who discouraged everyone but the most elite from seeking his help. Healing others was meat and bread to Ambrose, and the lack of use continued to dull and stifle his Gift.

Now, Ambrose couldn't even roam the palace grounds freely during the daylight hours. When Dylon slipped into the suite of rooms where his grandfather now spent most of his time, he found him a little more hunched, a little more pale, a little more weary. He was shriveling up, wasting away from disuse, and looked almost as old as he truly was.

Dylon wished for the first time he hadn't faked his death, to stay free of Maddix's spies and threats to force Ambrose to cooperate. He would march into his distant cousin's office right this moment and face him down, make him see the harm he was doing to Ambrose. The last time he had tried to persuade Maddix to give his grandfather his freedom, he had wanted to badger that false innocence and concern off Maddix's face and make him eat his lying words. Maddix continued to claim he was protecting Ambrose, that his life was more precious to him than any treasure Stonemount possessed.

That was the problem. Ambrose's Gift was nothing but a treasure, to Maddix. Something to horde for profit. Not something Yeshen had sent into the world to bless everyone.

~~~~~

Twenty members of one family waited for the guards at the border gate to swing the heavy iron barrier open in mid-afternoon that day. The

Stonemount guards tried to ignore the people, though a few cast envious glances at them; grandparents and mothers and fathers and children. The Westerland guards gave the ragged, footsore, hungry people pitying looks and one ran for the newly built storehouse. King Alix had given orders that anyone entering Westerland in need would be given decent clothes and medicine and enough food to get them to the farms that always needed more workers.

The ground began to vibrate several long moments before the thunder of hooves became audible. The people looked around in terror, then scattered with loud cries as Clancy and Baethon appeared through a gap in the forest, leading a troop of twenty elite guardsmen.

At the same moment, many miles away, Arden waited in the shade of the rear palace gates while the gatekeeper sent for Jason, the head gardener. She smiled at her daughter, who sat up by herself now and looked around at their new surroundings with interest. It was a pleasant enough place, Arden acknowledged. Wide stone benches in the shade and two trickling fountains furnished with cups so travelers could refresh themselves while they waited. Still, the blight that touched all of Stonemount reached even to the palace walls, visible in the stunted and dying plants in what were once ornate beds along the walls on either side of the gate. The dry twigs and colorless weeds hinted at the ornamental plants that had once graced this place.

The little man-door to the left of the gate creaked open and Jason stepped out. He was a big man, with a leathery face and wide shoulders and long, deft fingers. Arden wondered how he felt, watching his precious gardens dying little by little. Did he fight with his king over the cause? Did he protest even once when Maddix imprisoned her tree? Was he a new man, brought in because the last one protested? There was so much she didn't know, so much even faithful Rilling couldn't tell her.

"You are the woman seeking work in the gardens?" Jason looked her over, visibly dismissing her. He raked one hand through his sparse, red hair, pulling it over the bald patch running down the middle of his head and tried to smile through his regret. "We have no openings. Especially not for a woman burdened by a child. This is heavy work, and you're just not built for it."

"But you do have an opening, sir." She almost laughed, pitying him for his attempt at kindness. "The king needs someone to heal his apple tree."

"You? We don't need more farmer's wives making themselves nuisances."

"My husband was a soldier, not a farmer. I am plantwise." She stood, lifting Violet to perch on her hip, and met the man's eyes.

"Don't say that too loudly. King Maddix killed the last three who claimed to be plantwise and lied."

"I can prove it." She held out her hand, demanding he test her immediately.

Jason looked around at the stunted plants, the prickly bushes that held onto the soil with leather roots. He pulled a pod off one bush right next to the gate, so close that when it opened completely the wooden bars battered the poor plant.

"If you can make something of this…" He shrugged, trying again to smile as he put the pod into her open palm.

"Bittersweet." She smiled and glanced at Glynna, who hovered close by. "Appropriate."

"Indeed," the ghostly woman murmured.

Arden cradled the pod in both hands and sat down on the stone border of the flowerbed. Violet tried to get her little fingers between her mother's hands and chuckled with delight when Arden resisted her. Green-gold magic flowed out from between her fingers, a little brighter with every second that passed. Happy tears burned her eyes for the first time in months. She had truly feared she had lost her plantwise gift altogether.

"Hope does amazing things, my dear," Glynna murmured. "Your emotions were always too tightly woven into your magic."

Arden opened her hands to reveal the pod had sprouted several leaves and a delicate stalk. She shifted Violet back to her hip and got up, taking the seedling over to a spot by the closest fountain where it would get plenty of water without being splashed too hard. As she scraped at the soil with her fingers to make a hole for the seedling, she left streaks of green-gold magic that faded slowly into the soil. As soon as she planted the seedling, it put out more stalks and leaves.

"The job is yours," Jason breathed, hope lighting his face. "Heal the king's tree and he will give you half the kingdom."

"Right now, I need decent quarters for myself and my daughter."

Arden stood, fussing with Violet to hide the relief she felt, which threatened to turn all her joints to water. She reminded herself that she was no princess here and had no right to command.

"Granted. Food and a girl to bring you wash water morning and evening, and new clothes. And ten silver pennies every week."

"What if I don't heal the tree?" she couldn't help asking. She shivered a little, as it came to her how vicious Maddix had to be about his ailing tree, for this man to be so generous.

"Mistress, others have tried and the tree worsens each time. I always test them, as soon as they appear. But you—" He chuckled and spread his hands, indicating the answer was self-evident.

"Perhaps you should test me, first, before you show me my quarters."

"Very wise move, my dear," Glynna said. "Find out where the tree is, first. Find out if all hope is gone before you are too deeply inside enemy territory and trapped."

Arden felt the ailing tree long before she saw the stone wall that enclosed it. The tree should have stood taller than the wall, which was higher than Jason's head and topped with metal spikes slanting outward to discourage climbing. Arden couldn't see the tree's branches even from the top of the slight incline at the head of the path. She shivered and wished she hadn't taken her shoes off when she reached the palace gates, because she felt the silent whimpers of the tree's roots as it tried to suck nourishment in through the dead ground. There was stagnant water nearby and it fouled what little nourishment came in through the roots. The leaves were useless, taking more energy from the branches than they produced. Arden felt them, sickly yellow-brown, even before she reached the iron gate with its ornate curlicues and pouncing beasts and saw inside the enclosure.

It was all she could do to keep from crying out and yanking the keys from Jason's hands as he bent to unlock the gate. She set Violet down as soon as she stepped through the creaking gates and ran to the tree. Tears touched her eyes. Glynna was right. Part of the tree's illness was because of her, the bitterness and anger in her spirit. She nearly stumbled when a flicker of green-gold life danced across the tips of the outermost branches. Slowly, they rose, stretching out and upward like a dying man reaching for his sweetheart.

"Oh, I am here. It's all right. I'll make you well again," she whispered as she leaned against the naked, too-thin trunk. "I'm sorry. It's all my fault. But it's going to be all right now."

Golden-green magic flowed out of her in her tears, then spilled from under the kerchief covering her braided hair and down her arms and legs, soaking into the soil and the roots. The sparkles of magic danced up the branches, leaving a greenish tinge and suppleness in leaves that a moment before had been brown and crackled in the occasional wind.

Violet laughed and clapped her hands as magic skittered over the tree. Arden glanced over her shoulder through tearful eyes at her daughter and laughed. She had truly feared she would have no magic left, no sweetness in her heart, to bring about the miracle her child needed. As that fear died, leaves popped out all over the half-denuded branches, causing Jason to yelp and dance backward as if the sparkles of magic would reach out and bite him.

~~~~~

In the Westerland palace gardens, Alix sat at work under the branches of his sister's tree. He had promised to keep watch over the tree, so he had his people set up his study outdoors when the spring weather permitted. He was just looking up to thank Caitlin for the fresh pitcher of water she had brought him when a tingling raced up and down his arms. He looked at his hands, tinged with green-gold sparkles.

"Majesty!" Caitlin gasped and burst out laughing.

Alix looked at her, then followed her gaze. Above their heads, the tree burst out in pink and white and gold blossoms and tiny green apples the size of marbles popped out among the new flowers, with each kiss of a magic spark.

"She's all right. She's all right!" Alix roared. He leaped up awkwardly and grabbed Caitlin's hands to dance her around the tree in limping, giddy, joyous flight. Even when he stumbled and his bad leg gave out, they laughed and clung to each other. When he kissed her soundly on the cheek, Caitlin didn't blush or play coy.

As she helped him back to his chair under the tree, both of them breathless, Alix wondered if there was another magic in the air besides plantwise. He wisely kept his mouth shut, because there was only so much room in his heart for rejoicing.

~~~~~

Maddix sat in his study and tried to make pleasant conversation with Lord Anselm. It took all his skill in dissembling to appear relaxed and smile cordially. He barely tasted the rich red wine that Anselm sipped leisurely and rolled over his tongue with the enjoyment of a true connoisseur.

"Tell me, Majesty," Anselm said, "what progress have you made in obtaining the magic apples my king requires for his daughter?"

"Oh, we've had many offers of help." Maddix nodded, studying his face in the dark depths of his cup, and slouched a little in his chair. "It's very encouraging. I had no idea how much the people love me."

"They love the reward you offer, Majesty. Have you considered Princess Arden of Westerland? She is plantwise. And Westerland is an ally of long standing."

"Yes, but I hesitate to ask. Arden is having enough problems right now, governing Westerland while her brother is an invalid."

He silently cursed Alix for so very publicly refusing to consider the marriage alliance. Anselm had heard about it, and repeated Alix's words almost verbatim when Maddix had insisted he couldn't marry Princess Fiera because he and Arden had an understanding. He was simply waiting a decent period to allow Arden to mourn before they married.

"Yes," Anselm purred. "That unfortunate ambush. I had forgotten."

"I doubt Arden could help. After all, the tree was a gift from the wizards of —"

"Princess Arden made the tree. My people watched her as she created the tree. They saw your company flee the night it was stolen from the palace. And the wizards in question have no plantwise magic, even if they were inclined to gift you with such a devastating blessing. Which they most certainly are not."

"You must be mistaken." Maddix felt his tongue freeze in his mouth, along with his mind. Now, of all times, he needed a dozen glib answers. None came. And all the while, Anselm looked at him with that thin smile and his eyes big and dark and full of dangerous knowledge.

"No, you are mistaken if you think I will accept your habitual falsehoods. The reformation of the throne of Stonemount is required, not just three magic apples, before my king's daughter becomes your wife. You hesitate to ask Princess Arden for help because you don't know where she is."

"Well, she is somewhere in Westerland, I suppose." He shrugged and took a sip from his cup when he longed to down the contents in one gulp. "It's spring and she's a farmer at heart. I suspect she is out encouraging the crops for her people. It's part of her royal duty, of course."

"Of course." Anselm finally looked away, but somehow that was no improvement.

~~~~~

By the time Jason returned to the walled garden with Lord Jaygo, to report the visible improvement in the tree, Violet had fallen asleep in her traveling basket. Enrapt with the tree, Arden never reacted to the two men who stopped in the gate. Jaygo nearly laughed aloud as he recognized Westerland's princess. While he would enjoy her terror when she recognized him and realized her scheme had failed, he decided to ensure that never happened. The longer Arden was here, unknown, working in secret, the better for him.

Arden walked around the tree, sometimes ducking under its branches to touch the trunk, sometimes dancing back to the outer reaches of the branches and lightly brushing her fingers over the newly sprouted leaves. A trail of green and gold sparks like a tail of smoke from a torch followed her outstretched fingers. She had loosed her hair from her kerchief and braids so it streamed out behind her. Sparks of magic spun from her hair, rising up around the tree. The branches moved in a slow, stately dance in time with her movements, untouched by the errant
~~~~~

gusts of evening breeze.

"You have done very well, Jason," Lord Jaygo murmured. "I will see that you are properly rewarded. When the king presents the apples to his bride."

"You'll tell the king a plantwise woman has come?" the head gardener begged.

Jaygo respected Jason for his healthy fear, and his wisdom in always putting nobles between him and the king. That was how he had worked his way up to power, although it always galled him that those above him always took some credit for his hard work. Still, when something failed, they also took the punishment.

"Oh, yes, of course. Immediately," Jaygo murmured. He smirked as Jason walked over to join Arden.

He hadn't told Maddix about the last three contenders and had enjoyed threatening Jason in the king's name. He planned to keep the news to himself until he could decide how best to profit from it. Maddix deserved to be kept in the dark and worrying about his prey, he decided. For a while, at least. He had grown too cocky, thinking he needed no more guidance. Jaygo enjoyed the idea of watching Maddix panic and squirm, growing more desperate to find Arden. He would be properly appreciative when Jaygo revealed to him that his longed-for tool had been in his hands, almost in his pocket, for weeks.

CHAPTER NINETEEN

Olive, the palace's head cook, was a tiny woman, white-haired and red-faced, who insisted on wearing white no matter how messy her job became. She managed to be everywhere at once, tasting everything multiple times and yet never growing wider than she was tall.

She took Arden and Violet under her wing as soon as Jason brought them to her, making it totally unnecessary for the palace steward to become involved. Arden was grateful for that, and grateful for the private room for herself and Violet, the livery that would help her blend in with the servants, and most of all for the warm, savory meal Olive dished up for her, liberally sprinkled with palace gossip. Arden curled up in a corner of the kitchen and fed Violet while Olive worked on fancy pastries and preparations for tomorrow's cooking. She relaxed in the warmth of friendship, weariness, and a sense of having accomplished something enormous.

"You'll find yourself very popular, mark my words." Olive punctuated her words with a sharp rap on the worktable with her wooden spoon. "Even if you weren't so pretty and a widow and with such an adorable little poppet. Yes, I'm talking about you, sweetling." She wrinkled up her face at staring little Violet, who burst out laughing.

"I'm not sure I understand," Arden said. A sinking sensation put a lie to her words.

"It's the tree, of course. The king has been in a foul temper over it. When the tree gets better, why he'll be his old self and the rest of the palace can breathe easily again. All because of you."

"Is the tree that important?"

"The king needs those apples for Princess Fiera. It's very important to impress Brentonwald. We didn't do well in that silly war Westerland insisted on—"

"Maddix demanded the war. Westerland wanted nothing to do with it."

"No, dearie, you're mistaken." Olive gave her a puzzled little frown.

"My husband served with King Alix." Arden swallowed down her little flare of anger. It wasn't Olive's fault—she was only repeating the lies she had been told. However, Arden could do something about those lies while she was here. "He was there when they argued for peace talks instead of attacking Ambray. King Alix wanted peace and King Maddix was furious with him because he wanted war."

"Really? Now, isn't it amazing how we don't hear the truth down here? Tell me, since you were so close to the palace. Is Princess Arden really as ugly as the king said?"

"Ugly?" She sat up a little straighter, startled enough she didn't know whether to laugh or be upset. It wasn't like Olive had meant to hurt *her*, after all.

"We heard she pronounced a curse on King Maddix. It stands to reason, if she had the power to make the curse work, then she's a witch. And witches are ugly. Stands to reason." Olive emphasized her words with another sharp rap of her spoon, which totally delighted Violet. She giggled and wriggled on her mother's lap and snatched at the last spoon of soup, nearly upending it into her lap.

"Oh, no I've found that evil hides itself behind great beauty and charm. Only truth has the courage to present its real face to the world."

"Then you must be a very evil woman." Olive laughed when Arden blinked and shook her head, caught off-balance by the remark. "You have such a pretty face, it must be hiding a great deal of evil," the head cook explained with another chuckle.

"No." She forced herself to laugh and shake her head and at least appear to relax. "I'm nothing more than a soldier's widow, trying to take care of my daughter. I am here to heal the king's tree and take my reward, and then I can go home."

"It must be a sad place without you and your little one in it. Here, now, lad," she continued, turning toward the sound of a footstep in the doorway. "You didn't have to do that."

Arden caught her breath as the tall, lean form in the stairwell doorway resolved into someone vaguely familiar. She thought his coloring was wrong but wasn't sure why or how. She swallowed hard, praying those bright eyes would pass over her, and not see through her disguise. Any moment now, they would widen in surprise and recognition. What would she do if he demanded to know why the princess of Westerland was sitting in the kitchen, gossiping with the cook and wearing Stonemount livery?

The moment passed and the young man chuckled as he stepped across the room and deposited a tray of dirty dishes next to the washing barrel piled high with suds and dirty dishes. Arden knew she had seen him before, in Westerland. He was wearing livery, so he was some kind of servant. Had he come to Westerland in the service of Maddix?

"It gave me an excuse to come down here," the young man said, his voice rich and warm and low enough to send a shiver down Arden's back. A pleasant shiver. "I wanted to come see if the rumors are true." He winked at her and turned back to Olive, and Arden realized with a sudden sensation of weightlessness that he didn't recognize her.

"So, the stories have started already, have they?" Olive shook her head and went back to mixing the filling for her pastries. "Thirty years cooking for the palace, and I'm still surprised how quickly tales spread."

"For once, they're true. A maiden has come to heal the king's wretched tree and she's lovely and young and —" He stopped short as he turned back to Arden, a tiny frown wiping away his smile for a few seconds. "Don't I know you, mistress?"

"No, I don't think so." Arden shook her head, praying that her lack of flowers or jewelry and the black kerchief once again covering her hair would be a large enough difference to foil his memory.

"I never forget a pretty face, but I can't remember where I've seen you." He shook his head, that engaging smile returning.

"Wherever you've seen her, lad, she was probably already married when you met her," Olive said with a chuckle and a wink for Arden.

"Oh. Yes. My condolences on your loss, mistress. May I ask how long ago…?"

"In the war." She hugged Violet a little closer. The little girl watched the stranger with big eyes, considering him. Arden decided he was a good man because Violet was an unusually good judge of character and seemed to accept him already without any problem.

"Did he ever see his child?" He made a face at Violet and prompted a giggle from her.

"Oh, yes." She cuddled Violet closer. "He adored her. You just ruled your Papa's heart, didn't you?"

"Here, now," Olive said with a mocking growl and a sigh. "You won't leave until you get introduced, will you? Dylon, this is Maura and her daughter, Letti, of Westerland," she said.

Arden had added false names to their disguise. It would do little good to cut her hair and wear peasant clothes if a plantwise woman named Arden showed up at the palace gates with an ill little girl named Violet. Even the densest of Maddix's subjects would be able to put the pieces together and come up with trouble.

"Ah. Westerland," Dylon said. "That explains it. It's been years since I was able to travel to Westerland. A beautiful country, mistress. I miss it. Be warned. Your pretty face won't escape the king's notice for long. Take my advice and go home before you regret it."

"I came here for the king's reward," Arden said. "I have my daughter to provide for, now that her father is dead."

"Is half the kingdom worth the danger?"

"The reward I want and need is more than worth it." Yet even as she looked into his big, dark eyes, she felt a flicker of doubt.

~~~~~

Ambrose spent most of his days in his chair by the large open window that looked out over the palace gardens, lost in memories and trying to think of some new way to get past his too-vigilant guards for a few hours of freedom. Someday, Dylon promised, they would find a way to break free of Maddix and roam the world again.

As the months of his "protective imprisonment" turned into years, Ambrose explored the possibility that the only way to escape was to Gift himself to Dylon, and pray Yeshen helped his grandson escape Stonemount before Maddix realized what happened. He was too familiar with the treachery that filled the palace to hope that Dylon's faked death and dyed hair would protect them for much longer. Eventually, someone would betray them to win favor from Maddix, or more likely, to protect themselves from some injustice and cruelty. Dylon needed to flee Stonemount for good.

Ambrose wondered sometimes if his grandson realized how prophetic his words were, when he swore he would never leave Stonemount without his grandfather, free at last.

Tonight, he smiled despite his weariness and watched Dylon pace the length of the too-fancy sitting room. Did his grandson realize how quickly this plantwise woman, Maura, had captured his interest and sympathy? Was it his healer's heart guiding him, or something more personal?

"There's nothing I can do to persuade her to leave for her own good. Unless…" Dylon paused a moment, eyes darkening, mouth open on a word poised on his tongue.

"Unless?" Ambrose prompted.

"I think her child might be ill. She's an adorable little creature, but too pale. Maybe Maura is here to heal the tree, to get an apple to heal her daughter. Grandfather, it's easier for you to get down to the gardens at night. She's constantly with the tree. You could heal Letti and send Maura home tonight, couldn't you?" he hurried on.

"I could, but for her safety, it's best if she doesn't know who I am or what I've done. And then how do we persuade her to leave without that healing? If you're right."

"We have to try. If you can't escape yet, we can at least help others break free of Maddix's plots and lies."

"You're right. We can try. And ask Yeshen's blessing." He played with the idea that maybe he had found something to help him persuade Dylon to leave Stonemount for good, before their little deception was discovered. He would gladly accept years of imprisonment and fading away to nothing, to keep Dylon safe.
~~~~~

~~~~~

Ambrose walked slowly down the pathway strewn with crushed seashells through the center of the royal gardens. It had been so long since he had come outside during the day, he had almost forgotten what it looked like in sunlight rather than moonlight. On the whole, though, he preferred the nighttime garden. No over-anxious guards; no obsequious, sneering courtiers teetering on the knife's edge between keeping in the good graces of a Gifted healer and in King Maddix's favor.

The silver spill of moonlight across the gardens couldn't dim the green-gold glow of magic that rose up in the air like a dainty geyser, high over the spikes topping the wall around the tree. Ambrose took deeper breaths, invigorated by the magic vibrating through the ground and air. A tingling in the air filled his lungs. His heart picked up its pace and a few times he had to restrain himself from breaking into a mad dash of exuberance. Someone strongly Gifted in magic, plantwise magic, celebrated behind that high stone wall.

Ambrose later kicked himself for not realizing it could only be Arden's magic that he felt rippling through the ground and air. He saw Glynna, floating over sleeping little Violet, long before he saw Arden slowly weaving in and out among the shadows and the dancing branches of the apple tree. Ambrose stared at the spirit remains of the woman he had loved and cherished as a good friend long after the romantic fires turned to coals. Tears touched his eyes as years of memories crashed over him.

Glynna hadn't changed a speck in the years since he had seen her last. He knew that was to be expected, yet still it affected him deeply. He longed to call her name, to rush to her and take her in his arms and hold her close and hear her laugh at him and call him a worrywart.

He couldn't touch her. It was a miracle, a blessing amid his sorrows that his Gifting was still strong enough he could see her at all.

Ambrose chose to be grateful, though he wanted to take Arden and shake her and shout his furious fear for her. What foolishness had brought her here, in disguise, into the very jaws of that cruel, selfish, arrogant idiot, Maddix? He considered what he knew of his great-nephew's schemes and lies, and how he could protect Arden, while feasting on the sight of Glynna hovering protectively over the sleeping child. All the while, Arden worked her plantwise magic into the air and soil, eyes closed as she communed with the tree. It was still a part of her, despite Maddix's cruelty and lies and the poisoning and warping of the tree's magic.

Then Glynna looked up, as if the pressure of his gaze had become something tangible. Her eyes widened as her gaze went straight to him.
~~~~~

Ambrose stepped out from the useless shelter of the half-open gates and executed a deep bow to Glynna. Her hands went to her mouth and he nearly laughed at her surprise.

"Dear?" Her voice wavered with astonishment and a touch of nerves. "Violet is sleeping. Do you mind if I look around a bit?"

"Hmm?" Arden opened her eyes a moment, barely glancing at Glynna. "No ... that's all right ..."

Glynna darted past Ambrose, gesturing for him to follow. He had to run to keep up with her and they went a good twenty paces into the darkness before she stopped. From where they stood, they could still see through the gates, into the walled garden to where Arden slowly circled the tree and Violet slept.

"My dear, how good to see you again," Ambrose said, his voice strained with his delight and the effort to keep quiet.

It would be just his luck — bad — that tonight his lazy guards would decide to come looking for him. The last thing he needed was for them to catch him talking to no one in the dark. They would report it to Maddix and those vile herbs to make him docile and perpetually drowsy would return to his food. Little Prince Maxin was a healthy, relatively happy toddler now and didn't need his healing touch. The only reason Maddix made sure he was treated well was to control who received his Gifting, after all.

"How are you?" he added, fighting the need to reach out and try to take her hand.

"I'm useless and frustrated," Glynna cried. She at least didn't have to make any effort to keep quiet. "That's how I am. I wish I had a body again, just to spank some sense into that dratted girl."

"I can imagine. What in the world made Arden come here?" A dozen plans scampered through his mind, adapting his own plans for escape to help Arden flee the country before Maddix realized she was there.

"To find you. Ambrose, did you get any of her letters, the last two years?"

"Not a one. She got none of mine either, did she? Why does she need me?"

"Her daughter is dying. The warping of the tree's magic here and Arden's bitter spirit have made her own tree useless. And then we found poison in the roots of her tree, and poison in the palace well. We're sure Maddix did it, to force Arden to come to him. She's determined to win the prize he offered for healing his tree, and then she'll humiliate him in front of the entire world, if she can." Tiny green sparks shot out of Glynna's hair to punctuate her frustration and fear, just like they had done when she still had a body. It made Ambrose want to take her into his arms and laugh and kiss her soundly.

"Well, let me heal the child right now, and you three can head home in the morning." He bowed her toward the garden gate.

"Hmm ... I'm not so sure that's wise." Glynna's eyes narrowed as she glanced back toward Arden and her daughter. "She needs to be taught a lesson."

Twenty minutes later, Ambrose entered the garden, slowly, carefully, like the arthritic old man he had been an hour before. He didn't have to pretend the wonder and joy he felt at this display of Arden's magic, though it was dimmed by the things Glynna had told him and the risky decision they had come to and the plans they had made.

"Hello." He smiled when Arden stumbled and turned sharply, startled at his sudden appearance. "I didn't think anyone was awake at this late hour."

"Neither did I." Arden colored prettily and glanced at the bundle of blankets where her daughter lay sleeping.

"So you're Maura? That means Bitter, doesn't it? Why? You look like such a sweet girl." He bobbed his head as he had seen old gaffers do and hoped the princess didn't look past his outward appearance. He had to get her to trust him if he was going to help her, and looking old and harmless was the best way. Over Arden's shoulder, Glynna made faces, both teasing and encouraging him.

"Perhaps they could see into the future. Being a widow is surely bitter enough?" the young woman returned.

"Ah, but if that is your child, surely life is sweet?" He raised his eyebrows, asking permission.

Arden only hesitated a few seconds, then nodded. Ambrose's hands tingled with magic he couldn't quite repress as he bent to pick up the sleeping little girl. His entire body ached from the pressure of healing magic long unused that tried to come forth without his calling it. The child opened her big violet eyes at the first touch of his hands, and she smiled at him. Ambrose lost his heart to her at the first glimpse of the tiny white pearl in the center of her upper gums.

"Hello, sweetheart. And what is your name?"

"Letti," Arden supplied.

"Short for ... Violet? For your eyes?" He smothered a chuckle when Arden turned her face away, hiding her reaction. Glynna winked at him.

He half-closed his eyes, taking advantage of the mother's distracted moment. Silver sparkles enveloped his hands, flowing from them to cover Violet. Prickles of pain stabbed at his fingertips and palms as the magic told him what ailed the little girl. Ambrose frowned, a welter of negative emotions nearly overwhelming him for a few seconds. He recognized the poison, and it proved Glynna's words right. Only Maddix could have chosen such an insidious, rare poison to accomplish his end. Only someone who had given himself wholeheartedly to alliance with Durmad.

When Arden turned back around to face him again, he shut down the healing magic and pasted his harmless smile back onto his face.

"Now that you know us, who are you?" Arden asked, trying to smile.

"My dear, if you could call me Grandfather, I would be delighted. Everyone does. And please, don't tell anyone you met me." He shrugged and put on what he hoped was a guilty grin. "I'm not allowed out without a keeper. They think I'll fall and hurt myself. I wander at night because I just don't sleep anymore."

"Your secret is safe with me, Grandfather."

"Bless you, child. Will you be outside at night often? I'd be delighted if you'd let me come and spend some time with you. I get lonely so much, nearly a prisoner in my room."

"Yes ... " Arden looked up at the tree and sighed, but with a smile. "We'll be out here nearly every night. There is so much to do and so little time."

CHAPTER TWENTY

Ambrose didn't go to bed when he returned to his rooms more than an hour later. He had too much to do to waste time sleeping. A dozen plans raced through his mind, but this time they had purpose and meaning and weren't the dreams of a man who felt his life slipping away in uselessness. He roused Dylon from his restless sleep and told him to get ready for a long trip.

He was proud of his grandson's restrained reaction when he revealed that young, sweet Maura in the garden was Princess Arden. Dylon let out a muffled curse as he leaped to get dressed and obey his grandfather's orders.

Now, Ambrose sat at his table in front of the window where he had been dreaming his life away, writing by the light of the moon and three candles. His hand ached from the unaccustomed exercise, but time was of the essence here. There was more than just Violet's life at stake.

"All right, what were you able to do?" Glynna asked, floating in through the window to come to rest slightly above the chair opposite him.

"The poison accumulated slowly, and the healing must be done slowly, a little at a time, so Arden doesn't notice, but the child will not die." Ambrose barely smiled at the sight of her sitting there as if she had always done so.

"Thank you. Now, how shall we make sure Maddix doesn't win?"

"Brentonwald." He chuckled when she shook her head, confused. He muffled the sound quickly to avoid waking his guard. Ambrose could only press his luck so far, and tonight's comings and goings were near the safe limit. "Brentonwald is pressing Maddix for a marriage alliance. Their Princess Fiera."

"That poor girl."

"Hah!" He flinched, then grinned. "Her strong will and determination are greatly exaggerated by Lord Anselm, I suspect to frighten Maddix and others who think like him, that royal daughters are weapons against their brothers' thrones. I don't dare go to Lord Anselm directly, but I will ask for Brentonwald's help in getting Arden out of here safely. Once she's learned her lessons and repaired the damage she's helped Maddix do to Stonemount."

"May Yeshen guard us all," Glynna murmured.

Dylon entered the room, carrying his traveling sack, his steel-toed riding boots making sparks on the stone floor. His grim mouth and the tension radiating out of him drove away all Ambrose's other feelings in a surge of pride. There was still good blood in the royal family of Stonemount after all.

"Ready, Grandfather." He held out his hand for the packet of letters Ambrose hurried to fold and seal.

"Go directly to King Alix and show him these old letters from his sister, to prove you're a friend and coming directly from me. Tell him she's arrived here safely and so far no one suspects her true identity, and I will watch out for her to the best of my ability. I've given him several plans for how to prepare to sweep her away to safety, if the need arises. You need to find Rilling, who used to be a courier here, and get him to link you to his friends and contacts, so we can pass on information swiftly. If something goes wrong." He held up the last letter. "This must go to King Fallon of Brentonwald, to ask for his help. He knows my handwriting. Tell him whatever he wants to know, and return here in one piece, hear me?" He thrust the last letter into his grandson's hands.

"If only to spite Maddix." The young man grinned.

"Good boy. Now, go!" He stood, arms wide, and hugged Dylon hard, then cuffed the back of his head for good measure as his grandson turned to leave.

"I like that boy," Glynna murmured. "If only he were king instead of Maddix."

"Exactly what I was thinking." Ambrose shook his head, pushing away all thoughts of what might have been. There was too much to worry about in the present moment.

~~~~~

Arden settled into her new routine quickly. She found she rather enjoyed the hidden aspects of palace life, though in Westerland there wasn't such a great distance between the nobles and their servants as there was in Stonemount. She liked finding her own meals, always welcome in Olive's kitchen between the great noon and evening rushes for court meals. She liked wearing the palace livery and blending in with everyone, ignored by the nobles. She laughed when Stonemount diplomats and their wives who had been utterly obsequious to her in Westerland passed her in the gardens as if she were invisible.

The palace servants were a friendly crew when they weren't harried with the demands of their superiors, or dead tired. The women and girls doted on Violet and Arden was assured of a dozen nursemaids if she ever grew too busy tending the tree to watch her daughter. The men who weren't attached made it plain that as soon as she put aside her black mourning, they would pay her court. She was flattered, and it had been
~~~~~

a long time since she let herself be flattered. The attentions had to be genuine, she knew, because here in Stonemount she was no one and had nothing.

Most of all, she enjoyed spending long hours wandering the gardens of the palace without anyone calling her away to tend to this nobleman or that countryman needing advice. She started each morning by skimming through Olive's kitchen, gathering up bread and milk and fruit in the little basket the cook set aside for her, and took herself and Violet out to the tree. She examined it to see what growth and other changes had occurred overnight, snipping off more dead twigs and leaves, talking to the tree, praising it for the new leaves and buds that would soon become blossoms, stroking it and leaving streaks of gold-green magic sparkles that sank into the bark and drove away more of the poison. She brought water from the stream that flowed past the wall encircling the tree and attempted to dig a ditch to drain away the stagnant pool inside the wall. She dug around the roots to let air and water seep into the dead soil and employed every gardening trick she had learned in wandering the farms of Westerland all her life.

Common sense said she couldn't spend every hour of every day attending to the tree. Arden made herself popular with the servants by helping out with mending or washing clothes, doing small chores in the kitchen, or helping Jason gather flowers for decorations and arranging them. Violet was a favorite everywhere they went, and Arden was heartened by the new roses in her daughter's cheeks, the ready laughter when new friends tickled and jounced or made faces at her. Still, she reminded herself that Violet had rallied before in her long illness. This was only a change in climate and surroundings, and sooner or later the color would leave her daughter's cheeks and she would be too quiet again.

Glynna said nothing when Arden sighed her worries to her in the darkness, after they had met Grandfather in the garden and talked quietly in the moonlight for an hour or two before retreating to bed. Sometimes Arden wondered at the sparkle in her old teacher's eyes that could be mischief or tears, but Glynna had stopped lecturing her about the risk she was taking and for that alone Arden was grateful. She knew better than to push her luck.

She had a few special friends. Berneen, a lady's maid, gave Violet a rag doll. She sometimes came to sit with the little girl in the chill of the morning while Arden examined the tree and Berneen's mistress slept away her late evenings of dancing and wine. Anna, Jason's wife, brought pretty little dresses for Violet to wear and blushed when Arden thanked her and praised her needlework. They were only outgrown clothes of her own daughter, and shouldn't someone get some use out of them? And there was Olive, finding time in her overwhelming load of work to concoct special treats for Violet and Arden both, and regaling them with the newest palace gossip.

That gossip was a blessing and torment both for Arden. She learned when to avoid the garden so the nobles wouldn't see her and remark on her, and someone who was more alert and less self-absorbed might recognize her. And also when it was safe to dance and sing and spread her plantwise magic to all the trees and flowers. After all, the entire garden was affected in some way by the illness of the apple tree. Arden knew better than to believe her disguise of cut hair and peasant clothes would protect her forever. Eventually, someone who had traveled to Westerland would recognize her. The gossip helped her change her steps to avoid discovery.

The gossip also frustrated her. She knew better than to add to it, and she knew not to ask questions that would make people curious, wondering why she wanted to know one detail or another. No one would speak of Prince Ambrose, so how could she learn where he was, how to find him, if she didn't dare ask? For all she knew, Ambrose was dead and the people were afraid to say so because they feared the one who had committed such a horrendous crime.

Ambrose had to be alive and living imprisoned somewhere in the palace. His death would strike Stonemount with a curse far worse than the damage Maddix had done. And yes, the damage she had done with her bitterness and unforgiving spirit. Arden refused to ask Glynna to find him, because after being imprisoned so long, he likely had little magic left. Meaning he wouldn't be able to see or hear Glynna. What kind of torment would it be for her, to see her old friend and unable to speak with him? Arden didn't have the heart to ask such pain of her teacher.

Arden chose to believe Ambrose was alive, and everyone had been ordered to act as if he didn't exist. Just like most people acted as if the apple tree behind its wall didn't exist. How could they deny it, when the tree had grown so it reached three feet above the spikes on the wall? Because she spent most of her time with the tree, she became invisible in some ways. It exasperated her and made her head hurt, trying to understand how anyone could be anonymous when they were healing a magical apple tree. How could the entire kingdom ignore its presence? And yet, the blight brought by the tree had persuaded nearly everyone to act and speak as if it didn't exist. Her proof was that almost no one came to gawk at her as she worked. No one went through the gates except for herself and Violet, Jason and Grandfather. Whatever lay behind the wall was invisible.

Now, with the tree beginning to heal and green again, her biggest challenge was finding Ambrose. Preferably, before the tree produced apples. She had to let Ambrose know of her need, just in case Maddix tried to cheat her. He would if he could. She had ample proof of that.

Before she quite knew it, Arden had been two weeks among the servants of the palace. She had a set routine and friends and Violet continued to improve, if only gradually.

If not for her growing sense of guilt and shame over what she had done to both her apple trees, Arden thought she might have been persuaded to take Violet and flee Stonemount in the night. She had to heal the tree. Both trees.

And yes, she needed to reveal Maddix's evil to the world.

~~~~~

Midway through their third week in Stonemount, the three of them enjoyed a quiet evening in their little room. Violet was asleep, clutching her new doll and smiling that adorable little girl smile that made Arden's heart ache for pure joy and contentment. Glynna softly hummed the lullaby that had put Violet asleep nearly an hour before, and Arden brushed her hair. It still amused her how much less time the chore took, and how much more she enjoyed it.

"It's strange, Auntie," she murmured, still glancing around for the mirror that wasn't there. "In some ways, I think I've never been happier. I don't know why."

"Maybe because you can see the people of Stonemount aren't all monsters," her teacher offered.

"Just their king. Please, it isn't my imagination? Violet is getting better?"

"Oh ... I think any change of surroundings will cause an improvement." Glynna floated over to the other side of the narrow room to inspect the tiny pitcher filled with flowers that one of Jason's under-gardeners had brought by during dinner.

"A lasting one?"

"Time will tell. Fresh air and simple food are much better than relying on nasty-tasting potions that abuse the herbals Yeshen gave us." She sniffed her disdain, making Arden chuckle.

The sound stopped abruptly.

"Arden?" Glynna turned around, alarmed for a moment.

"That's it," Arden whispered. "Fresh air."

"What?"

She reached out as if she would hug her teacher. "The tree's healing is slow because of that wall. It holds the poison in, along with that bad
~~~~~

water. It's starting to blossom, but I'm afraid that is as far as it will get unless the wall comes down." She grinned. "We have to knock down the wall."

"How?"

~~~~~

Arden and Jason had never argued until that moment. He gave her every tool, every odd thing she asked for to aid in the healing of the tree. He would have given over his entire army of gardeners to her assistance if she had asked. But when she told him the wall had to come down, he refused flat out, trembling in fear.

"I just don't understand," he said after they had countered each other for nearly twenty minutes. He was almost whimpering, holding back words Arden sensed were there yet he could not speak. She suspected what he would say. "The tree looks much better."

"It won't get any better unless we knock the wall down." Her throat felt sore, her tongue numb from repeating the same words over and over.

"But—"

"Is a caged beast truly alive?"

"But it's only a tree!"

"It is alive. It feels and grows and reacts to everything around it." She swallowed her frustration. She couldn't exactly tell him the tree was still part of her, reacting to her heart and soul, without revealing who she was.

"But it's green and growing new leaves."

"It won't grow any further than that, unless we knock down the wall."

"She's right, Jason." Dylon startled them both. How long he had been standing in the gates, dusty with travel, Arden had no idea.

"But the king—" Jason choked, unable to finish the statement.

"Does he come to this part of the garden anymore? Does anyone? No one will notice the wall is down until they come for the apples for the princess, and by then the tree will be healed and no one will care." He spread his arms, inviting them to agree with him. "Am I right?"

~~~~~

Ambrose and Dylon were conferring, quietly, in his rooms, discussing the success of Dylon's mission when Glynna came through the wall. She flew a circle around them twice, wringing her hands and shooting out green-gold sparks.

"We're ruined! I should have warned her not to push so hard. Oh, that awful, nasty, sneaking little brat!"

"What is it?" Ambrose leaped to his feet.

"That girl is a spy for Maddix, just like I feared. She ran off to report about the preparation to knock down the wall, and now Maddix himself is on his way to the tree!"

"Go," Ambrose said, turning to his grandson, with more power in his voice and lungs than he had used in years. "Do whatever it takes, but protect Arden."

Dylon didn't hesitate but pushed aside the shutters and slid over the windowsill and leaped into the trees, to slide down to the ground.

"I don't dare go and reveal that I know she's here," he cried, and sank down to his chair, aching in his chest. He bowed his head. A cool touch startled him, and he opened his eyes to see Glynna caressing his face.

"Trust in Yeshen, my dear," she whispered.

~~~~~

Arden had left Violet with Berneen and Olive when she headed outside to confront Jason that morning. She was still alone after her morning chores with the tree and had settled down to rest and enjoy the increased sense of well-being radiating from it. She sat at the foot of the tree, head tilted back, eyes half closed, humming a soft nonsense song under her breath. It was the first time in months that she could remember simply enjoying being alive.

"Hide!" Dylon gasped as he staggered through the gates and skidded to a stop before her.

"Why?" She could only stare stupidly at him, half-inclined to giggle.

"The king is coming!"

For half a moment, his words made no sense. Hadn't he said just a short time ago that Maddix never came near the tree? Then Arden went cold as she realized the disaster about to happen. She hadn't planned on seeing Maddix face-to-face until she claimed her reward. What if he recognized her, despite her disguise?

Dylon grabbed her hand. They headed for the gate, but the approaching voices were too near. They couldn't slip out without being spotted. Dylon stared at her for half a second, then grabbed her shoulders and turned her around, nearly pushing her off her feet as they hurried back to the tree. Arden wished she could turn into a bird and fly away. What was the use of having magic if it couldn't protect her? Was this the time to pray her plantwise magic was so strong she could become one with her tree?

Yet what would happen to Violet if she vanished into the tree and couldn't get out again?

"Forgive me."

Dylon grabbed her shoulders and turned her around, knocking her
~~~~~

off balance. She snatched at him as he pushed her headlong into the stagnant pool. Dylon let out a shout as he went down with her. Arden yelped as she went to her hands and knees in the mud and floating debris. She closed her mouth just in time to keep from choking or being smothered.

She slipped as she struggled to her feet and rolled in the half-dry leaves and other debris sitting by the pond, waiting to be gathered up and carted away.

"What did you do that for?" She caught up a handful of mud and flung it at him. It hit him square in the face.

Dylon's eyes widened, then he grinned.

"You're brilliant. I adore you." Then he dug both hands into the mud and debris and flung the sloppy mess at her, spattering face and hair and the left side of her dress.

Arden muffled a shriek and lunged at him, fury making her careless. They went down. She sputtered and slapped at him, spreading more filth across his face.

Cruel laughter rang off the walls and Arden turned to see the four men she loathed most in the world standing in the gate; Maddix, Lord Jaygo, and Maddix's two henchmen. Dylon muffled chuckles as he struggled to his feet and helped her stand.

"What is going on here?" Maddix said through snorts of laughter. "That gate is supposed to be locked. Who are you filthy peasants, to come in here and make this your trysting place?" he ended on a roar.

Arden caught her breath, realizing in that moment what Dylon had done. They were indeed filthy. Spattered with mud and rotting leaves and dirty water. Entirely unrecognizable. She thought she would like to kiss Dylon.

"Majesty?" Jason hurried through the gates. He was pale, gasping, as if he had raced all the way here. "What happened? Mistress Maura, who did this to you?" He turned on Dylon. "What did you do to her?"

"She was in a plantwise trance," Dylon hurried to say. "I startled her. She ... fell, and we both lost our balance as I was trying to help her out of the mud."

"Plantwise?" Maddix sneered. "Surely ... not." His voice softened and his fury slowly shifted to wonder as he took a step back and his gaze traveled over the tree.

CHAPTER TWENTY-ONE

"Yes, Majesty. Mistress Maura has been here three weeks now," Jason said.

"Why did no one told me until now?" he demanded.

To Arden's relief, he wasn't looking at her at all, but at the tree.

"Majesty, I reported Mistress Maura's arrival the very night I hired her. I told Lord Jaygo." Jason hurried to say. He nearly stuttered.

"He did not! He brought her in secret to keep the reward for himself," Jaygo snapped.

Arden wanted to flee, but her legs nearly folded with the force of her terror. Jaygo knew all this time she was here? She could imagine a dozen vicious, cruel reasons for why he would keep the news from Maddix, all of them bad for her. Dylon caught hold of her hand and squeezed it tightly. His eyes were stern, and she hoped she was not imagining the promise of help she saw in them.

"Normally, I don't care about your little games," Maddix drawled, "but when it comes to my tree, no one lies to me. Is that clear?" He glared at the six standing around the tree. Then he focused all his attention on Arden. "So, I hear that someone, you I must assume, insists the wall must come down. Why?"

Her disgust with him, her fury, pushed aside the fear, allowing her to speak without trembling. How long that would last, she had no idea.

"Like a prisoner locked in a cell with no light," she said, the well-practiced words coming without a conscious thought, "the tree withers and dies from being locked behind these walls, with this stagnant water nearby. If you do not take the walls down, there is little more I can do."

"You have done miracles already. I see flowers trying to bloom."

"They will die soon. You will get no apples for your new queen, unless the wall comes down." Giddiness grew through her, as if each second she stood against Maddix without trembling was like a sip of potent wine.

"Indeed?" He looked her over once more, smirking at the mess of her clothes and hair and the mud plastered across her face, then turned on his heel and sauntered out through the gate. The others cast glances at him, then at each other, as they followed. In a few moments, Arden was alone again with Dylon.

"I'm sorry," he began when the sounds of footsteps on the gravel and shells of the pathways faded tway. "It was the only thing I could think—"

Arden flung herself at him, hugging him hard. She laughed and spun away and flittered around the tree in mad, giddy circles on her tiptoes. Her exuberant relief sent sparkles and swirls of gold-green magic spinning out of her fingertips to wrap around the tree. Branches lifted and the flower buds burst open, filling the air with a heady perfume like sweet wine. Dylon sank to his knees, his mouth falling open, and laughed with her.

~~~~~

That evening, a dozen soldiers surrounded the wall surrounding the tree and attacked it with massive sledgehammers. Jason supervised one of the gardeners, a girl Arden had disliked for no reason she could identify, making her clean out the stagnant pool, while the wall came down. Then Jason and three more gardeners dug a channel to reconnect the now clean pool to the stream. Arden and Glynna watched from their post at the base of the tree, and Violet slept in her mother's arms, despite the banging and ringing of metal on stone and crash of falling stones and the grunts of the soldiers.

A week later, the tree stood taller and straighter. No more branches drooped and every single one was thick with leaves and almost white with blossoms. Arden spent many hours each day leaning against the tree, eyes closed, feeling the life flow more clearly through the living heart of it with every day that passed. She was barefoot and streaks of green-gold magic flowed down her legs into the soil under her feet. She drifted in her mind, feeling the life and healing flowing into the tree, and back out of the tree to spread the blessing to the rest of the garden. She felt the healing extending across Stonemount, echoed and mirrored in the new life and vitality of her tree in Westerland. Arden knew every time someone picked an apple from her tree at home and felt it when two blossoms formed for every apple used to heal someone. If she could have stayed that way for the rest of her life, at one with her trees, she would have counted herself most happy.

Still, there was her daughter to recall her to reality and other joys. Violet was a little stronger, a little more lively every day and Arden sternly warned herself to be happy with each day as it came, no questions asked. She told herself to be grateful for every miracle and not look to the future or hope for what could not be. Violet would not be truly healed until Ambrose had touched her.

~~~~~

Tiny apples like round emeralds appeared almost the instant the blossoms started to fall from the tree. Arden made herself wait until all the blossoms had fallen, so the garden for fifty yards around looked like it lay under an early, sweet-smelling snow. Then, with Ambrose and Violet watching, she climbed up into the tree and slowly, cautiously, conferring all the while with Glynna, pruned away more than a third of the tiny apple buds so all the sweetness and life and healing power of the tree would be concentrated in the ones that remained. She did it at night to avoid questions. After seeing the conflict between Jaygo and Jason, Arden knew there had to be many among the seemingly friendly servants who would gladly carry tales to their king. She didn't want to risk another encounter with Maddix just to explain why she destroyed so many apples before they could ripen.

Arden was too caught up in her work and the gold-green sparkles of her own magic to notice the tiny flares and sparkles of silver magic as Ambrose healed Violet a little bit more every night. But the little girl saw them and she laughed and clapped her hands and tried to catch the bits of light before they vanished. Ambrose and Glynna smiled at each other over the child's head and talked softly of old times and friends.

With that pruning chore finished, Arden took the next night off and spent it chatting with Berneen and Olive by the fire in the kitchen. They sewed and sipped cider and nibbled on the crumbled ends of cakes and pastries that hadn't been pretty enough to be served at court dinner that night. Arden wished nights like this could last forever, for she truly was happy here if she took each moment on its own merit.

A page boy scurried in through the big doorway, from the hallway leading up to the court side of the palace complex. Arden went cold and knew disaster had struck even before the boy opened his mouth and gasped out, "His Majesty wants you in the gardens. Now!"

What could she do but obey? Arden snatched up a shawl for protection against more than the chill night air. As she went, she cast a pleading glance at Olive. But what could her friend do to rescue her? She didn't want to be alone with Maddix for one moment, but she had no power to deny him what he wanted. Not even if she revealed her true name.

To her relief, she found she wouldn't be alone with Maddix. A bright light blazed in the garden, visible from over the hedges and fountains and miniature hills. Arden smelled the smoke of perfumed oil lanterns and torches. What were Maddix and his nasty courtiers going to do to her tree?

The tree seemed unharmed, but she felt its discomfort with the bright light and warmth and dozens of perfumed bodies standing around it in a wide circle. Arden stepped through the circle and went to her tree and leaned against it, giving it comfort with her touch and presence. She found Maddix and watched him from the corner of her eye as he walked around and around, studying the tree. His smile of satisfaction grew wider with every circuit and he nodded.

Jason came running, tucking his shirt into his trousers, obviously roused from retiring to bed early. He gaped at the courtiers who had never come into this part of the garden before, then gathered up his courage and pushed through the circle to stand with Arden.

"Yes," Maddix said at last. "Very good. I am pleased, Mistress Maura. You have done well. I hope you continue to do so well."

"I have done everything I can. The test of the cure is in the apples when they are ripe," she responded.

"Then you must make sure nothing goes wrong. Mustn't you?"

"I will be there, Majesty, when you put the apple into your bride's hand and she takes the first bite. I will claim my reward from her hand."

The thought of Maddix's dismay and embarrassment when she revealed the truth cheered her and helped her speak with a steady voice.

"Will you? And what is wrong with mine?" He snatched a lantern from one of his followers and stepped closer. The light felt like a physical blow, fully illuminating her. Arden refused to flinch away, though she wanted to hide or slap at him. His smirking inspection of her felt like a chill hand touching her where he had no right.

"Yours, Majesty?" she managed to say, keeping her voice from trembling even then.

"What will you do when you have claimed your reward? I'm sure there is other ... work for a beautiful woman."

Arden's face burned, knowing exactly what he implied. She was grateful for the protective touch of Jason's hand as he rested it on her shoulder; especially knowing what it cost the man to stand up to his king even that little bit. Maddix chuckled and turned to leave. Soon all the light vanished as the courtiers walked away with their lanterns and torches and Arden blinked hard as her eyes adjusted back to moonlight.

"He might not be able to find you," Jason murmured, barely above a whisper. As if the trees around them could hear and report their words. "If you left right away. Before he decides what to do with you."

"No." She shivered. How many times had she wrestled with fears like this in the dark hours of the night? The need to heal her child and her anger at how Maddix had gone on so long without punishment kept her here. "I need the reward."

"Maura, you are a friend. Your child is the darling of the servants. Olive won't know what to do without you to make her laugh. But no one can stand between you and the king if he takes a fancy to you."

"Thank you, Master Jason. You're a dear friend. Everything will be all right. Don't worry about me."

She turned back to the tree and stretched out one hand to lovingly brush her fingers across a few outstretched leaves. Arden knew she was safe as long as Maddix needed her to heal his tree. She had to plan her steps well and never give him a moment to strike at her, once the day of revelations came.

Glynna appeared out of the darkness as Jason vanished into it.

"Well, you at least got Maddix to admit you're beautiful," she said with a sigh.

"Auntie!" After everything that happened, Arden had the most awful urge to giggle, but she feared what sounds would emerge from her strained body and heart.

"Jason is right, you know. The servants fear the king more than they love you. You should leave for Violet's sake."

"It's for her sake I'm here!"

"Is it? Really?"

"When I claim the healing and reveal Maddix's evil to the world, Maddix will want people to stand between me and him."

"Maura?" a man called through the darkness.

"Grandfather?" Arden called back, hearing the familiar heavy tread on the gravel and seashell pathway.

Ambrose appeared in a spill of moonlight and looked all around as he made his slow way to the apple tree.

"I heard the king was here. Are you all right?"

"I'm fine. Thank you."

His concern comforted and warmed her. It didn't matter that the elderly man could do little against Maddix's wickedness. She stepped up to the tree and wrapped her arms around the trunk and pressed her face against the smooth bark, taking comfort from the throbbing of life and magic deep inside.

"That girl is going to get herself hurt," Glynna murmured so only Ambrose could hear. "And sometimes, I think she doesn't care."

"I can protect her," he said, reaching out a hand as if he would grasp her filmy shoulder. "Maddix won't dare act against me."

"You hope."

"He wants my magic too desperately to harm me."

~~~~~

Maddix chuckled as he settled in behind his desk, finally free of the tedium of the morning council meeting. Someday, he wouldn't have to keep up the pretense to make the nobles think he valued their opinions and insights. For now, he played the game that his father had so foolishly taken seriously and welcomed the silence of his office when the meetings were over. Then Jaygo came into his office, holding the papers he had
~~~~~

been writing on during the council meeting. Did that pompous old fool think he was any more valuable than the nobles who made their suggestions and complaints and requests? Maddix knew what he had to do and how to do it, and he trusted the servants who worked in secret and darkness far more than the ones he kept around for show and pretense.

"Who would have thought little Arden would have that much courage and guile in her? She came all this way in disguise, too proud to let people know she had to mend my tree. Probably because the two are tied together, just like Uncle Ambrose always said. The only way Arden can have her tree healthy is to mend whatever damage she did to mine. I could almost admire her."

Jaygo shook his head as Maddix spoke and slowly paled as he sank down into the chair in front of his desk. "Arden? The plantwise woman? Surely you can't believe—"

"Oh, yes, that's Arden. I didn't recognize her without all that lovely hair. And so pale. Black just isn't her color, nor is my livery, more's the sorrow ... You know, Jaygo, I rather believe I'm being given a second chance. There's nothing I can do to avoid marrying Fiera, but who says I can't have Arden, too?"

"Her brother must know she is here. And why would she accept you after what you've done to her?"

"What I've done to her?" For a few heartbeats, he struggled between amusement, amazement and fury, that anyone, even Jaygo, would accuse him of any crimes against silly, rustic Arden. "What have I done? What proof? Unless someone is telling tales out of school?" He smiled a little wider when Jaygo flinched and looked away. "No, even if Alix knows she's here, there's nothing he can do. No proof she ever got here. I can keep Arden here to take care of my tree, and I can use her brat to make sure she's ... agreeable in other areas."

"Princess Fiera won't like having a rival."

"Fiera doesn't expect me to love her. My little campaign of secret wooing is making headway. We've agreed on that, and quite a few other things. As long as she has the title and I don't embarrass her in public, why can't I have my fun? You, old friend, are responsible for Arden's safety. And her ignorance. Understood?" He stared at the older man until he straightened and looked him in the eyes again.

Maddix sighed, feeling much put-upon at the realization that faithful old Jaygo truly had outlived his usefulness. When should he dispose of him?

~~~~~

Jaygo called Clancy and Baethon to his rooms very late that night,
~~~~~

to confer with them. It was an unusual enough occurrence. They rarely spoke to each other even in Maddix's presence and never socialized. He looked down on them as ruffians, and they sneered at his refined manners and sneaking ways and roundabout plans that took three times longer than they thought necessary to achieve Maddix's goals.

When he explained that they had to protect Arden from notice and slowly easy her out of the life of the palace servants, they only stared at him, as if he spoke a completely different language. Even when he explained who she was under her false name and shorter hair and widow's clothes, they just shook their heads and gave him those frowns that clearly said they thought he was daft. Jaygo was ready to shout for pure frustration.

"I don't get it," Clancy said. "The tree is almost healed. Why let her live any longer?"

"The king wants her as a plaything when Princess Fiera isn't agreeable." Jaygo sighed. He had said that already, hadn't he?

"I know how to make women agreeable all the time," Baethon said with a sidelong glance at his cohort. They both rumbled hungry laughter and licked their lips. Jaygo wanted to vomit.

"Your job, the two of you, is to make sure Arden sends no messages to Westerland. Make sure no one here knows who she is. If they do, you know what to do."

"The best solution is silence everyone now. Maddix is ruining everything with Brentonwald, playing both sides."

"He's not playing both sides, you moron!" Jaygo winced as his voice rose. At this time of night, there would be no one listening, but it never hurt to be careful. "All along, the goal is to get what Maddix wants for Stonemount and the rest of the world can suffer."

"Did he just call us morons?" Clancy turned to his friend, huffing slightly. "We don't like that."

"No one cares what you like. You'll do as you're told."

"No." He grinned.

"What?"

"Maddix told us a long time ago," he said, leaning closer to the old counselor so that the beer from his dinner blew sour in Jaygo's face, "our job was to look after him, no matter what it took. We're allowed to deal with problems the way we think best." He nodded to Baethon, who stepped around behind Jaygo.

A shiver of apprehension went up and down Jaygo's back and he turned to follow Baethon's movements. Clancy stepped up behind him and drew a long, gleaming, curved knife; a present from Maddix, with tiny rubies in the hilt.

"Killing is not always the best solution to a problem," the old man croaked.

He gasped as Clancy wrapped a beefy arm around his neck and jerked backward, making him arch his back painfully. Baethon licked his lips and stepped up so his breath gusted in Jaygo's face.

"Really? It always works for me."

~~~~~

"Please. Please," Arden whispered to her tree the next morning.

She shivered, feeling again the tremor of darkness and threat that had twanged through the ground last night. Something evil had reverberated through the healing tree and set every nerve in her body on edge. She longed for Westerland, which seemed a lifetime away now.

"Be magical again. Only another week and the bride will be here and then I can go home."

From Ambrose's window, Glynna and Ambrose kept watch. Even from so far above her, they could tell the change that had come over her, the fear that had chilled the edges of her determination. Both their hearts ached and both felt a little relief. Perhaps their plan was working after all.

"I think she's starting to learn that lesson you wanted to teach her," Ambrose murmured. Glynna sighed and nodded and their eyes met for one long moment.
~~~~~

CHAPTER TWENTY-TWO

Four nights later, Arden was up in the highest branches she could reach in the tree, checking the apples, which had started showing signs of gold and red among the green only a few days before. Ambrose sat a short distance away, amusing Violet with a puppet he had brought, by the light of a lantern. Arden let out a cry of dismay that brought the man to his feet and startled Violet's giggles into silence. Glynna arrowed down out of the night sky to hover near the ground and look up into the branches, as if waiting for Arden to come tumbling down and break an arm or leg.

"What's wrong?" Ambrose demanded as Arden slid abruptly to the ground, holding onto the tree with one hand and clutching three apples against her chest with her other arm.

Her face was far paler than the moonlight and lantern could account for as she held out the apples. All three were spotted with dark holes. As they watched, a worm appeared in one hole, waggled its blunt end around, then retreated.

"This shouldn't be happening!" Arden moaned.

"It's rather symbolic, my dear, of the rot at the heart of your healing," Glynna said softly.

Arden glared at her, but she couldn't retort because the man she knew as Grandfather couldn't see or hear the woman. Ambrose smothered a grin and pretended not to have heard.

"Surely not all of them are bad?" he asked.

"No ... not all." Arden dropped the apples to the ground and stepped back to study the entire tree. She absently scrubbed her hands against her apron. "But I have to drive the worms away and get rid of the bad apples."

"What are you going to do?"

She frowned and stared at the tree, already so deep in thought she didn't hear him. Glynna gestured for him to step away and leave her be. He returned to little Violet, who was trying to make the puppet move and talk to her.

"It's not too late, my dear," Glynna said. "Go find Ambrose, ask him to heal Violet, confess your deception -- "

"No!"

"Is your revenge so much more important than your safety and Violet's health? If you fail, do you think the king will hesitate to punish you?"

"But I'm—" Arden went white, visibly swallowing the words she had been about to speak.

"You are in his power. He wants Violet dead, so your brother has no heir!"

"Alix will—"

"There is nothing your brother can do to rescue you if you don't escape the palace while Maddix's back is turned. He will make you both disappear."

Arden shuddered, blinking hard against tears. Then her mouth hardened and she knuckled away her tears, took a deep breath and straightened her shoulders.

"Then there is no choice," she said, and nodded at the tree as if it had spoken to her.

"Yes, we will go find Ambrose—"

"I will work night and day to drive away the worms and have the perfect apples for Fiera." She wrapped her arms tight around herself as her new resolve slipped for a moment. "Then I will take my reward and hurry home as fast as I can."

She picked up Violet and hurried away from the tree. Glynna and Ambrose sighed in unison as they watched her vanish into the streaks of moonlight and darkness.

"Well, she's starting to learn," Glynna murmured. "I just hope it isn't too late."

An hour later, Arden had marshaled Olive's help and the palace kitchen was turned into an apothecary's shop, full of herbs and extracts and old tomes with half-forgotten knowledge, discarded by the nobles above stairs and retained by the servants in case they were ever needed again. Olive threw herself wholeheartedly into the project of finding something to drive away the worms without tainting the apples or harming the still-healing tree.

It was nearly dawn when Arden took a pinch of the end result of hours of testing and tasting and consulting the old books and tossed it into the fire. Gray-blue billows of smoke erupted for a few seconds. Despite their speed in jumping back, wisps of smoke caught both Arden and Olive, making them choke and cough and brought tears to their eyes. Through their tears, they grinned at each other in success.

~~~~~

Arden only allowed herself a few hours of sleep before taking her precious concoction out to the garden and setting up tiny smudge pots in a tight circle around the tree. For the rest of the day, she went in a slow circle, adding a little more fuel, a little more concoction, wreathing the
~~~~~

tree in gray-blue smoke until it was hardly visible. A few noble ladies dared to complain to Jason when a stray breeze brought the acrid-smelling smoke to their windows, but they went no further when he explained that it was for the sake of the king's apple tree.

Ambrose and Dylon watched from Ambrose's window, ignoring the bitter-acid scent, knowing by the taste it gave the air what Arden was doing. They were cheered to know that she had found the right concoction to achieve her purposes. Still, knowing wasn't good enough for Dylon. He watched and wondered and waited with his grandfather until just before noon. Then he stalked out of the room. Ambrose watched him, a bemused smile on his face, which only grew wider when Dylon appeared in the garden five minutes later and joined Arden in her circuit of the tree. Glynna appeared in Ambrose's window moments after Dylon joined Arden and the two old friends smiled at each other.

Dylon made Arden stop to rest and eat and drink. He brought damp cloths to wipe her smoky, hot face and kept up the rounds of the smudge pots so the thick smoke never wavered or thinned.

~~~~~

"What are you going to do when you have your reward?" Dylon asked as he finished his latest circuit of the smudge pots and came back to Arden's resting place. "Besides go home to Westerland, I mean."

"I really haven't thought about it," she said after a moment. A dry chuckled escaped her when she realized she hadn't thought of her life in general beyond the all-consuming goal of Violet's healing for weeks, maybe months. Did she really want to go back to Westerland? It was her home, yes, but suddenly it felt small and lonely, despite everyone she loved waiting there for her. Why was that? "I rather like traveling. I've never been far from home before."

"I like the life of a traveling healer. I've been thinking of returning to that work," he hurried to add. "We would make a good team. Come with me."

"What could I do?" Arden's heart skipped a few beats. "I mean yes, I can see how having a plantwise with you to grow fresh herbals you need for healing could be useful, but if we don't have the seeds or scraps of the original plant, I'd be useless." She sighed, smiling wearily. "Sometimes I feel entirely useless, about so many things."

"You know you don't know things, so that means you can learn. I'm sure wherever you go, you will be cherished." Dylon paused in scooping up more mixture to add to the pots, and their gazes locked.

She opened her mouth to respond. The wind shifted, tearing the curtain of smoke and swirling it into both their faces. They laughed and choked and waved the blue-gray wisps out of their faces. Arden jumped
~~~~~

up to take up the chore. She staggered a little as she sprinkled more of the worm-killing mixture into a pot three steps down from Dylon. He hurried and caught hold of her by her elbow before she quite lost her balance. A single spark of magic passed between them. She told herself it was his healing talent at work. Only his healing talent, and not something that made her feel rather weak with longing for more, and to understand what that spark promised.

"You haven't been taking care of yourself," Dylon said with a frown. "What good are you to anyone if you fall ill?"

"There are other things more important ... But right now, I'm so tired I can't really remember what they are!" she added with a chuckle. They made another round of the smudge pots, adding fuel to some, powder to others. When she was quite sure the pots would smoke adequately for a short while without her tending, she sat down again. It was like his words were a cork pulled from a barrel that let her strength drain away. More than anything, she wanted to curl up and sleep for a week. Dylon sat with her through the day, making her rest every other time she tried to jump up to tend the pots again.

His care enabled her to have the strength to climb into the tree that night to inspect the apples by magic and moonlight. Arden was disappointed that Dylon's duties took him away, and he couldn't be there. He was a palace servant, after all. But Ambrose was there, holding Violet up so the little girl could see what her mother was doing. They and Glynna were all the company and audience she truly needed.

She picked three apples, from the three places that had seemed most infected by worms in the tree. Then she climbed down and examined the apples again. She threw one aside, finding a tiny mark where a worm had started to eat its way into the apple but stopped, dissuaded by the smoke, she prayed. The second apple was untouched but didn't quite meet her expectations. The third, Arden rolled between her hands several times, loving the smooth feel of the ruby skin. Then she took out her pruning knife, wiped it thoroughly on her apron, and cut the apple in half. A golden spark of magic burst from it and she nearly burst into tears in relief and pride. She cut one part in half again and handed it to Ambrose.

He thanked her with an exaggerated bow and took a bite. Golden sparkles of magic lingered around his lips for a moment. His eyes widened and he smiled as he chewed. Violet laughed and snatched at the piece still in his hand and he gave it to her. The little girl giggled when more sparks of magic flared at her first taste of the apple.

Laughing, Arden snatched her daughter from the old man's arms and did a little spin in celebration, then stepped back and looked up at the tree. In the moonlight, it glowed with health and life and renewed magic. She gloried in weary satisfaction that she had healed the damage both she and Maddix had caused it.

She could admit freely now that her own bitterness and anger had hurt her tree just as much as Maddix's lies and selfishness. Whether the tree would continue to flourish was not up to her, once she left Stonemount. Could Maddix be taught the error of his ways? Arden doubted that. Not even with Fiera's influence. She had heard good things about the princess of Brentonwald, but she also knew how unreliable gossip was, especially when it swirled around royalty. Fiera was strong-willed and outspoken in obeying Yeshen's teachings, but how much of that was by her own choice, how much of that was unthinking obedience to her father and his standards, and how much was carefully guided and nurtured public image? She could be an intolerable brat, once she left her father's kingdom behind and joined forces with Maddix. She could be a puppet and figurehead, or a shrew, and be totally useless in reforming Stonemount.

"My efforts could all be wasted, turned entirely around the moment I leave Stonemount," she whispered. Her elation drained away under the chill wind of unpleasant facts and unknowns.

"You could feed Violet a few of those apples and she would be just fine," Glynna said softly. "No need to stay here any longer."

"I know, but ... I've worked too hard for this triumph," Arden said, forgetting for a moment the old man holding Violet. Sometimes, she had moments where she could have sworn that Grandfather, as she knew him, had been exchanging glances with Glynna , or she came back from circling the tree and interrupted a whispered conversation. That was impossible, she knew. He couldn't hear Glynna or see her. Although she wished he could, because that would mean he had magic, and he could understand a little more what she faced, what she could and couldn't do. If he had magic, he could have helped her locate Ambrose, and determine if he was here in the palace, and maybe, at long last, talk to him and have him heal Violet.

If she found him... if Violet was healed at long last, cleansed of the poison ... maybe she would consider leaving Stonemount without unmasking Maddix at long last?

"Sometimes what we think we want isn't what's best for us, child," the old man said.

"What?" There it was, another moment when it seemed he knew what Glynna had said.

"Go to bed, sweetheart," he said with a chuckle. "You've certainly earned it. Rest, relax, enjoy yourself. The bride isn't due for two more days."

"I know. But I can't. Too many of those apples are rotted. I have to get rid of them before someone eats one."

"In the morning." He grasped her by her shoulders and steered her away from the tree, toward the doors into the palace. They laughed together as she made a small, token resistance, then headed down the path on her own, clutching Violet close and chuckling in weary triumph.

"She still won't give up her need to punish Maddix," Glynna whispered.

"I don't blame her." Ambrose settled down at the base of the tree and leaned back against it with a deep sigh. "I want to see that nasty little snot humiliated, too. She's a great deal like you at that age."

"I know. That's why I worry." She settled down almost on the moss next to him. For a moment, it seemed like the days of their youth, when they met in their wanderings and shared the shade of a tree together in perfect peace and contentment.

~~~~~

The next morning found Arden hard at work, inspecting every apple and yanking the bad ones off, tossing them to the ground and marking the best ones in her memory, to help her decide which ones to pick for Maddix when the bride arrived. Berneen came out to help, but Violet made a pest of herself, trying to climb up into the tree to be with her mother or trying to swim in the renewed stream. Arden and Berneen both agreed the young maid was more help keeping Violet company and out of trouble, rather than studying apples.

Just before noon, Dylon came out to see how they were doing. "I just heard the good news. Yet here you are, tossing apples away as if they were nothing but ... well, apples!"

"Just the bad ones. I don't want to take a chance and have someone get a mouthful of worm."

They laughed together.

"You're making an almighty mess. Maybe you should gather them up as you pick them and cart them away."

"Oh, dear, I hadn't thought of that. I was so concerned about getting rid of the bad ones..."

"That's what happens when you concentrate on the evil instead of the good, my dear," Glynna commented from her hovering perch just above the highest branches. "Narrowed vision."

Arden grimaced and tossed a wormy apple at the woman. It flew straight through her. Glynna chuckled wickedly and flew out of her reach.

"What are you going to do with all these?" Olive asked when she
~~~~~

came out to check on Arden an hour later. She gestured at the apples scattered across the moss.

"They're spotted and bad and wormy." Arden sighed, hating the waste. "Nothing to do but throw them out."

"I could cut around the bad and save the good. Think of all the lovely apple pies and cakes I could make. And think about everyone enjoying apples from this tree when the king has forbidden it." The head cook chuckled, sounding a little too much like Glynna for Arden's comfort.

"But—the worms, the bad spots—"

"You've been looking at worms for so long, that's all you see," her teacher piped up again. "Look at the good in the apple for a change."

"We'll need baskets," Arden said with a sigh. Her back ached from just thinking of all the bending and picking up and hauling away that lay ahead of her.

As proof of the restored magic of the tree, the abundance of apples produced in a matter of a few weeks was staggering. More than three normal trees together could produce. That worked against her now.

"You leave that to me." Olive nodded for emphasis and stalked away. Likely she was in search of Jason, to make him hand over baskets immediately.

~~~~~

The afternoon was nearly done by the time most of the apples rejected so far had been gathered up. Olive stayed to help only until she had two basketfuls. She commandeered Dylon to carry one while she manhandled the other into the kitchen, so she could get to work on the forbidden treats. Then, Berneen had to return to her duties. She took Violet indoors for her nap, leaving Arden alone. Dylon returned and carried baskets of apples to the kitchen as they were filled.

With the first streaks of sunset, they only had two large baskets of bad apples left. It amazed Arden how many bad apples one tree, even if it was magical, could produce. She wondered if it was another of those subtle lessons from nature Glynna kept telling her to look for.

She found a few more bad apples still in the tree and climbed up and out on a limb to get them. There was no use in waiting for someone to happen by and pick a bad apple. She reached out and caught three of the four but lost her grip when snatching at the last. Dylon darted over and caught her. For a moment they hung there, frozen in time and lost in each other's eyes again. His hands were strong and warm and she swore she could feel his pulse through the thin fabric of her dress.

"I think you've been working too hard," Dylon said, his voice a little too soft, as he put her down securely on the ground. He was slow to take
~~~~~

his hands away and Arden thought perhaps he had moved too quickly at that.

"It's almost over." Her voice echoed with portent and she felt a throb of sadness that made her turn her head and brush away a few inexplicable tears almost before they formed.

"We should celebrate. You stay here, and I'll sweet talk the first apple cake from our dear Olive." Dylon dashed away almost before she could smile and nod agreement. She had to laugh at his eagerness.

"The more I see of that boy, the more I like him," Glynna said.

Arden nodded and sat down, leaning her weary back against the baskets of bad apples. She wondered if Dylon would come visit her in Westerland. She hoped their friendship wouldn't change once he knew her true name. Would he be hurt by her deception? She hoped not. His offer to join him on his healing rambles was tempting, but she knew it could never be. She had responsibilities to Westerland, to her brother, to her daughter.

"Always to everyone else," she whispered, so softly not even Glynna heard. "What about my responsibilities to me?"

~~~~~

Ambrose was at his table, writing in his journal when Glynna floated in through the open window. He smiled at her and slowly closed the book and slouched a little in his chair. The two old friends shared a long look, full of weariness and satisfaction, just touched with dreams that still held strong despite the years and changing circumstances.

"Things seem to be turning out just fine, aren't they?" he said, and held out his hand. She brushed her spirit hand against his, and it sank through his more solid flesh. Their smiles faded.

"I would give anything just to be able to touch your hand, one more time," she whispered.
~~~~~

CHAPTER TWENTY-THREE

When Dylon returned to the tree, his arms loaded with a skin of wine, cups, cheese and warm apple cake, he found Arden asleep. He stood a few moments simply drinking in the sight of her. It amused him to realize she seemed so much smaller when she sat still; no bright energy and constant movement making her seem so much larger. He wanted very much to kiss her, but he feared it would wake her like in the old tales of magic spells. The healer in him demanded Arden be allowed to sleep as long as possible.

Instead, he set their treats down on his handkerchief, then took off his jacket and spread it over her to keep her warm. Just one more day, he told himself, and this charade would be all over. Arden would have her reward and Ambrose would reveal his true identity. Half the battle would be won once they had smuggled Arden out of the palace. Then it would be a race to the border where her brother had stationed soldiers to watch for her.

His grandfather had bluntly told him to be ready to leave Stonemount and not return. Dylon could only hope the king of Brentonwald had responded to Ambrose's request for help, and the protection of Lord Anselm and Princess Fiera would free his grandfather at long last.

Dylon gave himself permission to dream and plan for the future. Possibly with Arden. He couldn't really know until there were no more false tales between them. What would she say when she knew he was Ambrose's grandson? For the first time in his life, he wished his grandfather had held onto the throne, so he could offer Stonemount to Arden.

"Master Dylon!" Olive waddled down the path, waving her arms, her hair flying from her exertions and her face red with effort. "Your grandfather needs you now!"

He cast one glance back at Arden and ran to meet the old cook. She was one of the few trustworthy palace servants, and she had supported his grandfather's deception with a smirk and a chuckle. She had recognized Dylan when he first appeared in disguise, slapped him for being cheeky, and hugged him with tears in her eyes, glad he wasn't dead as all the stories said. For her to be worried enough to speak about Ambrose where anyone could hear, something was deathly wrong.

"The bride is coming," Olive gasped, and nearly collapsed into his arms.

"A day early!" The next moment, Dylon nearly burst out laughing. He hoped Princess Fiera kept Maddix guessing like this for their entire marriage. His obnoxious cousin deserved all the trouble the Brentonwald princess could give him.

"Master Ambrose needs you. He says its urgent."

Dylon hesitated. Should he wake Arden? Then the next moment he knew it wasn't necessary. It was far too late in the day for more than welcoming Fiera to Stonemount and settling her into her rooms for the night. The grand ceremony to present the magic apples would have to wait until morning. And Arden most certainly needed her sleep. He wrapped an arm around Olive to support her back into the palace. His mind raced, speculating on how he and Ambrose would spirit Arden away to safety.

He had barely stepped into the palace when Maddix, Baethon and Clancy hurtled down another pathway toward the apple tree and Arden. Maddix led the way, fists clenched, forehead creased in fury, swearing under his breath as he stomped his way up the path. His henchmen hurried to keep up, grinning at his discomfort.

"I should have known she'd do this to me. I'd kick her high-bred rump if I didn't think Brentonwald would declare war over the insult. Arriving a day earlier than we agreed. She lied to me!" he snarled between his teeth.

"You have to admit," Baethon said with a badly repressed chuckle, "she's a wife to match you."

Maddix turned his head and opened his mouth to retort, but they had reached the tree then and the sight of Arden asleep among the baskets of apples startled them all.

"You!" the king roared. "On your feet!"

"Majesty?" Arden yelped, nearly reaching her feet before her eyes were fully awake. "What's wrong?"

"My bride is here. She'll be at the palace gates at any moment. I need your wretched apples now!"

"Yes, Majesty. I marked the perfect ones this morning. It will be only a moment." She ran to the tree and started climbing.

Clancy sauntered over to the tree and bent down, turning his head to try to look up her skirt. Maddix slapped the back of his head hard enough to push his face into the trunk.

"Leave her be," he growled under his breath, the fire in his eyes real enough to make Clancy blanch. "I don't share."

The sound of trumpets and cheering drifted on the evening breeze to them as Arden made her way to the top of the tree where the three most perfect apples waited. Their perfume made her mouth water and the golden glow of magic around each apple was visible in the dim evening light.

"That sounds like trouble," Clancy said. Drums could be heard now.

"She's taking too long." Maddix paced a circle around the base of the tree, cursing under his breath.

"These apples down here look just fine." Baethon gestured at the basket of rejects.

"She's sabotaging me!" Maddix gasped. "She's taken the best apples off the tree already, and now she's making me late." He snatched three apples from the basket. His face twisted into a fierce mask and he reached up to shake the trunk of the tree, making the topmost branches where Arden perched sway abruptly. "It's too late to cross me. You've failed!" He laughed as she shrieked and slipped and barely caught herself with her knee hooked around one branch and her hands desperately snatching at others.

"No!" Arden wailed, breathless. "You can't! The best apples are still on the tree!"

Laughing, Maddix led the other two at a run, leaving Arden to struggle out of her awkward position. She slid and scratched herself and caught her dress on a branch, tearing it, and tore the palms of her hands in the fight to keep from falling and seriously hurting herself. Glynna appeared as she landed on her knees on the ground and burst out in wracking sobs.

"Child, what happened?"

"Auntie, everything is ruined!"

~~~~~

Maddix ignored the triple rows of torches and the Guardsmen in straight lines with gleaming uniforms, the servants in pressed, bright livery, the nobles in their jewels and silks and velvets, the avalanche of flowers and the thick, plush red carpet that lay without a wrinkle all the way from the wide, double doors of the palace down to the spot where Princess Fiera would step from her carriage. He fumed and snarled silently, his face a serene stone only betrayed by the fire in his eyes. Fiera had arrived a day early and though everything was exactly as arranged he raged inside because it was on *her* schedule, not on his. Well, he would have to teach her very quickly that in Stonemount, the king ruled in everything no matter who his wife's father might be.

He cast narrow-eyed glances at Baethon and Clancy and wondered yet again what they had done with Jaygo. All anyone knew was that the irritating old fusspot had vanished overnight. No body. No outcry. Not even a spot of blood or a sign of struggle to indicate where he had died.
~~~~~

Maddix knew his two henchmen had done it. They had been itching to remove the old man and his precautions for years.

While he didn't mind finally having Jaygo and his frequent lectures and precautions and criticizing glances removed once and for all, Maddix resented the abruptness of it. He wanted the old man to know he was being removed, and why. He wanted to see that flash of realization and despair before the blow that shut his mouth once and for all.

What he resented most was having Jaygo gone when he could have laid the blame for any failures and disappointments tonight on him. Curse them both, Baethon and Clancy should have notified him what they were going to do. They had probably acted without thinking. That was their usual pattern, after all.

Maddix wondered if he should punish them immediately for their inconvenient timing. Maybe he would let it build up for a while, prolong their agony. If he got rid of one of them, the other one would be more loyal and might learn to think before he acted.

At least he had the apples. He almost smiled as he looked down at them gleaming red and gold, smelling sweetly like new wine in the silver bowl he held in both hands. He almost laughed, remembering the little shriek Arden made as she fell. He hoped she wasn't too badly hurt, because he planned to rip away her little charade tonight and enjoy himself. She wouldn't be any fun in bed with a broken arm or leg, and if her pretty face was marred that would reduce some of his pleasure.

But Arden and Clancy and Baethon would have to wait. He had to deal with Fiera right this moment.

Ambrose appeared on the steps, pushing his way through the gathered nobles at the same moment the royal carriage of Brentonwald appeared in the palace gates. He appeared entirely unimpressed by the eager, breathless nobles in all their finery. He wore no jewels, nothing to make him stand out among them, except by his very simplicity of dress, and the silver sparkles of magic swirling through his hair. Maddix fought down a shiver of portent. Ambrose hadn't stirred up his magic so strongly, to be that visible, in years. What was the old man up to?

~~~~~

Dylon stayed in his grandfather's shadow as he searched the crowd for tall, dark, gaunt Lord Anselm, Brentonwald's ambassador. He silently begged Yeshen that Maddix wouldn't look directly at him. Much as he despised his cousin, he knew Maddix wasn't so much a fool he wouldn't recognize him, despite his dyed hair and his beard, and believing Dylon had been dead several years now. Everything was poised to go utterly wrong. He could only hope that his grandfather's
~~~~~

requests had been granted by Brentonwald, and Anselm would be a shelter and ally if things started falling apart very publicly in the next few minutes.

His gaze landed on Maddix, much as he didn't want to look at him. Dylon nearly stumbled off the step when he saw the apples and silver bowl in Maddix's hands. Everything had indeed gone wrong. When had the king changed the order of ceremony for welcoming Fiera? They were to have a grand procession out to the tree itself, to pick the apples in Fiera's sight, to prove the apples did come from that tree.

Why had Maddix changed things? Where was Arden? Wasn't she to be allowed to present her apples to Fiera?

Horrid suspicions washed over him. Was Maddix reneging on his vow to reward the one who had healed his apple tree? Had Arden been discovered, or had Maddix simply made her vanish when no one was looking?

Fiera's carriage rumbled up the long cobblestone road to the palace steps while Dylon hurriedly whispered his suspicions to Ambrose. The old man nodded, looking concerned, but not concerned enough for Dylon's tastes.

"I will take care of that, lad, never fear," was all Ambrose would say.

Anselm stepped through the crowd, reaching the bottom of the steps at the very moment the carriage smoothly slid to a stop. The stiffly dressed noblemen waiting there stepped up and opened the door and folded down the steps. Four maids in the deep green of Brentonwald stepped out, followed by four guards, stiff and tall and dark-skinned. Then Fiera emerged, dressed in dark green, sparkling with emeralds and diamonds, tall and coldly beautiful. The sharpness in her eyes made Maddix stand up straighter, tilting his head back.

Despite his worries, Dylon grinned. Perhaps his royal cousin had found a real challenge in this bride. He rather hoped the princess made Maddix suffer for a while.

Anselm gave his hand to Fiera and helped her down the steps. They exchanged small nods, and one corner of her mouth quirked up in a flicker of a smile. Then Fiera gave a shallow curtsey to Maddix and held out her hand.

Not to beckon with sweet coyness for her bridegroom to come to her, Dylon realized. And from the new flash of fire in Maddix's eyes, the king knew this too. No, Fiera held out her hand for her apples. She would not move one step until she got what her father demanded. Proof that the blight affecting Stonemount, which everyone believed had killed Queen Bianca, despite all Maddix's efforts to kill the rumors, had been cured.

Maddix barely refrained from stomping down the steps, slowly, prolonging the moment as a new kind of silence fell over the watching crowd. Not even the torches crackled in the waiting anticipation that washed over them all.

Glynna appeared, sparkling green and gold with agitation.

"Ambrose! Stop her! That idiot Maddix took the wrong apples," Glynna cried, wringing her hands and flying circles around him. In her agitation, she flew through several courtiers. They all flinched.

"What?" Ambrose groaned. As one person, he and Dylon and Glynna turned to see Maddix hold out the bowl with the apples.

"He decided Arden was taking too long to climb up and pick the best ones. He took bad apples!"

"Maddix!" Ambrose shouted. Ripples of astonishment nearly knocked some of the courtiers off their feet. "Nephew!"

Princess Fiera's hand hovered over the apples.

"In a moment, Uncle Ambrose," the king sighed, not even looking at him.

"For the sake of all you hold dear," Ambrose cried, as he pushed through the astonished, overdressed nobles and petrified servants. "Halt."

Fiera glanced at him, then at Anselm. The ambassador frowned, then tipped his head slightly to one side. His eyes narrowed as he looked at the apples.

An impish smile touched Fiera's lips. She picked up the apple and held it out to Maddix.

"After you, my lord."

~~~~~

Arden limped down the pathway of crushed seashells and sparkling gravel, blood on her face and hands, her kerchief torn off her hair, her dress torn in several places, nearly blind with tears. She had to get to Violet. She had to get out of the palace. She had to find a place to hide. Where was Glynna? Where was Dylon? Surely he would help her. Everyone lived in fear of Maddix. Oh, why hadn't she listened to Glynna's warnings and advice? Like a fool, she had trusted in justice and astonishment to paralyze the court and halt Maddix's retribution.

And now look what happened.

Maddix would kill Violet. Arden didn't care what Maddix would do to her, because she would die inside the moment he harmed her child. Derrien's child. But she cared what Maddix would make Alix do for her sake. Why had she risked so much? Why had she been so proud?

Then suddenly Ambrose and Dylon were both there, trying to hold her and guide her to a bench to sit and she couldn't resist them, could
~~~~~

barely speak for a moment.

"It's ruined!" she finally sobbed into Ambrose's shoulder. "Everything is ruined. Auntie was right. Grandfather, what have I done? Why was I so stubborn?"

"Shhh, child. It will be all right." Ambrose smiled at Dylon over her head.

"No, it won't! I lied. I played by Maddix's rules and look what it has done to me! If only I had listened to Auntie and simply asked for Ambrose and left as quietly as I came!" she wailed, shaking her head.

"Why do you need Ambrose?" the old man asked, with a touch of laughter in his voice.

No, that couldn't be laughter. The old man was too kind, he wouldn't mock her in her hour of despair. He knew something, though. Arden sensed it. A shiver went through her magic, a warning, anticipation of something about to happen. Yet how could she expect any sympathy, any help, any sacrifice if she wasn't entirely honest, if she didn't drop all her deception right this moment, and face the truth?

She lifted her head and knuckled away her tears and withdrew just enough from his supporting embrace to see his face.

"Let the truth begin now. I am Princess Arden of Westerland. My daughter is dying and I asked to come see Healer Ambrose, to save her life. Maddix refused. It was the last insult and injury I could take from him. I came here and I lied. I planned to take the reward for healing the tree he stole from me. I planned to reveal the truth to shame him once and for all. But he took wormy, rotten apples to give Fiera and when he finds me—oh, what will happen to Violet?" Her voice cracked but she didn't break out in fresh tears again.

"You've been so busy plotting your revenge, my dear, you never realized that I already healed Violet."

"You knew? All along?"

"Of course they did," Glynna said from over their heads. "Ambrose and Dylon can both see me, and he knew exactly who you were."

"Oh, Auntie ... what am I going to do? You were right."

"If it means anything, Fiera made Maddix take a bite first, and the look of disgust on his face was almost worth it." Dylon grinned despite their glares. He grinned wider when Arden gasped and the reality of it all struck her hard.

"You're Ambrose? You knew what I wanted all along? Oh, I could just—" Now she did burst into more tears.

"Come, child. We don't have much time." Ambrose stood and raised her to her feet. "When Maddix finishes his temper tantrum and trying to recover his dignity—"

"He'll be much too busy trying to think his way around Fiera," Lord Anselm said, appearing out of the gathering darkness from another direction. "You have been playing a dangerous game, Princess."

"Haven't I been able to keep a secret from anyone?" she cried. She felt her mouth twist into a crooked grin, just for a moment. Someday, if she lived that long, she would appreciate the irony and the ridiculousness of this moment.

"Maddix always looks for someone to punish when he plays the fool," Ambrose said.

"I can't get out of Stonemount quickly enough."

"Too late," Dylon said, pointing in the direction of the palace and the hints of torches, meaning people approaching through the gathering darkness. "Grandfather, what can we do?"

"Trust me. I know how to settle Maddix once and for all." Ambrose took hold of Arden by her shoulders and turned her to face the crowd with Maddix, Clancy and Baethon at their head.

"Uncle?" Maddix gasped, skidding to a halt. "What are you doing here? What has this lying little slut told you?"

"Princess Arden has told me the truth. Which you never did. For shame, Maddix, poisoning the entire palace to kill an innocent child."

Arden clasped Ambrose's hand a little tighter but said nothing.

"Uncle, I assure you—"

"No more lies, Maddix."

"She is the liar! She said the tree was healed, but every apple is rotten!"

"Only bad apples fall from that tree, Maddix," Arden said quietly. "The good ones are still on the branches."

"If only I could be sure of that." He pulled himself up taller, his mouth twisting with disdain. "Your game is up, Arden. You have lost. Everything."

"Wrong," Ambrose said, his stern expression relaxing into a weary, sad smile. He freed his hand from Arden's clutch and placed both hands on her shoulders as he closed his eyes and bowed his head. Silver sparks appeared in his hands. A silver nimbus of magic sprang up around Arden.

CHAPTER TWENTY-FOUR

In the Westerland palace gardens, Caitlin and Alix shared a very late dinner together under the apple tree. He read to her by lantern light and she gazed at him with affection both of them had only recently discovered, to their surprise and delight. Their quiet picnic ended in a blaze of silver and green light bursting from the tree above them. The tree shuddered. Silver and green magic flowed over the tree in waves as it stretched out its branches, exploding into flowers and golden fruit and adding several feet of new branches in all directions.

The two new sweethearts stared up at the tree in open-mouthed astonishment for several seconds. Then they laughed and hugged each other and struggled to their feet for a victory dance, needing no music but the happy beating of their hearts.

~~~~~

"No!" Maddix roared. "You can't give her my Gifting!"

"It was never yours," Ambrose said.

Arden was too stunned by the magic flowing into her from Ambrose to speak or even blink. Somewhere in all the chaos, she had finally recognized Dylon. He was Ambrose's grandson, a healer in his own right. Shouldn't the Gifting be going to him?

Ambrose stepped back as the glow of his magic faded and the flow slowed to a trickle. Arden turned, staring, tears in her eyes as he stepped back toward Glynna and faded a little more with every step. As he reached her, he was fully transparent and his feet left the ground. They joined hands, smiling, and faded from sight.

"Good-bye, Grandfather," Dylon whispered.

"He's not gone. He'll be with me..." Arden's voice cracked. "Forever."

"Arden—my princess," Maddix said in a choked voice. He held out both hands to her. "Forgive me. Think of our childhood love. Remember our plans to marry! I have always adored you."

She jerked away, out of his reach. She wanted to laugh, wanted to scream, overwhelmed by sudden fear for Violet. Yes, she had a healer's Gifting now, and the traditional protection granted to healers, by Yeshen's decree, but Maddix could still hurt Violet.

"Marry me. Let me repay you for all you have suffered." His voice throbbed with longing, but Arden knew better. He had never felt a single pure emotion. "Join Westerland and Stonemount into one nation as our
~~~~~

fathers dreamed."

"It's too late, Maddix." The calmness in her voice startled her. "I know all your dirty tricks, all your lies. But do you know something amazing?" She laughed a little breathlessly. The ready-to-fly feeling inside wasn't just from the magic churning through her as it made itself at home. "I'm not going to tell anyone. The truth has a way of coming out no matter what we do. I won't use your tricks any longer. I'm going home."

With a smile that was almost friendly, she turned to leave. Maddix reached to stop her, but Anselm and Dylon moved as one person to block him.

"A word of advice, King Maddix, if you would remain king." Anselm's quiet, pleasant voice wiped the growing rage from Maddix's face and turned it white. "Make peace with Princess Fiera. It's the only way to survive." He nodded and turned to go, then looked back over his shoulder. "Oh, and learn how to tell the truth. It's a valuable talent."

Dylon didn't even look back as he hurried after Arden.

~~~~~

Jason brought Arden a horse; a big, young, healthy gelding that chomped at the bit with eagerness to run, provided by Lord Anselm, complete with a sack of silvers and coppers to help pave her way home. Olive packed her food for the trip to Westerland. Berneen brought her new clothes, to disguise herself a little on the journey to the border. She worked in silence to help Arden pack for the trip. All her friends among the servants came to say good-bye, their faces alight with wonder and amazement and some little fear.

Arden wished she could take all her friends back to Westerland with her, but she couldn't if she wanted to leave quickly and quietly. Maddix would seethe for a time and then he would move against her. She couldn't count on the ancient inviolability of healers to keep her safe against his revenge. What she could count on, though, was for gossip to spread the word so that the sooner everyone knew what had happened and who she was, the more quickly Maddix's hands would be tied. Her friends would gladly spread the tale she knew, without her even asking.

The moon had risen before she and Violet were mounted, their provisions safely tied to the horse. They made their last farewells at the back palace gate where they had entered so many weeks ago. There were no guards, no one to witness their farewells. If Jason had arranged it that way or the guards had begun to revolt, Arden neither knew nor cared. All that mattered was being able to leave the palace without interference.

Olive gave Violet one last kiss and put the little girl into her mother's arms, then stepped back, tears in her eyes.
~~~~~

Now, Arden let herself look for Dylon. Berneen had told her about how he had faked his death and worked from the shadows to help Ambrose, and how glad so many nobles were that he had returned from the dead. He would be busy, forced back into his former role as a member of the royal family, likely dealing with so many people who had lost some of their fear and respect for Maddix. She knew he was busy, yet she wanted so very much to see him, to ask him to go with her, and ask how long he had known her secret. All they had been allowed was one hurried moment in the hallway, when he urged her to leave and promised he would catch up with her. Eventually.

"And to think that the Princess Arden worked in my own kitchen," the cook murmured for the dozenth time.

"If you ever come to Westerland —"

"I might at that. Do you need another cook in your palace, Princess?"

"I need my friends. All of you. When you see Dylon..." Arden couldn't find the words. She reached down for Olive's hand once more, squeezed, and nudged the horse to get it moving. Time was on her side, but not for long.

~~~~~

Mid-afternoon the next day they reached the border of Stonemount and Westerland. A far smoother, more comfortable, faster trip than she had the first time. The gate hung open, which was a marked change she wondered at. Had something happened she didn't know about, immured in the palace? Word of Maddix's defeat and embarrassment couldn't have reached here already, could it?

The guards of both sides lounged against the poles supporting the gate, talking to each other, looking bored. The traffic flow was all in one direction, Stonemount to Westerland. That, at least, hadn't changed.

Just before she dismounted to approach the gate on foot, Arden felt what she could only describe as a nudge, and a silent whisper telling her to turn and look. She saw a boy sitting by the side of the road, flushed with fever, his left leg bound with splints and blood-spotted bandages. Before she quite knew it, she slid off the horse and brought Violet down with her, set her daughter on the ground, and knelt next to the boy. The well-trained horse stayed with her. She barely noticed in the overwhelming, totally new compulsion to reach out and help.

But how? a voice asked inside her head.

It's easy, another voice said, laughing, and Arden suddenly knew exactly what to do.

Violet toddled off toward a mud puddle where other children were playing. Arden reached out both hands to touch the boy's leg. He stared
~~~~~

at her, his wariness turning to wonder as her hands glowed silver, and the glow spread to his leg.

A few travelers saw and came over to watch. Murmurs of astonishment brought more people to watch. Arden ignored the gasps and new voices and the people calling for others to come see. All that mattered was somehow being able to see under the bandages with a kind of sight that was rooted in her fingertips. She knew what needed to be done, how to guide her own strength and health to clean and seal the boy's badly gashed leg.

As she unwrapped the dirty bandages, the murmurs turned to shouts and laughter and the sound of running feet from both sides of the gate.

"Princess?" a familiar voice called. Bardon, a good friend of Derrien's, crossed over from the Westerland side of the gate. He led four more Westerland soldiers, all of them with the same expressions of wonder that the Stonemount border guards wore. "Are you all right?" He gestured at the men behind him. "We're here to take you home."

"Home. Yes, please." She blinked tears from her eyes.

"Mistress, can you help my wife?" a Stonemount gate guard begged as Arden stood up from her very first healing. "She's been that sick for three days now."

"I will help everyone who needs me." She looked around at the crowd and knew what to do. She smiled and raised her voice to call out, "Tell everyone you meet. Princess Arden says there will be no more border and no barriers to keep Stonemount and Westerland separate. I will build a healing house nearby and anyone who wants may come to me and I will help them."

Then she gestured for the guard to lead the way. He shucked his helmet and sword and reached out to take her hand and lead her at a run.

~~~~~

That night, frustrated by ambassadors who no longer toadied and servants who smiled instead of quaking in fear, Maddix drank himself dizzy in the hopes of escape. He only grew queasy and more angry. He found a long-handled axe—he couldn't quite remember where—and staggered out to the gardens.

It was the tree's fault.

The tree was part of Arden, wasn't it?

He could still hurt her, even if everyone kept telling him he didn't dare touch a healer who had been Gifted by the great Ambrose.

The tree drew back its branches when he got within ten feet of it, just like a dowager pulling up its skirts at the approach of a rat. Maddix
~~~~~

shuddered, nauseated by the image of a fat, greasy, filthy rat. Anger thudded through his swollen head as he realized *he* was the rat. He imagined the axe hitting Arden as he stepped forward, hefted it and raised it and swung with his entire body.

Green-gold light spurted from the wound as the axe bit in with a glancing blow. The wound in the bark sealed up a moment later, with a sound that was half harp chord and half hissing. Maddix's stomach writhed at the clash of sounds and sensations.

"Don't be an even greater fool, Maddix," Ambrose called, and faded into sight a moment later, bobbing slightly in mid-air in front of the tree trunk. He chuckled and shook his head when Maddix gaped at him. "Forgotten me already?"

"You're dead. Arden took your life."

"I *gave* Princess Arden my magic, and I am far from dead. I've come to say good-bye, Maddix. Don't try to hurt the tree, if you know what's good for you."

He held out his hand, and Glynna faded into sight as she gave her hand into his. They smiled at each other like young sweethearts.

Maddix staggered back two steps as he recognized the woman from Arden's christening day. The day he had lowered himself to feel jealous of a baby; the day he decided he would have Ambrose's Gifting someday.

But Arden had it all now. Despite everything he had done, she had won. He just couldn't understand.

"No! It's not fair!" he roared as the two spirits rose slowly through the air, passing through the branches of the tree.

He snatched up the axe again and swung, hitting the trunk hard enough to knock himself off his feet with the rebound. The tree shrieked with a sound that went higher than a falcon's scream and deeper than the rumbling of an earthquake. Green-gold magic burst out from every leaf and branch, enveloping the entire tree in blinding light. Maddix screamed as if his head would split open from the brightness and fell to his knees.

When the light faded, the tree was gone.

"He never did know what was good for him," Ambrose murmured from far above the highest towers of the palace. "Shall we go, my dear?"

In mid-air, he leaned forward and kissed Glynna with all the passion of their long-ago youth. They faded into the night quiet with a spattering of sparkles of magic brighter than all the stars.

~~~~~

The palace garden in Westerland had two apple trees, and as a result, the harvest gave signs of being triply abundant that year, as if to
~~~~~

make up for the paucity of the spring. Arden stopped from time to time and silently apologized to the trees, to Westerland, and to Yeshen, for her bitterness and lack of forgiveness, that had started off the year so bleakly.

Then she threw herself gladly into the preparations for Alix and Caitlin's wedding celebration, to take place at the end of the harvest.

Violet became a handful for her mother, making up for the many months of listlessness. Arden hired two new nursemaids for her daughter. After all, once construction began on the healing house near the border, she would need her hands free both for teaching and healing.

If she had no help, of course.

For the first week after returning to Westerland, every time a visitor was announced, Arden looked up with eager expectation of seeing Dylon's face. Each time, she was disappointed and she scolded herself not to invest so much of her heart into waiting for him. He had responsibilities to Stonemount, after all. The rumors and official courier packets coming from Anselm and other ambassadors hinted that a growing number of people wanted Dylon to claim the throne. She wondered what all the political chaos and court intrigue was doing to him. She prayed, asking Yeshen to protect him, and scolded herself not to be selfish. Maddix had been right about the higher duty of the nobility, although his interpretation of what that meant had always been questionable.

If Maddix had killed Dylon, how would she know?

Ambrose assured her, the few times he and Glynna became visible, that he would know if Dylon fell into danger. Arden had to be content with that.

Brentonwald was strangely silent, and there was no sign Princess Fiera would be going home. Arden felt sorry for her, being sent to Stonemount to correct Maddix. She hoped the princess had many friends and allies to support and protect her.

She tried not to imagine Fiera marrying Dylon, if he was persuaded to take back the throne.

~~~~~

The royal family spent nearly every late afternoon under the apple trees, just the four of them, relaxing and talking and taking a respite from the press of court life. Violet's favorite new game was to snatch sweets from under her doting uncle's hand and make him chase her to get them back. Today, she climbed up into his lap as Caitlin held out the plate to him with the last piece of pastry filled with late berries. She caught the treat in both hands and squealed her glee as she turned to flee. And kicked King Alix in the stomach. He *ooph*ed his surprise, tumbled
~~~~~

backwards, and stared, open-mouthed, as the child scampered across the grass with lightning speed.

"If you don't catch her now," Arden said, laughter tears in her eyes, "you'll never live it down. She'll only get worse if you don't stop her."

Muttering, Alix got to his feet and lumbered after the child. Caitlin leaped at his arm to stop him. Laughing, he wrapped his arms around her waist and spun her around several times, then put her down so quickly she stumbled. Freed momentarily, he raced after Violet, who was halfway across the garden by now and shrieking laughter.

A rippling sensation went up Arden's back, stopping her laughter in her throat. The knowledge inherited from Ambrose told her that was the feeling when one healer sensed another. She turned to the garden gates, and there he was.

"It's about time that boy got here," Ambrose said. He and Glynna preferred to be invisible as they watched over the family.

"I think his timing is perfect," Glynna said with a chuckle.

Dylon didn't move until Arden got to her feet and started toward him. He crossed the garden grass in long, smooth, quick strides, meeting her under the very edge of the second apple tree. He smiled with only his eyes as he caught hold of her hands. Neither of them could speak for several seconds. Arden thought she would choke on her questions and the strange longing to laugh and cry at the same time. Then Dylon grinned and she realized how silly they both had to look, and they laughed quietly together for a few seconds.

"I hear you're starting a school for healers," he said, and tightened his grip on her hands.

"Grandfather says a gift hoarded becomes evil. I have a lot of Maddix's evil to make up for."

"Is there a place for me?"

She smiled and swirls of green-gold magic intertwined with the silver of healer's magic spun through the leaves of the apple trees.

END

Author's Note:

Plantwise may feel familiar to some of you who have read my earlier books. This is a *revised* and *expanded*, and *much darker version*, of a novel called *Bitter Sweet*, originally published by Mundania Press.

I changed the names of most of the main characters, but left some names of countries and characters the same. I've revised the magic system, changing names and colors, in anticipation of greatly expanding the entire series. Plus, I've added an ongoing war for domination of the world and all the magic and magic-users in it.

There were originally four books, loosely connected in two couples. *Bitter Sweet* and *The Wolf That Was* took place in a fantasy world. *Wolves on the West Side* and *Shatter Scatter* took place in the present in our world. Children who were descendants of *The Wolf That Was* were thrown into our world, and forced to survive high school before they could trigger the magic that sent them home, to fight the evil magic-users who tried to kill one of them ten years before.

Many of those names and characters and large chunks of history will be revised, deleted, or expanded to create the new, much larger series, **Steward's World**. For example, in *Bitter Sweet*, Princess Fiera was originally Princess Sorcha, and she and Maddix, originally Fallon, were spoiled brats and most certainly deserved each other. I made Maddix much darker, more evil, bordering on psychotic. Now, Fiera is a much more important and pivotal character in the ages-old war with the scheming despot called Durmad, the nemesis of Steward. She has been sent to reform Maddix. Will she succeed? You'll have to find out in the next book, originally called *The Wolf That Was*.

Keep in mind that Fiera has some magical traditions working against her, starting with the ugly tendency for royal stepmothers to turn evil. Maddix's little son, Maxin, needs defenders and good influences in his life if he isn't going to turn into an even worse brat and schemer than his father!

Will Durmad show his ugly face? I haven't decided yet. (I have to write the next book in **The Enchanted Castle Archives** before I can start revising *The Wolf That Was*. I have two series going on my storytelling podcast, **Ye Olde Dragon's Library**.) There's an evil enchanter already involved in the story, who has been torturing innocent travelers by merging them with wild animals, to make the ultimate warriors in the coming battle between the forces of Durmad and the allied kings under the guidance of Steward. Some of them escape, and meet a maiden currently named Tyrian, the daughter of a wise woman. To save her life when she was an infant, her mother merged her with a wolf cub. Hence the current name. I have many ideas for the new title of the book. Maybe **The White Wolf**?

Right now, I'm planning on at least four more books, to expand the series to eight titles, bridging the gap between *The Wolf That Was* and *Wolves on the West Side*, and then following up after the events of *Shatter Scatter*. Who knows? I might have so much fun in this world, with these characters, I'll keep writing!

I hope you'll keep watch for the next book to come out. There are several ways to stay on top of developments:

My blog: *www.MichelleLevigne.blogspot.com* – click on one of the links to get a free short story ebook, and automatically sign up for my newsletter.

The publisher's blog, at *www.YeOldeDragonBooks.com*

My website: *www.Mlevigne.com*, where you can also sign up for my newsletter.

And the podcast: *Ye Olde Dragon's Library*. That's where you can listen to chapters delivered twice a week of a fantasy novel, either in the **Steward's World** series or **The Enchanted Castle Archives** series. And more to be created. **PLUS: interviews with authors of fantastical fiction.**

And if you join the **Ye Olde Dragon's Library Patreon group**, you'll get sneak previews, chances to snag free ebook short stories, sample chapters in audiobook, and opportunities to pre-order upcoming books at a discount. Please consider joining and supporting the podcast?

Thanks for reading. I hope you're as excited about upcoming books in this series as I am!

Michelle L. Levigne

About the Author

On the road to publication, Michelle fell into fandom in college and has 40+ stories in various SF and fantasy universes. She has a bunch of useless degrees in theater, English, film/communication, and writing. Even worse, she has over 100 books and novellas with multiple small presses, in science fiction and fantasy, YA, suspense, women's fiction, and sub-genres of romance.

Her official launch into publishing came with winning first place in the Writers of the Future contest in 1990. She was a finalist in the EPIC Awards competition multiple times, winning with *Lorien* in 2006 and *The Meruk Episodes, I-V*, in 2010, and was a finalist in the Realm Awards competition, in conjunction with the Realm Makers convention.

Her training includes the Institute for Children's Literature; proofreading at an advertising agency; and working at a community newspaper. She is a tea snob and freelance edits for a living (MichelleLevigne@gmail.com for info/rates), but only enough to give her time to write. Her newest crime against the literary world is to be co-managing editor at Mt. Zion Ridge Press and launching the publishing co-op, Ye Olde Dragon Books. Be afraid … be very afraid.

And please check out her newest venture: Ye Olde Dragon's Library, the storytelling podcast. Each week, listeners are invited to join Michelle on her blog to ask questions and give feedback and suggestions. Interspersed between the chapters will be interviews with authors of fantastical fiction. Listen to the podcast on your favorite podcast app or listen on the website: www.YeOldeDragonBooks.com, and click on the Ye Olde Dragon's Library link. Then go to her blog to interact: www.MichelleLevigne.blogspot.com

www.Mlevigne.com
www.MichelleLevigne.blogspot.com
www.YeOldeDragonBooks.com
www.MtZionRidgePress.com

Look for Michelle's Goodreads groups:

Guardians of Neighborlee
Voyages of the AFV Defender

NEWSLETTER:
Want to learn about upcoming books, book launch parties, inside information, and cover reveals?
Go to Michelle's website or blog to sign up.

Thanks for reading!
If you enjoyed this book, would you help Michelle by posting a review on Goodreads?

Are you a member of Book Bub? If so, please follow Michelle on Book Bub, and you'll get alerts when new books are coming out.

As a way of saying thanks, Michelle invites you to the Goodies page on her website. It will change regularly, offering you a free short story, a sample audiobook chapter, sneak peeks at new cover art, inside information on discounts and new release dates, etc.

Please go to: Mlevigne.com/good-stuff.html

Also by Michelle L. Levigne

Guardians of the Time Stream: 4-book Steampunk series
The Match Girls: Humorous inspirational romance series starting with **A Match (Not) Made in Heaven**
Sarai's Journey: A 2-book biblical fiction series
Tabor Heights: 18-book inspirational small town romance series.
Quarry Hall: 11-book women's fiction/suspense series
For Sale: Wedding Dress. Never Used: inspirational romance
Crooked Creek: Fun Fables About Critters and Kids: Children's short stories.
Do Yourself a Favor: Tips and Quips on the Writing Life. A book of writing advice.
To Eternity (and beyond): *Writing Spec Fic Good for Your Soul.* A book defending speculative fiction.
Killing His Alter-Ego: contemporary romance/suspense, taking place in fandom.
The Commonwealth Universe: SF series, 25 books and growing

The Hunt: 5-book YA fantasy series
Faxinor: Fantasy series, 4 books and growing
Wildvine: Fantasy series, 14 books when all released
Neighborlee: Humorous fantasy series
Zygradon: 5-book Arthurian fantasy series
AFV Defender: SF adventure series
Young Defenders: Middle Grade SF series, spin-off of *AFV Defender*
Magic to Spare: Fantasy series
Book & Mug Mysteries: cozy mystery series
Quest for the Crescent Moon: fantasy series starting in 2023
Steward's World: fantasy series reboot and expansion
The Enchanted Castle Archives: fantasy series, Liars' Quest, 1st book in the
Ye Olde Dragon's Library podcast